STEPHEN

Missing Joe

SCEPTRE

First published in Great Britain in 2001 by Hodder and Stoughton
A division of Hodder Headline

A Sceptre Paperback

2 4 6 8 10 9 7 5 3 1

A CIP catalogue record for this title
is available from the British Library.

ISBN 0 340 75149 5

Printed and bound in Great Britain by
Clays Ltd, St Ives plc

Hodder and Stoughton
A division of Hodder Headline
338 Euston Road
London NW1 3BH

For Lucille Thompson

BEFORE

It had been a long flight, over nine hours, and Joyce was feeling jet-lagged and irritable. This was her first visit to Jamaica in four years, Cyrian's first visit ever.

Outside the airport she hailed a taxi. A toothless old man, who'd been leaning against his battered Ford Anglia, acknowledged her wave and stepped forward.

'Where you want to go, moom?' he asked.

'Downtown,' said Joyce.

The taxi-driver picked up her two suitcases and ferried them to his car. Joyce was then accosted by another man, who was naked from the waist down. He asked, politely, if she could spare a dollar. Joyce ignored him. Wounded, he muttered something about the stinginess of foreigners, then set off to prey on some other new arrival. Cyrian tried not to stare at his sunburnt genitals.

Arriving downtown, they got out of the taxi and stretched from fatigue. While Joyce was busy reacquainting herself with the surroundings, the taxi-driver unloaded her suitcases. Cyrian craned his neck every which way, like a tourist.

'Right,' said the taxi-driver. 'Six hundred dalla, please.'

'What?' said Joyce. 'Is what you take me for, man? A damn fool?'

'All right, all right,' said the taxi driver, looking about furtively. 'Keep you voice down. Pay me 'alf.'

Joyce paid him, but felt compelled to say: 'You lucky you get that.' In addition, she advised him to carry out what she thought were some much-needed repairs to the bodywork and engine of his vehicle. The taxi-driver grumbled and sped away.

They'd been deposited outside a busy street market. They entered it, pushing past hordes of shoppers. Reggae music blared from mobile record booths elaborately decorated in red, green and yellow. Men, women and raggedy children sat or stood about eating sugar cane and other foods, their faces blackened by the sun. Mangy dogs scavenged in the stinking, litter-clogged gutters.

Emerging at the other end of the market, they came to a halt outside a bus terminal. Here they were met by an even larger group of people, all waiting to be transported to various parts of Kingston. A bus crawled noisily from the depot. The driver – young, shirtless, cocky – insisted that those wishing to board must form an orderly queue. The passengers ignored him and clambered aboard willy-nilly. Shaking her head at the scene, Joyce gave thanks that she lived in England. These people, she thought, they're so uncivilised.

They'd only paused here for the opportunity to catch their breath, rest their weary arms, and soon they were pushing on down a narrow pavement lined with higglers of every persuasion. '*Gleaner!*' 'Nuts!' 'Kisco-Pop!' Joyce waved them away, kissing her teeth. Used to rejection, the higglers stepped aside in readiness for the next passer-by. Up ahead was a small knot of women, huddled around their wares. They were much more sedate than the boisterous lot outside the bus terminal. Joyce was happy to see them, for like her, they were unmistakably country folk. She checked with one of them and was assured that, yes, she was at the right pick-up point for the bus to Cascade.

It was an old bus, in need of a thorough sweep and a wash. Some of its windows were missing and it tilted to one side. In every nook and cranny there were either chicken feathers or goat droppings. It also had a musty scent of stale sweat and rotting vegetables.

The bus left the city limits and poked its nose into suburbia. Joyce immediately relaxed, for she hated Kingston, and only a shortage of available flights had prevented her from flying in to the more laid-back Montego Bay. Settling into her seat, with Cyrian pressed up next to her, she feasted her eyes on the landscape, at once familiar and strange. Gone now were the ramshackle lean-tos and zinc huts of downtown Kingston, replaced by farms and sugar-cane plantations and hillside dwellings. Along the way, the bus passed numerous weather-beaten figures walking leisurely along the roadside with farming tools thrown casually over their shoulders. The driver, familiar with one or two, would acknowledge them by honking rhythmically on his horn.

The farther inland they drove, the greater the signs of poverty: half-naked children, bad roads, deserted filling stations. At times skeletal dogs ran out into the road, narrowly escaping with their lives. Some hadn't been so fortunate, for there were carcasses dotted all along the route, decaying and giving off a pestilential stench that penetrated the bus and forced Cyrian to cover his nose. Vultures would soon be in attendance, and in a few days all that would remain of these wretched creatures would be sun-dried hides and brittle skeletons.

The bus stopped on a couple of occasions, letting a few people off and giving some of the other passengers a chance to relieve themselves in roadside bushes. Cyrian was embarrassed at the sight of grown women hitching up their skirts, his own mother among them.

Cascade was a backwater, arguably the most remote district in the entire parish of St Ann. Electricity had only recently been installed, there were no phone lines, and the whole area was served by a single road, which, in bad weather, was often impassable. The locals made the best of it. Poor but resourceful, they lived off the land. Needless to say, religion featured prominently in their lives. The district was divided into four villages: Greentown, Mount Moriah, Borobridge and Wild Cane. Of the four, Mount Moriah was by far the most important. It had a post office, a school, a church, and more shops than its three neighbours put together. When the bus finally reached it, Joyce heaved a sigh of relief. Many of the locals had come out to witness the return of friends and relatives. Meanwhile, the busboy, who had snoozed for most of the journey, was perched precariously on the roof of the bus taking instructions from the impatient passengers below. Those who had already received their belongings made their way into a nearby bar. Cyrian, standing obediently beside his mother, assumed they sought refreshments from a man called Sam, whose name was painted in bright yellow above the door.

Finally, the busboy hurled down their suitcases, which landed with a thud on the pebbled roadside. Joyce immediately checked them for damage, berating the busboy throughout. Satisfied with her inspections, she turned to Cyrian and said: 'Come.'

They'd been walking for about twenty minutes, via a short cut which saw them trying to avoid cowpats, when Joyce suddenly stopped and said: 'Hold on a minute, Cyrian. There's somebody me have to see in there.' They were standing in the middle of a patch of scrubland. Straight ahead was a sad-looking wooden house with a veranda. Partially obscured by trees, it was the only house visible in the immediate vicinity.

They ambled up the footpath, to the right of which were three tombstones. Neville saw his visitors approaching, but made no attempt at a greeting. He was sitting on the veranda, hunched over a mound of sweet potatoes, busy scraping them with a muddy cutlass. Dressed in a tatty string vest and a pair of dirty black trousers, he looked sweaty and harassed, and kept scratching his groin. His visitors climbed the small set of steps to the veranda and stood before him. Without looking up, he said, 'Joyce,' then carried on scraping his potatoes.

'That's it?' said Joyce. 'Me don't see you for four years and that's the welcome me get?'

Neville lifted his head, regarded her coolly. 'Listen, Joyce,' he said, 'not because you can tek plane like taxi an' waltz in an' outta here when you feel like, don't mean de res' of we 'ave to jig an' dance an' kiss you foot, you know?'

'Oh, shut up,' said Joyce. 'You too damn miserable.'

Neville stood up, dwarfing Joyce. Cyrian feared for his mother's safety and he tensed up, ready to defend her.

'Look, woman,' said Neville. 'Do me a faiva. Jus' don' come 'ere and provoke me, all right? Ah beg you, please.' He sat down again. Joyce kissed her teeth, unimpressed. They'd had countless arguments in the past, and she'd always held her own. She may have spent years abroad, but Neville was a fool if he thought that they had softened her in any way. She gave Cyrian a conspiratorial wink, then said: 'Oh, Mister Miserable, so that mean you don't want the present me bring for you?'

'Wha' kin'a present?' said Neville, inclining his head to one side, suspicious.

'No, no, no,' said Joyce, smiling at Cyrian, who was sitting on the veranda railing. 'You say I must leave you alone. Come, Cyrian, make we leave the gentleman alone.'

Neville shook his head. 'You see? Da's what ah taaking about. You say you bring a present for me, but is like you want me to beg you for it. Is like you want me on all fours. Well, it not gwine 'appen, Joyce. You hear me? It not gwine 'appen.'

Joyce smiled. 'But surely you can't want anything me bring for you.'

'You hear me say dat? Eh? Dat's what you saying, not me. Kin'ly don't put words into me mout'.'

'Sound to me like you change you tune.'

'Me do nutten of de kin',' said Neville. 'Me not too proud to accep' a present from you. Da's all me saying. Dere's no "change choon" in dat. Ah simply don' . . .'

'All right, all right,' said Joyce. 'Mind you bite you tongue, man. Here.' She delved into her handbag for his present, shooting a quick glance at Cyrian. He didn't notice, too busy looking around. He saw that the yard was littered with rubbish, mostly Dragon Stout bottles. The trees encircling the house were enough to induce claustrophobia. As for the house itself, it looked old, mournful, and was, Cyrian thought, obviously haunted, probably by those whose names he could just about make out on the tombstones: Granville Forbes, Barbara 'Bunty' Forbes, Charmaine Forbes.

Neville examined his watch, fiddling with the plastic strap.

'You like it?' asked Joyce.

'Is very nice,' said Neville.

Joyce helped him fasten it to his wrist. Cyrian noticed how intimate they'd quickly become, and it made him uncomfortable. He thought about his father, and tried not to picture him with another woman. Neville wrapped a few choice potatoes into some old newspaper and handed the package to Joyce.

'And what me must do with these?' she asked.

'Mek Adlyn cook dem up for you later, of course.' He turned to Cyrian. 'So is de las' one dis?'

Joyce nodded.

'Come 'ere, bwoy.'

Cyrian slid down off the railing and walked over. Neville studied him a while, then said: 'Sowhademcallyou?' That's how it came out, as one word.

'I'm sorry,' said Cyrian. 'I don't understand.'

Neville raised his brows. 'But you does taak very nice.' Joyce beamed with pride. 'Ah mean what you name, young sir?'

'Oh, Cyrian.'

'Well, Ocyrian. Is very nice to meet you. Me and you madder go way, way back, so you and me is practic'ly fam'ly, you hear?' Cyrian nodded. 'All right, den. Good.' Relieved, Cyrian went back to sit on the railing.

'So,' Neville asked Joyce, 'how dem odder ones doing?'

'Oh, you know, busy, busy. Too busy to visit them own mother, sometimes. Donovan wife expecting. Again.'

'Stop!'

'True. And Michael just get promoted. Earning more than all of we put together.'

'Da's good,' said Neville, nodding. 'Da's very good.' He thought a while, then added: 'And how work treating you?'

Joyce wasn't comfortable talking about her job. She was a supermarket supervisor, and could never find anything interesting to say about it. 'Work is work.' She shrugged.

Neville shot a quick glance at Cyrian, seemed about to address him, but instead said: 'A hear dat you see Joe.'

In a letter to Adlyn, three years previously, Joyce had mentioned seeing Joe. They'd bumped into each other in the street. She'd been surprised to see him, given that he no longer lived in London. They'd exchanged numbers, but failed to keep in touch.

'Yes, me see him, for about five minute.'

Neville said he was worried that something might have happened to him.

'Why you say that?' asked Joyce.

'Is over two years now since me hear from him. Ah write a coupla letter in dat time but ah don' get no reply.'

'P'raps him move.'

'Maybe. But surely him would write an' tell me?'

Joyce thought for a while then started shaking her head. To her, it was unbelievable that Joe hadn't visited the island since leaving more than thirty years earlier. Was he so blissfully happy living in the English countryside that he couldn't tear himself away? It would appear that way, said Neville; from his letters, at any rate. In them, Joe had often mentioned his wife and son, and said what a good life they had. Joyce had her doubts. Being cut off from your own people was not her idea of a good life.

'Well,' said Neville. 'At leas' him sekkle down.'

'True,' said Joyce. 'And who would have believe that?'

Neville explained that he was thinking of going to England to look for Joe. Joyce laughed.

'Wha'?' asked Neville.

'Oh, just you in England.'

'Da's funny, is it?'

Before she could answer, Joyce noticed that Cyrian was becoming restless. 'Look, Neville,' she said, 'me have to go and see Mama now. Make we talk later, all right?'

'You know where me is. How long you here for dis time?'

'Two weeks,' said Joyce, and left.

'Boy-oh-boy,' said Joyce. 'It hot is a shame. Phew!' She put down her suitcase and started fanning herself.

'Mum,' said Cyrian, grumpily, 'how much further?' He was feeling hot and faint.

'Don't worry,' said Joyce. 'We reach.'

Cyrian was perplexed. Reached where, exactly? They'd come to the end of a dirt track. He looked to his right and saw a dry river-bed, beyond which was a small plot of sugar cane. Turning to his left, he saw a craggy hill with a footpath zigzagging its way to the top. There, at the top of the hill, stood a whitewashed shack with a pyramidical zinc roof, which Cyrian could barely look at for it glistened so brilliantly in the sun.

'We're not going all the way up there, are we?' he asked, wearily.

'You young people nowadays,' said Joyce, shaking her head. 'I use to run up that hill as a girl. Come.'

They struggled up the hill, weighed down by their suitcases. When they reached the summit, as if from nowhere, a tall old woman appeared. A faded, multicoloured headscarf inadequately covered her grey plaits, a few of which were poking out at the edges. Mud-splattered wellingtons housed her feet, with holes cut into the sides for the comfort of her corned little toes. A lacklustre, floral-patterned dress met the wellingtons at her knees. There were beads of sweat on her nose and forehead, and traces of mud on her skeletal hands. She'd obviously been working.

'Praise de Lawd!' she said, throwing her arms around Joyce. Moments later she came out of the clinch and rounded on Cyrian. 'And dis mus' be Cyrian. My, what a 'andsome young man, what a truly 'andsome young man. How ol' him is now, Joyce?'

'Thirteen,' Joyce replied.

'My. T'irteen. Big, big man. Come give you granny a hug, bwoy. Standin' dere like dat wid you big 'andsome self . . . Come 'ere!'

She stretched out her arms. Cyrian walked into them, and was surprised by the strength of her embrace. Joyce took a moment to absorb the surroundings, which hadn't changed since she was a child. There, adjacent to the house, was the sooty wattle-and-daub kitchen, and next to it the tiny wattle-and-daub latrine.

'T'ank God unnu reach safe,' said Adlyn, releasing Cyrian. 'But how unnu tek so long? Look from when me see bus go up.'

'We pass by Neville on the way,' said Joyce. She smiled, then added: 'You know that man never going to change?'

'Oh, chuh!' said Adlyn. 'Dat cantankerous ol' fart. Hones'ly, Joyce, ah don' know why you bodder wid him.' She kissed her teeth.

Joyce smiled and said: 'You not fooling anybody, you know? The whole world know you love him like a son.'

'Lawd, child, stop you foolishness. A cruff like dat? My son?'

They laughed. Feeling left out, Cyrian let his eyes wander. He noticed three tethered goats, a donkey, a pig, and two sly-looking curs of indeterminate breed whose ambiguous welcome had consisted of a simultaneous snarling and a wagging of their tails. What a place, he thought. It was difficult for him to imagine that his mother came from such humble beginnings. Thank God they were only staying two weeks.

The following afternoon, Joyce went back to see Neville. This time he was nowhere to be seen, so Joyce stood in the yard and called his name. Moments later he emerged, his face puffy with sleep.

'Sorry to wake you,' said Joyce.

'Da's all right,' said Neville. He stretched and yawned, invited Joyce to join him on the veranda. 'Ah would awks you to come inside, but . . .'

'I know, I know,' said Joyce, interrupting. 'The house not tidy.' She climbed the steps to the veranda and sat on a rickety old chair.

'You want somet'ing to drink?' asked Neville.

'Water, please. With ice, if you have any.'

Neville disappeared inside. While he was gone, Joyce gave the place the once-over. 'My God,' she whispered.

Presently Neville returned with two tall glasses of water. He handed one to Joyce, then went and sat in his wife's old rocking chair. They sipped their water and looked out across the yard. After a time Joyce said: 'You know what, when me really stop and consider it, this place was like a second home to me.'

'Can say dat again.'

Joyce turned and faced him. 'What you mean by that remark, Neville Forbes?'

'Ah mean we could nevva get ridda you.'

'I see. It all coming out now. Didn't realise you wanted to get rid of me.' She stuck her nose in the air, looked away from him.

'Not me, of course. It was mos'ly Joe. You know him nevva did like you.'

'Only 'cause him was jealous.'

Neville was embarrassed. Joyce realised her error, and sought to make amends. Looking out at the tombstones, she said: 'I was really sad to hear about Charmaine.'

Neville shrugged and said: 'In de midst of life . . .'

'I hear she get a good send-off. Sorry I miss it. Just couldn't afford to . . .' She trailed off.

Neville didn't say anything. Charmaine had been gone only two years and the memory of her death still pained him. Joyce studied his profile. The grey-flecked beard, the sullen mouth, the paunch. Bereavement had aged him, she thought. He was only forty-eight, same as her, but he'd acquired the ravaged features of a much older man.

The mood had become depressing, so on a lighter note Joyce said: 'What ever 'appen to that swing?'

'How me mus' know?' said Neville, and he tutted.

'All right, all right. I was only asking. Jesus.'

Neville downed the rest of his water then hurled the unmelted ice out into the yard. Joyce knew he was upset, and she regretted mentioning Charmaine.

'You don't get lonely out here all by youself, Neville?'

'Not really.' His tone sounded more even. 'De boys dem does pass by from time to time.'

Joyce kissed her teeth. 'You and you "boys".'

A lizard appeared in the yard, its throat inflating and deflating, like a frog's. Neville started looking around for something to throw at it.

'No lady friend?' asked Joyce, playfully.

'Don't be impert'nant, Joyce.'

'See anything of Brenda these days?'

'Who?'

'Stop pretend. You know exactly who me mean. Brenda Emmanuel. You one-time sweetheart.'

Neville wasn't listening. He'd found a clump of dried mud under his chair. Taking careful aim, he flung it at the lizard, missing by some distance.

11

'God blin' it,' he cursed, and immediately began searching for another missile.

'Man, leave the lizard alone. It troubling you?'

Sensing danger, the lizard scurried to the edge of the clearing and disappeared among the bushes. Joyce shook her head.

'Still 'fraid of duppie, eh? Big man like you.'

Neville didn't rise to it.

'Superstitious and backward,' said Joyce.

'Ah beg you pardon?'

'You deaf?'

Neville stared at her, outraged. He wanted to come back with something, but words failed him. Joyce handed him her empty glass and said: 'More ice this time, please.' Sighing heavily, Neville grabbed the glass and went inside. Joyce tittered to herself.

The day began early, all three of them rising at six. Neither Joyce nor Cyrian had slept very well, owing to the dogs barking all night. Sharing a bed hadn't helped either.

Washing took place outdoors, much to Cyrian's embarrassment. A few jugs of cold water, standing in a metal washbasin, to the rear of the house.

After breakfast it was time to get the glad rags on. Adlyn wore a plain purple frock, stiff with starch, and a matching hat with a fake feather. Joyce was resplendent in a cream trouser suit, accessorised by her shiny black purse. Cyrian wore a green double-breasted suit, with a handkerchief tucked into the outside breast pocket. Then off they set, down the hill, across the dry river-bed (known locally as Dry-Gully), around Ned Knight's 'cane piece, then along a well-worn track that brought them out on to the main road. From there it was but a few hundred yards to Mount Moriah Square.

As they neared the church, they noticed quite a few of the congregation milling around outside, clutching Bibles and tambourines. The men wore dark suits, the women hats and frilly dresses. Adlyn turned to Joyce.

'But would you jus' look at Polly Danville in all dat jewellery. And where she t'ink she going wid all dat make-up?'

Joyce pinched her mother. 'Behave.'

There was organ music coming from within. Adlyn groaned and said: 'I don' know who teach Gladys Reid to play organ. Lawd 'ave mercy on me ears.'

Joyce sniggered. The whole idea of church amused her. She only ever went when she was back in her village, and then merely as a form of entertainment. Of course, as a child, it had been as much a part of her life as breathing. Every Sunday without fail. All those Bible stories learned by rote. All those hymns sung without feeling or understanding. All those hours spent daydreaming. After so many years of religious indoctrination, secularised England had come as something of a relief. In recent times, however, as she moved into the final phase of her life, she found herself thinking more and more about those early days.

Bishop Douglas was also outside the church, meeting and greeting the faithful. He was wearing a white suit, which contrasted starkly with his black skin. Indeed, he was so black he glistened, from whence came his nickname, 'Shine'. Not yet in the pulpit, and already he was sweating.

'Mawning, sista Lou. Mawning, bredda Harol'. Praise him, praise him on dis glorious day. Mawning, sista Adlyn. And who's dis? Well, well. Nice to see you again, Joyce.' He looked at Cyrian. Unsure who he belonged to, he said: 'Mawning, young sir. Suffer de likkle children to come on to me. Not my words, but de Lawd's.'

The church was an elongated hut on stilts, with windows along both sides. There was a plaque nailed to the front, with the words Mount Moriah Pentecostal Church written in gold biblical lettering. Next to it was a loudspeaker, it too nailed on, erected so that, on Sundays at least, the unbelievers in the district couldn't fail to hear the gospel. Inside there were rows of wooden benches, many without backs. Up front was a podium, with benches on one side for the all-female choir (most of whom had already taken up their seats) and plain wooden chairs on the other side for the various church officials. Gladys was at the organ, practising her scales. Dominating the podium, naturally, was the pulpit.

The service began with a few rousing hymns, so that the congregation might warm up. Not that they needed to, sweltering as it was. Many people were already wilting. Adlyn whispered to Joyce: 'Wid all de money we t'row in collection every week, you t'ink we would have a ceiling fan by now.'

Cyrian was not having a good time. He'd not been to a church service before, and hadn't wanted to go that morning. Joyce had insisted, determined to expose him to all aspects of life in the village. As well as the heat, he had to contend with the awful singing. Then there were the deafening tambourines, plus the tuneless organ. It was all too much, and he had to refrain from covering his ears. But as the service became more spirited, he found himself gripped by the antics going on around him. Men, women and children were thrashing around and talking in 'tongues', their eyes rolling back in their heads as though they were having seizures. Many of them had to be prevented from hurting themselves as they collided with the furniture and each other. It was a real spectacle, and Adlyn, one of the few not possessed by the 'holy ghost', couldn't help herself. She nudged Joyce and said: 'Pure put on. Ah mean, look at Cleveland over dere. If only de man would show de same energy wid him grung!' Joyce almost laughed out loud.

When things had calmed down, Bishop Douglas stepped up to the pulpit. After a few praise-hims and hallelujahs, he quickly outlined the theme of his sermon: the final days. It had been heard many times. Bishop Douglas was from the old school, a Bible-thumping fire-breather who ended every sentence with 'can ah get a amen?' He'd work himself into a state of exaltation, carrying his flock with him almost into the promised land itself. Then, with their very souls in the palm of his hand, he'd lead them in prayer. Afterwards, he'd invite the 'unsaved' to approach the podium. On any given Sunday, he'd be lucky to rescue a single soul from Satan's clutches. Yet week after week he beseeched his flock. 'Knock and de door shall be open unto you. Seek and ye shall find. Step up. Step up and confess.' Which was merely the first step *en route* to being saved. Later came the baptism at the local river.

On this particular day, two people approached the podium. A ten-year-old girl bullied into it by her parents, and a man in his mid-thirties who'd been saved before but had since 'back slided'. Once again Adlyn had a comment to make. Exaggerating the facts, she said to Joyce: 'Fourt' time dis year. De man's a sinner, pure an' simple.'

Taking her cue from Bishop Douglas, Gladys began free-wheeling across the organ keys – making sounds, any sound, striving for mood. Adlyn gnashed her teeth. Pastor Morris made man and child kneel at the podium, before laying a hand on each of their heads. He then invited the congregation to join him in yet another prayer. Next came the collection, the duty of Gladys's husband, Eric, a wizened old man with few teeth. With a silver salver in his hand, he wended his way along the pews. Bishop Douglas, meanwhile, was urging everyone to 'give generously'. When Eric reached Adlyn, she deposited a single coin, then whispered to Joyce: 'It all right for him to taak about "give generously", wid him big house and big car.' Joyce smiled and put a few notes on to the salver. When Cyrian tried to do the same, Joyce put out a restraining hand. 'I put for you as well,' she said. Cyrian was crestfallen.

The service had been a long one and the congregation was now flagging. After a couple more hymns, and a final prayer, Pastor Morris thanked everyone for coming.

Outside the church, Joyce got a chance to exchange a few words with a childhood friend, a timid woman called Lulu. She

STEPHEN THOMPSON

wanted to know when Joyce would be coming home for good.
Joyce smiled non-committally. Bishop Douglas was standing
at the church doorway shaking hands and receiving praise
for his sermon. Eventually the three took their leave, Adlyn
commenting on how starving she was, a sentiment echoed by
Cyrian. They laughed and set off home.

A few days later they took a day trip to Ocho Rios, sight of
the world-famous Dunns River Falls. Joyce rented a car for
the six-hour round trip, and persuaded Neville to come along
and share driving duties. Adlyn didn't want to go, but was
badgered into it by Cyrian.

They paid their entrance fee, had their hands stamped,
and went in. Whitewashed boulders lining the walkways,
manicured lawns kept moist by sprinklers, neat flower-beds,
fat Americans pursued by higglers.

They made their way down to the beach. Adlyn and Neville
were adamant that they wouldn't be entering the water. Joyce
called them killjoys, then dragged Cyrian off to find the
changing rooms. Adlyn and Neville hurried to a remote corner
of the beach, to a patch of shade provided by an overhanging
rock. There they spread a towel, on to which they laid out all
the food they'd brought. Neither was particularly hungry, it
was just something to do.

Some time later Joyce and Cyrian re-emerged: she dressed
in an unflattering one-piece, he in a pair of knee-length
shorts. Cyrian ran straight into the water. For a while Joyce
watched him splashing around in the shallows, then went off
to find Adlyn and Neville. 'What you two doing all the way
over here?'

'Too much white people over dere,' replied Adlyn.

'Don't make them bother you,' said Joyce. 'Is your country,
after all.'

'Is it?' said Neville. 'Not from where I sitting.' They looked
along the beach, which was lined with sunbathers – a few on

16

towels, most on loungers. Beyond them, holding hands for safety, others were waiting to be guided up the falls, wearing colourful wraps, sunhats, shades.

'Well, I not going to let them ruin it for me,' said Joyce, and she went off to join Cyrian in the water. When she'd gone, Adlyn and Neville began to whine.

'Ah don' know why we couldn't go to Runaway Bay,' said Neville.

'Or Discovery Bay,' said Adlyn.

'Both of dem closer to where we live.'

'An' a darn sight less busy.'

'But you headstrong daughter mus' get ar own way as usual. Once she mek up ar mind to do a t'ing . . .' he trailed off, shaking his head.

'Wha' you know 'bout anyt'ing?' said Adlyn.

Neville mumbled something, which Adlyn didn't catch. She asked him to repeat it, but he refused. She asked him again, and before long they were bickering. They'd stopped by the time Joyce and Cyrian came over to eat, but the tension between them was palpable.

'You two,' said Joyce. 'You like a coupla love bird.' She smiled and nudged Cyrian, who was busy tearing into a fried fish.

When they'd all finished eating, Joyce was about to nod off when Cyrian started tugging at her arm. 'Come on, Mum,' he said. 'We're going up, remember?'

'Bwoy, leave you madder alone,' said Adlyn. 'You don' see she tired?'

'Why you don' go on you own?' said Neville.

'Is all right,' said Joyce. 'I promise him.'

Cyrian hauled her to her feet, almost putting his back out. They went and joined the queue for the falls. Cyrian took the hand of the person in front of him, an old American woman with freckles from head to toe. She turned and smiled condescendingly.

It transpired that the linking of hands was only necessary to negotiate the first stage of the falls, where the rocks were most slippery. After that, you were free to ascend as you saw fit. On the advice of the stewards, the majority took the safe option and crawled up on hands and feet. The others, Cyrian and Joyce among them, chose a less bestial approach.

During the ascent, Cyrian was struck by the beauty of the setting. There was a powerful central spray that forced everyone to keep to the sides. At each new plateau there were rock pools, which, surprisingly, contained fish. Trees lined the edges, with overhanging branches, through which the sun filtered to create a dazzling light show. And then there was the noise, a combination of rushing water, wind and birdsong.

It was clear to Joyce that Cyrian was having a good time, and this made her happy. She'd been meaning to take him to Jamaica since he was a child, but had been prevented from doing so by financial constraints. With his brothers such regular visitors, she knew that it hadn't been easy for him. Now that he'd finally sampled it, would he want to come back? Joyce wasn't sure, not from what she'd seen so far. Yes, he was enjoying himself at the falls, but she knew that Mount Moriah was boring him to distraction. Still, he had to experience it. Perhaps now he'd appreciate the privileges he enjoyed back in England.

They were almost near the end of their climb when a steward, sunning himself on a boulder, asked to see their stamps. Joyce immediately got angry. 'Why you don't pick on these white people? Eh? Why you bothering you own?'

The steward tried to speak, but couldn't get a word in.

'Is fool like you,' said Joyce, jabbing her finger in his face, 'who sell this country down the river. Shame on you.'

She spat at his sandalled feet, just missing them. She and Cyrian then headed for the nearest exit.

It was dark when they got back, and late. Cyrian was

asleep, his head in Adlyn's lap. Driving through Greentown, they noticed a large group of people huddled around Gladys's doorway, their faces lit up by the lamp burning within. Neville slowed the car to a crawl, but Adlyn ordered him to stop completely. He obeyed, and they all got out and walked up to the house, which was set back from the road on a slight incline. It didn't take long for them to discover what the commotion was. Gladys was dead, passed away that afternoon while having a nap. When Adlyn heard she widened her eyes and put her hand over her mouth. Neville looked heavenward and whispered: 'In de midst of life . . .' Joyce was dumbfounded, and she grabbed on to a still-sleepy Cyrian. Eric was said to be inconsolable. Standing on tiptoe, Adlyn tried to get a glimpse of him, but there were too many people, so she asked for her condolences to be conveyed, after which she and the others quietly withdrew.

In the car they began to whisper, as though Gladys were eavesdropping near by. Joyce expressed sympathy for Bunny, and wondered if he'd heard. Neville thought it unlikely, given that he lived in Kingston. Adlyn felt sure that the message was on its way. Cyrian yawned involuntarily, which was the cue for them to get going.

Bunny arrived the following night, with his wife and three children, and immediately assumed responsibility for the funeral arrangements. Eric was happy to delegate, since there were any number of things to be done, none of which he had the stomach for. It was Bunny, then, who decided what his mother would be wearing when she went to her grave. It was he who decided on the coffin, the wreaths and the tombstone. It was his decision that there should be an official 'file past' viewing, at the church, giving loved ones the opportunity to pay their last respects. And it was he who decided that there should be a procession from the church to the grave site. The only thing that he consulted his father on was the choice of hymns, which included Gladys's favourite: 'Rock of Ages'.

The nine-night was spread over three nights, though it should have been nine, hence the phrase. Wakes of that length were a drain on resources, and Bunny couldn't afford it. Nevertheless, over the three nights he managed to lay on enough of a spread to keep everyone happy.

Adlyn and Joyce turned up on the second night, for it was considered rude to show up on the first, which was set aside strictly for members of the family. In any case, it was understood that anyone too eager to visit a 'dead yard' was acting from morbid curiosity and nothing else.

They arrived to a full house. As well as Bunny and his family, there was Ned Knight and his wife Gwen, Sister Lorna, Mother Smith (Adlyn's best friend), Deacon Danville and his wife Polly, Les the postie, Neville and his friend Sam and his wife Mable, Elder Walker, JP, and Bishop Douglas.

Not much happened. There were hymns and prayers, but mostly there was idle chitchat. Bunny, however, wasn't happy. He hated the way Bishop Douglas was shamelessly holding court, taking the spotlight away from his family. At every opportunity he, Bishop Douglas, tried to make light of the proceedings. He told bad jokes and tried to jolly everyone along, insisting that Gladys would have wanted it that way. Bunny was also galled by the fact that Neville had had the temerity to step foot inside his parents' house. There was an enmity between them dating back to when they were at school together. Most of those gathered were aware of it, and it made for a lot of tension. Of the two, Neville was the more willing to let bygones be bygones. But Bunny was having none of it, and whenever Neville tried to make conversation he was openly snubbed. Joyce, too, was snubbed; partly because of her association with Neville, and partly because Bunny thought that she'd acquired airs abroad. Then there was Cyrian. Bunny was angered by his refusal to talk to his own children. They asked Cyrian any number of questions about England, all of which he stubbornly refused to answer. The wake was set to last all night, and Bunny wondered whether he could hold his tongue that long.

It would take at least five men, working in tandem. Neville could be relied upon, and he could always rope in some of his 'boys'. Thus ran Adlyn's thinking, as she decided on the best way to slaughter the pig.

The men showed up early, just after eight. Neville had brought along his two best friends, Sam and Freddie, plus a couple of his regular drinking companions, Ralph and Lance.

They were all excited about the kill, and were looking forward to taking home some choice bits of meat. There'd certainly be enough to go around, for the pig was a monster, a huge fat sow with teats so long they were practically scraping the ground. She was standing in her bamboo pen, mud-spattered, with a sly look in her eyes. The men couldn't wait to get their hands on her.

'Ready, boys?' said Neville. The others nodded their assent, and they climbed into the pen.

The sow became immediately nervous. She started grunting and snorting as the men advanced on her. Felling her would be difficult, they realised, so they improvised a strategy. One leg per man, with the spare man grabbing the neck, to which a length of rope would be attached. After that, it was simply a question of throwing the rope over a tree branch and throttling the animal to death. That, at least, was the theory. In practice, the pig gave them a torrid time. She was just too strong for them. Bucking and kicking and thrashing, she refused to be upended. Each time the men thought they had her secured, she'd wriggle out of their grasp The mudbath of a pen wasn't helping either, and the men slipped about and crashed into each other and started arguing. With their frenzied barking, Ringo and Rex were simply making things worse.

Adlyn and Joyce, standing outside the pen, were trying hard not to laugh. Cyrian, on the other hand, was wetting himself. At one point Neville said to him: 'If you had any use, bwoy, you would get in here and help. Instead you out dere, wid de women, skinning you blasted teet'.'

Cyrian laughed even louder.

Meanwhile, the pig had decided that there was nothing for it but to escape, and was now desperately trying to scale the fence. Time and again she launched herself at it, and each time she bounced off. But her attempts were having a destabilising effect on the pen, and the men realised that if she wasn't caught soon she'd simply ram it down and flee, the consequences of which didn't bear thinking about.

It was time for the women to get involved. They questioned whether the men were up to the job, called them useless, and threatened to take charge of proceedings themselves. In all their born days, they said, never had they witnessed such incompetence. Perhaps they should send for clubfoot Harold, for even he could do a better job. It was a worthwhile ploy. The men redoubled their efforts, and eventually, exhausted and covered in mud, they managed to get the rope around the pig's neck. Now it began to squeal, a sound that stifled Cyrian's laughter and sent a shiver down his spine. He suddenly remembered what he was witnessing, and from that point on he watched with his mouth agape.

It took the combined efforts of five grown men to hoist the pig into the air. As the rope tightened around its neck, it stopped squealing and its eyes began to bulge. Then, as the blood supply to its brain was slowly cut off, its death throes began. It kicked and jerked and twitched, and, after a few final spasms, was still.

The men slowly lowered it to the ground, sweat running off them. Joyce went to fetch them cold drinks from the kitchen, while Adlyn teased them about the comedy in the pen. The dogs had seen enough, and went off to find a patch of shade.

Cyrian, though, couldn't take his eyes off the carcass. He experienced a morbid desire to walk over and prod it. Adlyn thought that he'd been idle long enough, and she told him to go and fill three buckets of water from the drum at the back of the house.

'What for?' he whined.

'Nevva you min',' said Adlyn. 'Jus' do it.'

Using a razor-sharp knife, Neville made a small incision in the pig's throat, then stepped back out of the way. Moments later, a jetstream of blood shot out across the yard. Cyrian gasped, provoking laughter among the adults. Putting her arm around his shoulders, Adlyn said: 'Nice bit of hog foot for me gran'son later, yes?'

Cyrian gagged.

The 'draining' completed, Neville ran the knife along the pig's stomach and opened her up. Her innards came spewing out, hot and squelchy and rotten smelling. Adlyn gathered them up, then went and fed them to the dogs. Cyrian watched them wolf down the treat, then ran to the back of the house and vomited. When he came back, he saw that Neville was in the process of severing the pig's head. He couldn't watch any more, and ran inside the house and closed the door. Laughter all round.

'Dat bwoy is a real joker,' said Neville.

'You leave him be,' said Adlyn.

Neville wouldn't let it drop, and soon he and Adlyn were trading insults. Joyce smiled, then used the buckets of water to wash away the mess.

By mid-afternoon the guests had arrived. There weren't many. Despite pressure from her mother, Joyce had insisted on keeping the numbers down. The chosen few were Neville, Mother Smith and her daughter Daisy, and Lulu.

Most of the pork had been salted and stored away. The rest had been cooked in a variety of styles: jerked, deep-fried, and boiled. There was rice and hard food to go with it, and home-made lemonade. Everything was on a table in the yard, attracting flies. Paper plates and plastic forks were the order of the day. Self-serving was encouraged.

Surrounded by so many women, Neville couldn't relax. He tried talking to Cyrian, but found him monosyllabic and standoffish. He'd met Joyce's other two sons and liked them, but he thought Cyrian was rude. The women, meanwhile, were in free flow. Daisy (at thirty, the youngest of the women) was talking about the differences between New York and London. She had lived in the one and visited the other and thought they were similarly unfriendly. All in all, she preferred the Caribbean. Lulu just wanted to travel, it didn't matter where to. Jokingly, she said she was still waiting for Joyce to invite her to England. Joyce said that she was welcome any time. Mother Smith said that her days of travelling were long past, and that the only place she wanted to visit was the promised land, to be near her beloved husband. Adlyn laughed and told her that she'd have a long wait, at least another twenty years.

'Don' be so sure,' said Mother Smith. 'Gladys was a pickney nex' to me, and she gaan areddy.'

'True,' said Lulu, 'and she wasn't even poorly.'

'She get a good send-off, anyway,' said Joyce.

'Is Eric I feel sorry for,' said Adlyn. 'De poor man don' know if him coming or going.'

Neville and Joyce started making eyes at each other. Cyrian noticed, and scowled. Neville then went off to the toilet. When he came back, he found the women still discussing Gladys. They paid him scant attention; so, irritated, he walked over to the table and helped himself to a plate of food. He was soon joined by Cyrian, who looked at the food but didn't try any. The slaughter was too fresh in his mind, and he wondered whether he would ever eat bacon again.

'Don' be a eediot, bwoy,' said Neville. 'Eat a piece of de meat. It won' kill you.'

Cyrian turned up his nose and went and sat on a flat rock

by the kitchen. Ringo and Rex approached him, wagging their tails. He put an arm around each, and they tried to lick his face. Neville looked over at the women. He tried to catch Joyce's eye, but saw that she was engrossed in the conversation. She had her arm linked in Adlyn's, and it made Neville yearn for his own parents. He quickly finished eating, then walked over to the women. 'Well, ladies, is time ah was getting along.'

The women protested, for form's sake.

'Sorry, but ah must go home and work. Not all of we can stan' aroun' all day gossiping.'

The women were outraged. Neville laughed.

'Well, Joyce,' he said. 'Dis is goodbye, I s'pose. Tek care of youself, you hear? See you in . . .' He paused. '. . . whenever.'

Laughter. Joyce said: 'You will see me a lot sooner than that, mister. Tonight, in fact.'

The other women pricked up their ears, as did Cyrian.

'Tonight?' said Neville.

'You going to Sam's tonight, right?' Neville nodded. 'Well, I coming to have a farewell drink with you.'

'But is wha' get into you?' said Adlyn. 'Sam place? Dat den of iniquity?'

'Oh, shut you mout', Adlyn Young,' said Mother Smith. 'Mek she go and enjoy arself. You ac' like you nevva have a drink in you life.'

Adlyn sputtered, 'But . . . but . . . but . . .' then threw her arms in the air and gave up.

'See you later, den, Joyce,' said Neville, and he bid them goodbye and set off down the hill.

Once he'd gone, the women got comfortable. Adlyn brought out some chairs and they arranged themselves around the table in the yard, where they remained talking and eating till dusk. Cyrian found the experience mind-numbingly boring, and was relieved when, finally, Mother Smith and Daisy said that they were leaving. Before they went, Mother Smith made everyone

join hands and bow their heads. Mercifully for Cyrian, the
prayer was short. Mother Smith asked God to look after 'Joyce
and Cyrus' and to smooth their passage back to 'Inglan''.
There were hugs, then mother and daughter left. Soon it was
time for Lulu to get going, but not before Joyce had given her
a cardigan and some money. 'God bless you,' she said. 'Tek
care of youself till we meet again, awright?' Joyce hugged and
kissed her and she left.

Neville, Freddie and Lance were in a corner playing dominoes.
Nearer the entrance, Ralph and Barsey were at a table playing
cards. Sam and Mable were behind the counter, sitting quite
some distance apart, looking bored.

When Joyce walked in she got a round of applause. 'Oh,
shut up,' she said, then walked up to the counter. Leaning
across it, she said: 'Sam. Mable. How things?'

The couple shrugged bashfully, clearly honoured by her
presence. She looked across at Neville. He said: 'One minute.
Mek ah just finish dis han'.'

'No rush,' said Joyce. 'Evening, boys.'

'Evening, Joyce,' the men chorused.

They were all drinking Dragon Stouts. Joyce bought them
a round. While Mable served the drinks, she started looking
around the place. It was as dark and cavernous as ever, with
the same old almanacs and Pepsi-Cola signs and sparsely filled
shelves. Mischievously, she said to Sam: 'All de money you
mek down de years, you can't do up de place, Sam?'

'Awks him again,' said Freddie.

Sam smiled. Mable said: 'So you leaving tomorrow?'

Joyce nodded and sipped her Red Stripe, which Mable had
poured into a glass. The men all drank from bottles.

Neville finally left his game and joined Joyce at the bar.

'Da's right,' said Freddie. 'You sweetheart here now, so you
don' want to know we no more.'

He nudged Lance and chuckled. Lance said: 'Yes, Mr

Neville, but remember, when she back in Inglan', is we same one you going to crawl back to.'

Neville shook his head and said: 'Grown men. Grown men acking like pickney. Come, Joyce, mek we go over here where dem can't bodder we.'

The others laughed. Neville and Joyce went and sat at a secluded table near the back. In fact it wasn't a table, but a downturned barrel, with two high stools placed next to it.

After a couple of false starts, the conversation got under way. Joyce wasn't relishing going back to work, and wished that she could be staying longer. Neville was now seriously concerned about Joe, and had all but made up his mind to pay him a visit. 'Somet'ing just not right, Joyce. Ah can feel it.'

Joyce told him that he must follow his instincts, and invited him to stay at her place. He nodded, but didn't actually accept. There were issues between them, they both knew it, and his staying with her might complicate them. The truth was, if and when he did arrive in England, he was banking on being able to stay with Joe. Joyce, for her part, found it amazing that he should be acting so coy. Circumstances had conspired to give them another chance, yet once again he seemed bent on squandering the opportunity.

They'd been childhood sweethearts, and it had been expected, not least by Adlyn, that they would eventually marry. It wasn't to be. After school, Joyce had been determined to start a new life in England whereas Neville vehemently opposed the idea. It caused a lot of quarrels between them and in the end, likening Neville's obstinacy to that of a 'jackass breed by a mule out of a donkey', Joyce had emigrated alone.

While disappointed there hadn't been a wedding, Adlyn respected, and indeed admired, her daughter's decision, and she heaped abuse on Neville for not grabbing the chance to go abroad and 'better' himself. Suspecting a conspiracy, Neville became bitter towards both women.

Years later he married Charmaine, the daughter of his

parents' closest friends. He had been happy enough, if only because Charmaine hadn't spent her time dreaming of foreign lands, the fascination for which he had never understood. After all, a lot of these places were said to be cold enough to 'freeze eye water', as Sam had once put it.

His had not been a love marriage. It had been commonly known (and neither he nor Charmaine had said anything to the contrary) that he still carried a torch for Joyce. Nevertheless, when Charmaine finally lost her fight against breast cancer, not even the most cynical in the village had questioned the depth of his grief.

He had lost all pride in himself and had taken to wandering the village dirty and unshaven, his hair greying prematurely. He wallowed in self-pity, became sullen and grumpy. Naturally cantankerous, he started to fly off the handle at the slightest provocation. A farmer by trade, he abandoned his crops to thieves and weeds, and sold what little livestock he possessed for next to nothing. The house his father had built he allowed to fall into disrepair. And on top of everything, he started drinking.

He carried on in this vein for close on two years. Adlyn finally intervened, feeling he'd mourned long enough. She paid him regular visits and verbally slapped him around. 'Get over it, man,' she ordered him. 'Do like me. Busy youself. Do some work. Your problem is you too damn lazy. Stop feeling sorry for youself de whole time.' When her bullying tactics failed, she appealed to his vanity. She told him that he'd become the laughing stock of the village, and how rumours were rife that he'd been 'obeahed'. That had done it. Within weeks Neville had managed to pull himself back from the precipice. He felt indebted to Adlyn for all her help, and they'd since become close; but he could neither forgive nor forget the part she'd played in Joyce's leaving.

It was gone midnight when they left Sam's, and they were light-headed without actually being drunk. Although it took him out of his way, Neville insisted on walking Joyce home. It was a fairly long walk, most of it completed in silence. At one point, Neville felt an urge to take Joyce's hand, but he feared looking silly, and so resisted. Joyce detected his hesitancy, and, for the second time that night, was annoyed that he wouldn't seize the initiative. A little while later, they arrived at Adlyn's. A dull lamplight burned in her window at the top of the hill.

'Adlyn waiting up,' said Neville.

'I know. You'd think me was twelve.'

They stared into each other's eyes. The moment was perfect, the setting flawless: moonlight, twinkling stars, a chorus of crickets.

And yet . . .

'Well, goodbye, Joyce.'

'Goodbye, Neville. Was nice seeing you.'

'Who knows, we might see one anodder again soon.'

'I hope so. You take care of youself.'

They found it difficult to part. Finally, Joyce turned and started climbing the hill. Neville watched her for a while, then said: 'Have a safe trip.'

Without looking round, Joyce said, 'Mind the duppie man on the way back,' then carried on up the hill. Neville smiled, shook his head, then left. When he got home, he sat up for a while drinking and thinking. The thought of Joyce returning to England made him feel sad and lonely; and, as often happened whenever he felt lonely, his parents came to mind.

He'd always been very proud of his parents, proud of the way they had risen to become two of the most prosperous people in the village. Through sheer hard work they'd managed to build themselves a decent house, owned a vehicle, and could even afford to send their children to school. Consequently, there had been some in the village who thought they had airs. Aware of the talk, they kept themselves to themselves, which, of course, simply confirmed what was being said. From a very early age, then, Neville had been aware of what his parents called 'bad-mind people'.

Their routine was simple. They owned a few acres of fertile land and would work it from dawn till dusk. That was one of Neville's most abiding memories: his parents, in the field, hoeing and digging and planting, aided by himself and Joe. Depending on the season, they grew almost everything: yams, sweet potatoes, dasheens, cocos, okra, skellion, tomatoes, thyme, peppermint, sorrel, bananas, sugar cane, lemons, avocados – not in any great quantity, but more than enough to feed the family. They also had some livestock – chickens, goats, pigs.

So food was never a problem, but money was a constant worry. There just never seemed to be enough, and Neville could remember how his parents were forever dreaming up schemes to earn cash. His mother made dresses for the village women. His father hired out his pick-up. They sold surplus crops. And still they had struggled to make ends meet. Neville remembered the day that his mother hit upon the idea to start selling their goats' milk. Immediately she had risen in the family's estimation, for in the village this was definitely a niche market. The word quickly spread, and for a time they had done really well. Most of the villagers were sick to death of condensed milk and before long they were lining up outside the Forbes' roadside stall, which Neville and Joe would man on occasion, after school. The success of the venture had surprised the family no end, and Neville could recall how his parents used to genuflect nightly to give thanks and to ask for continued prosperity. Ironically, the money they earned was used to buy (among other things, such as rice, flour and granulated sugar) condensed milk.

For about a year the business had flourished, but gradually it began to founder from too much credit and talk that the Forbes, in a greedy attempt to maximise their profits, were watering down the stock. Neville remembered how angry his

parents had become when they heard the baseless ru...
and how quickly they had closed the business. He could
hear the exact words that his mother had used. 'Dat will teac...
de ungrateful so-and-sos a lesson.' Of course, money had once
again become a problem, especially for the boys. They saw
their pocket money halved, and treats, such as only money
could buy, were once again denied them. Neville and Joe had
argued for the reopening of the business, but their parents had
been resolved, united in the belief that a degree of privation
was nourishment to the soul. And that was how Neville liked
to remember them: as proud, defiant, God-fearing people who
didn't suffer fools gladly. How he missed them. He wondered
whether Joyce knew how lucky she was to have at least one
parent still alive.

Once her luggage had been loaded onto the roof of the bus,
Joyce was anxious to be on her way. But Adlyn was bent on
delaying the moment for as long as possible. It was always
the same. The tears, the overlong hugs. Cyrian, already in
his seat, wondered if he might ever get back to England. He
liked his gran, but she was making a spectacle of herself. It
was the driver who rescued Joyce. He honked impatiently on
his horn, and she used it as her excuse to tear herself away.
Adlyn was left snivelling at the roadside, waving frantically as
the bus moved off. Staring at her through the window, Joyce
was heartbroken . . . again.

CHAPTER ONE

Dilys had just left work. She'd had a hard day, spent most of it on her feet. One service wash after another had left her worn out. She was in a hurry to get home. It was important she got in before Sean. There was his dinner to cook, his bath to run. To save time, she took the short cut through the town centre.

She arrived home and quickly set about her evening tasks. To combat the damp smell, she went around opening all the downstairs windows. Afterwards, she made herself a cup of tea. She'd barely finished it before she realised that it was time she got the dinner on. 'No rest for the wicked,' she muttered to herself. Once she had the food (beef stew) simmering on the cooker, she went upstairs to run Sean's bath. He came in moments after she'd turned the taps off. Her timing, as usual, had been perfect.

Sean had evidently been gardening. There was caked mud in his hair, on his face and arms, and under his fingernails. Dilys was having a hell of a job scrubbing him clean, and wasn't helped by his fidgeting and squirming and splashing water everywhere. 'For heaven's sake, Sean, keep still.' She lathered soap into his face. 'How the Bishops can have the gall to send you home looking like this, I just don't know.' The doorbell rang. Sean immediately tried to leap out of the bath. 'You stay right where you are,' said Dilys, drying her hands. 'Now who on earth . . . ?' Curiosity getting the better of her (she never had callers), Dilys fairly ran down the stairs. When she opened the door she almost fainted. Just then Sean appeared behind her, wrapped in a towel, dripping water on to the already musty old carpet. Within seconds of seeing the visitor his eyes rolled in his head, his body began to convulse, and he collapsed in the hallway.

'Wha' de raas . . . !' Neville shrieked. Sean began to kick and twitch and groan, frothing at the mouth, his face ghoulishly contorted. Instantly, Dilys pinned down his arms and legs, made sure that he didn't swallow his tongue. Neville stood gawping, incredulous. 'Anyt'ing me can do?' he asked. She ignored him and attended to Sean. It was a full couple of minutes before Neville realised that he was still holding his two suitcases. He quickly set them down, as though, under the circumstances, it was the right and proper thing to do, the respectful thing. He felt useless. He kept turning in circles, looking about for anyone that might be happening along. Then he saw that Sean's eyes had returned to normal, that his convulsions had all but ceased.

'Anyt'ing me can do?' he repeated.

'Yes,' said Dilys. 'Help me carry him upstairs.'

Half an hour later they were having tea in the living room.

'Well, ah mus' say, Beelzebub himself woulda feel hurt by a welcome like dat. Him going to be all right?'

'Yes,' said Dilys. She quickly changed the subject. 'Why didn't you let us know you were coming?'

'You right. I shoulda drop you a line.'

And yet he hadn't. Why? Had he seriously expected to find Joe at home? That's what he'd hoped for, though he had known all along that it was unlikely.

'Him not here, is it?'

'No,' replied Dilys, and she went on to explain that she hadn't seen Joe in more than two years, and had no idea where he was. He'd simply upped one day and left, or rather he'd gone to work one day and not bothered coming home. She neither knew where he was nor cared. She meant no offence, but if she never saw him again she'd die happy. And in case he, Neville, was wondering, no she hadn't gone looking for Joe, or reported him missing to the police.

'You serious?'

'Yes.'

'But why not, for heaven's sake? You don' care dat somet'ing mighta 'appen to him?'

'No.'

Neville looked at her, incredulous.

'My God. T'ings mussa been really bad 'tween de two of you.'

'That's putting it mildly.'

They stared at each for a few seconds before Neville looked away, towards the window. It was not a pretty view outside. A jungle of tall weeds blocking the light. When Neville turned round again, he caught Dilys staring at him. She seemed spooked. 'Unbelievable,' she said.

'Beg you pardon?'

'The likeness.'

Neville ignored the reference. In the present context, it seemed inappropriate. He thought a while, his eyes fixed on the grey carpet. He wasn't exactly warming to Dilys, and more than anything wanted to tell her so. Dilys searched for something in the room to look at other than his balding pate. She settled for the flying ducks above the mantelpiece, made a mental note to straighten the one second from the left. In fact she was suddenly conscious of the state of the entire room: the threadbare carpet, the bare bulb dangling from the ceiling, the moth-eaten net curtains. One of these days she would get around to . . .

'An' you have no idea where him is?'

'None whatsoever.'

'So mek ah get dis straight; you saying him jus' up and leave?'

'Would appear so, wouldn't it?'

'But surely him wouldn' do dat. Him wouldn' jus' run out 'pon him own family.'

'Really? And when did *you* last see him?'

Neville averted his eyes, became pensive. Thirty years. Thirty long years. He didn't know what to say, or do. He felt foolish, angry. He rose to leave, gathering up his suitcases. Dilys thought that he looked pitiful. 'Where are you going?'

'London.'

'Got family there, have you?'

'Not exac'ly. A frien'.'

'This friend expecting you?'

Neville shook his head.

'You're welcome to stay the night.'

'Oh, no. Ah wouldn't want to impose.'

'And I wouldn't let you. Just seems a bit silly you travelling all the way up to London tonight.'

Neville weighed up his options. What if he did go to London and Joyce wasn't in? He could always phone and check. But did he really want to speak to her at that moment?

'Well, if you don' min',' he said. 'P'raps ah could stay jus' de one night.'

Later that night in bed, in the spare room, he tried to formulate a plan of action. He would find Joe if it was the last thing he did. But where would he begin his search? He had practically nothing to go on, and decided to sleep on it. Much to his frustration, he couldn't get off. The unfamiliarity of his surroundings was keeping him awake. In the country not even a day and already he was itching to leave. This was his first trip abroad and he was feeling desperately homesick. He missed the boys, he missed Adlyn, and he wondered what they were up to back home.

As he struggled for sleep, other thoughts came to him. From his initial impression, he didn't think much of Dilys. She'd shown not the slightest bit of concern for what might have happened to Joe. Perhaps it was this very cold-heartedness that had driven Joe away. The marriage must have been in tatters for years. Yet in his letters Joe hadn't mentioned it at all. In fact, he'd led Neville to believe that his marriage was a model of stability. He hadn't told the truth about Sean, either. Neville had met a shy, epileptic simpleton, but had expected someone confident, healthy and bright. No wonder Joe had ignored all requests to bring him to Jamaica for a visit. He was obviously ashamed of him, ashamed of his own son. And judging by the looks of her, he couldn't have been that proud of his wife, either. What a life, thought Neville, as he drifted off.

CHAPTER TWO

Neville came down the next morning to find a note from Dilys on the kitchen table. *Gone to work (Sean, too). Hope you had a good sleep. Make yourself at home. See you this evening. D.* Neville was confused. There was not a trace of hostility in the note. Perhaps he'd misjudged D.

Once he'd showered, dressed and had some breakfast, he found himself at a loose end. He'd woken with the notion that he might visit his brother's old workplace. Since they were supposedly the last people to see him, he was hoping that Joe's former work colleagues could tell him something – anything. But without an address his hands were tied, and he couldn't contact Dilys for it because she hadn't left the number, or the address, where she worked. So there he was, stuck in the house, with the entire day ahead of him, and no thought as to how he would spend it. He thought about calling Joyce, but somehow the timing didn't seem right. For something to do, he went on a tour of the lower part of the house.

He began with the kitchen, which had access to the back garden. It was in a terrible state. The lino was cracked and peeling and turned up at the edges. The units were decades old, with doors hanging off their hinges and drawers missing. Neville dared not touch the work surfaces, which were coated with a thick layer of congealed grease and what looked alarmingly like mouse droppings. The sink was encrusted with limescale, as were the taps. And to cap it all, there was a heavy smell of gas in the air, which Neville traced to the ancient cooker. He wondered how anyone could prepare food in such a place. It was a far cry from what he'd expected, and it was difficult for him to imagine Joe living in such squalid conditions.

Covering his nose, he looked through the window. It was a sunny autumn morning, so he decided to get some fresh air. The moment he stepped outside, a huge Alsatian pounced on him. Barking, growling and baring his teeth, he backed Neville up against the low garden fence. Terrified, Neville stood perfectly still. No sudden movements, he told himself. No sudden movements. It occurred to him what a pair of harmless creatures Ringo and Rex were.

Just when he was beginning to think he'd be stuck in the garden all afternoon, the dog calmed down, and even began to wag his tail. Realising that he was being mistaken for Joe, Neville made his move. He reached forward and gingerly stroked the dog on the head, while at the same time tiptoeing round it and heading stealthily for the back door. Just before he entered the house, he suddenly felt as if he was being watched. Because he wasn't yet free of the dog, he waited till he was safely ensconced inside before he turned and looked back through the kitchen window. A woman was standing in the garden next door staring at him, her expression totally inscrutable. Neville was convinced that he was looking at a 'duppie', and he lowered his gaze and said a quick prayer. When he looked up again the woman had gone. Just then he noticed two wooden platforms atop a couple of poles. Strange that he hadn't seen them earlier. He couldn't work out what they were. He was about to step away from the window when, out of the corner of his eye, he caught sight of something else, propped up against the garden shed. 'Good God in heaven!' he cried, and fled the kitchen.

He'd barely reached the hallway when the doorbell rang. He froze, trying to decide whether to answer it. He could see the front door from where he stood. It had two frosted glass panels, and the person's outline was clearly visible. Which meant they could probably see him as well. As if to confirm this, the doorbell rang again. Collecting himself, he went and answered it. When he saw who it was, his heart leaped from fear. It was the woman in the garden.

'Hello,' she said. 'I'm Valerie.'

Neville didn't respond in any way, merely stared.

'I had to come over.'

Still no reaction.

'You're Neville, right?'

That snapped him out of his trance, but still he said nothing.

'Joe mentioned you.'

'You know my bredda?'

She paused before responding. 'He was my neighbour. We said hello.' She shook her head slowly, then added: 'The likeness is amazing.'

Neville studied her. She was dressed frumpily, but wasn't bad looking. In fact, compared to Dilys, she was quite pretty. Guessing at her age, he reckoned early fifties at the most.

'You're on your own at the moment, right?'

Neville nodded. Valerie smiled and said: 'Don't talk much, do you?'

'Wha' you want me to say?'

Neville knew her type. The nosey neighbour.

'Look, if you get lonely, pop over for a cuppa.'

'A what?'

'Cuppa tea.'

'Oh. T'anks very much, but . . .'

Valerie was already walking away. Neville watched till she reached the other side of the hedge that divided the front gardens. Before going in, she smiled and said: 'Maybe I'll see you later, then.' Neville didn't respond, so she opened her door and went in. For a moment he stood there, looking at her house. Though identical in style, it was in a much better state than Dilys's, the front walls covered in wisteria. Neville tried to picture the interior, but no image came to mind. Feeling slightly chilly, he stepped back inside and shut the door.

He went upstairs to his room to unpack. He could have murdered a Dragon Stout, even at that early hour. Distractedly, he began putting his things away in the various storage spaces: chest of drawers, bedside cabinet, wardrobe. He then squeezed his battered suitcases under the bed out of the way. He was determined, at least while he was staying with Dilys, to make an effort at tidiness.

It had never been his strong point, unlike Joe, and as a child his parents had lectured him about it constantly. Adulthood had brought about no change in his conduct. Clearing away his mess had almost driven Charmaine insane. For a time, after Charmaine died, Adlyn had tried to shame him into cleaning up his house, all to no avail. 'You can't teach old dawg new trick,' she said. But her efforts had not been completely wasted, for it made him realise just how much she cared for him.

With Dilys not due home for at least another five hours, Neville, becoming increasingly bored, decided to go snooping in the upper part of the house. He went first into Sean's room, situated at the front. He discovered nothing in it of any interest. It was a depressing little room, monastic, with hardly anything in the way of possessions. He walked over to the window to assess the view. The house (the last in a row of eight) stood on the edge of a busy road, which had vehicles speeding along it in both directions. On the far side of the road was a field, fringed by a long hedge. To the left was the town centre, just about visible through a cluster of trees. To the right was more open land, patches of it cultivated.

Next came Dilys's room. It was at the back of the house, and therefore quieter than Sean's. Neville stepped inside, closed the door behind him, then stood with his back against it taking in what he saw.

The room was twice the size of his own, with considerably more light. It was also very tidy. The bed, for instance, had been made with the kind of attention to detail that he associated with hotels – neatly arranged white pillows, evenly hung quilted bedspread. There wasn't a thing out of place on the dressing table. The lace curtains, drawn wide apart, framed the window with near-perfect symmetry. The sky-blue carpet, though faded and threadbare in parts, was without blemish, and had clearly been vacuumed that morning. The row of shoes in the gap under the wardrobe appeared to have been arranged according to colour – browns, blues, blacks. The one photograph in the room (framed, black and white, showing a stern-faced man and a pale, timid-looking woman) was positioned dead centre on the left bedside cabinet. An ornate carriage clock was placed with equal precision on the right, next to a volume of verse: Emily Dickinson's complete works. Even the wicker chair in the far corner looked as though it had never been sat on. It was the kind of room in which a burglar might defecate.

Neville walked to the window and looked down on the back garden. The Alsatian was having a snooze, his head on his huge front paws. He was a beast of a dog, with long matted fur, and Neville decided not to go near him again. Summoning his courage, he looked again at the thing propped up against the shed. Second time around, it didn't appear so frightening. Studying it more closely, he realised that it was a half-finished wood sculpture, a bird of some sort, frozen in animation. One leg had been completed, plus the tail and half of one wing, but nothing else, rendering the whole thing macabre, monstrous. Over four feet high, it dominated the back garden like a hideous mythological sentinel. Neville presumed it to be Sean's handiwork. What a strange boy his nephew was. He'd clearly been touched; though by what, Neville couldn't say.

He looked beyond the perimeter fence. Immediately the other side of it was a copse, and after that a meadow. He looked into Valerie's garden. But for the clothes on the collapsible washing line, it was neat and tidy, with a patch of lawn surrounded by wilting flowers. Farther along, the other gardens were done up in various styles. One had a greenhouse. Another had a patio. There were two with artificial ponds. And a couple had decking. And what did Dilys's have? Crazy paving.

Coming away from the window, he opened the wardrobe and peered inside. An overpowering smell of mothballs forced him to pinch his nose and step backward. There was a shelf at eye level, on top of which were four stacks of towels. Hanging below the shelf were maybe a dozen frumpy-looking dresses. On the wardrobe floor, taking up more or less the entire space, was a metal trunk, or chest. Crouching, Neville ran his palm across the lid, disturbing a thin layer of dust. As he did so, he saw her in his peripheral vision, standing behind him, slightly to his right. He pretended he hadn't, buying time to think up an excuse. None came to him. It crossed his mind how absurd he must have looked, on all fours, with his nose in the wardrobe. He felt undignified. There was only one thing for it – move, get up. He started to do so and she hit him. Twice. Although he knew that he'd been struck, and where (at the back of the head), the force of the blows didn't really register, neither did the pain. In fact, as he toppled over, just before the darkness closed in on him, he had but one thought on his mind. Joe.

When he came to he was lying on his bed. His immediate thought was to wonder how he had got there. Surely she hadn't carried him. She might be strong, but ... He felt the back of his head. Oddly, there was no pain. A dream, then. A vivid dream. He checked his watch. It was showing six o'clock. Impossible, he thought. He couldn't have been asleep for eight hours. Then again, he'd hardly slept a wink the night before. He felt his head again, this time kneading it thoroughly with his fingertips. Definitely no pain. And yet he couldn't believe he'd been dreaming. One by one, he went over the morning's events. He was certain that everything up to and including his unpacking actually took place. To make doubly certain he sidled across to the edge of the bed and felt under it. There they were, his two battered suitcases. He was less certain about what had happened after he'd unpacked. Did he lie down? Was it then that he started thinking about Adlyn? How long was it before he fell asleep? Did he fall asleep? Or did he . . . of course, he thought, and he leaped out of bed.

Outside Sean's room he paused for a moment, composing himself. After a couple of deep breaths he slowly pushed the door open. Teenage clutter, lots of glossy posters featuring birds of various species, a caged bird with a splintered wing cheeping feebly. He'd dreamed the whole thing after all. Relieved, he leaned against the doorpost and smiled. Just then he heard the front door slam. His old fears instantly returned. He stood still and silent on the landing, immobilised by a premonition that some evil was about to befall him. Dilys shouted his name three times. Panicking, he crept back to his room and quietly shut the door. He heard Dilys mounting the stairs, her footfalls heavy, ominous. He heard her walking along the landing. She shouted his name again. He didn't answer. He couldn't, no more than if he were mute. His heart almost gave out when she rapped on his door. He prayed she wouldn't open it. She didn't. He heard her carry on down the landing. Although he knew that she'd gone, he was compelled to check. Gingerly, he opened the door.

'That you, Neville?'

This time he had to answer. 'Yes,' he croaked.

'Thought you were asleep. Come down here, tell me what sort of day you've had.'

It was an order. He started dragging his feet along the landing, as though he were lame. He finally reached Dilys's room, but he couldn't see her, even though she was directly in his line of vision, sitting on the edge of her bed, hunched forward slightly, putting on her slippers. He felt like running, but his legs had gone, turned to jelly. He had to grip the door frame to stay upright. He couldn't believe his eyes. The room was exactly as he'd seen it in his dream, right down to the dust motes.

He heard her voice. It sounded far away, getting stronger by the second. She kept repeating the same word over and over. Devil! Devil! Devil! Then he sensed himself being shaken, violently. Weak as he felt, he offered no resistance. Her voice again, bellowing now. Devil! Devil! Neville!

'Huh!'

'For God's sake,' said Dilys, fraught. 'What's wrong?'

'Huh?'

'Right. Let go of that.'

With some difficulty, she prised his fingers from the door frame. His knees wobbled.

'Steady now. Lean on me.'

She put his arm around her broad shoulders. He felt her power as she wrapped one arm around his waist.

'Can you walk?' He nodded, uncertainly. His head felt light, swimmy, as if he'd been drinking. He could have been on his way home from Sam's. 'Come on,' said Dilys. 'Let's get you downstairs. Cuppa tea's what you need, Mister.' They staggered off down the landing, she propping him up like a wounded soldier on his way to the sick bay.

It was an accumulation of things. He was jet-lagged, unaccustomed to flying, had had very little sleep the night before. Shaky, but it was the most plausible explanation he could invent. He had to keep the truth from Dilys. He didn't trust her. More than that, he feared ridicule. Dilys knew that he was lying, but she kept up the pretence anyway, played the game.

Neville told her about his near-fatal encounter with the dog. She laughed, and told him that his attacker was called Major. He was pleased that she'd seen the funny side. It relaxed him, to the extent that he felt able to tell her about Valerie.

'You spoke to her?'

'Yes,' said Neville. Anticipating the next question, he said: 'In de garden.'

'Nosey cow. She's got far too much time on her hands, that woman. Was different when Harry was alive.'

'Harry?'

'Her husband. Dead. Prostate cancer.'

That word. Cancer. Even now, after hearing it so many times, it struck terror into Neville's heart. He asked Dilys about the two wooden poles.

'Sean. He's a bird-lover. Leaves food out for them.'

Neville thought that it was a strange hobby. Where he came from people killed birds and ate them. Here, people fed them. Where was the fun in that? He asked Dilys about the thing that he'd seen propped up against the shed.

'Oh, you saw that? Scary, eh? Sean's been chipping away at it since he was a child. One day he might even finish it.'

Just then Sean burst into the room, bristling with youthful energy. He'd forgotten about Neville, and when he saw him he lowered his eyes and slunk back out.

'Be patient with him,' said Dilys. 'He'll get used to you.'

'Poor bwoy. Must be very strange for him.'

'It's a strange situation for all of us,' said Dilys. She let Neville think about it for a while, then said: 'You know, I just can't get over the likeness. Joe used to say that if you two were standing side by side no one could tell you apart. Now I know what he meant.' Neville smiled, as though he'd been paid a compliment. 'Anyway, if you'll excuse me, I must go and run Sean's bath.'

'You mean him can't run him own bath, big grey back bwoy like dat?'

Dilys smiled and left. While she was out of the room, Neville fell to thinking about Sean. Imagine a child his age being so heavily dependent on his mother. As far back as Neville could remember, he and Joe had fended for themselves. Their parents had encouraged it. By age ten they could wash, cook and iron. Sean probably couldn't boil an egg. Neville had seen his type before. Back home they called them simpletons. There was

47

probably not that much wrong with him. He just needed some company, a friend his own age, or a brother, someone with whom he could while away the hours. Neville tried to imagine what it must feel like to be an only child, and couldn't, since Joe featured in all his earliest memories.

In many ways theirs had been an idyllic childhood. In the absence of a TV, they were driven outdoors and forced to devise their own entertainment. If allowed to roam, they'd get into all sorts of mischief. So mostly they had been confined to the yard, where they'd play marbles, or cricket, using dried lemons for balls. Once they even constructed a swing, out of an old tyre and some rope. Not that they used it much. Joyce had made it her own. If they tried to get her off it, she'd run crying to their parents, who were very fond of her. As she was an only child, they encouraged her to come by as often as she liked. Not a day passed when she didn't pay them a visit. She had the run of the place, and would invariably stay over. Often she'd stay for days, and Adlyn would be forced to come and check on her. At other times, her surrogate parents had to remind her that she actually lived somewhere else. They used to leave it as long as they could, not wanting to hurt her feelings. But she was an extra mouth to feed, and they were not made of money. Deprived of Neville's company, she'd be heartbroken for days, and would only perk up when she would next be allowed to stay at his house.

Later that night, after dinner, they settled down to watch TV. Dilys and Sean were cuddled up together on the sofa, like a couple. Neville was soon restless, having a very short attention span. What he wouldn't have done for a few bottles of Dragon. He pictured Sam's bar, could clearly see the boys lined up along the counter, the kerosene lamps swinging from the sooty beams above their heads.

Dilys brought him out of his reverie. Would he like her to change the channel? No thanks. In fact, if it was all the same to her, he thought he might go to bed. But it was not even ten. True, but he was planning an early start in the morning; which reminded him, was there any chance he could get the address of the factory where Joe used to work? She had a better idea. Why didn't they go into town together; that way she could point him in the right direction? He didn't want to put her out. He wasn't, though she did think that he was wasting his time.

'Maybe. Well, goodnight, den.'

''Night.'

'Goodnight, Sean.'

Sean kept his eyes on the TV.

Neville hadn't gone to bed to sleep. His intention was to clear his head, sort out some of the issues swirling around inside it. He thought about Joyce, and decided that he must call her the very next day. Her offer to put him up was now looking very attractive. He couldn't spend another night under Dilys's roof. She was finding his presence in the house too upsetting; though, to her credit, she was doing her best to be accommodating. She really was a strange woman. What had Joe seen in her? She was hardly attractive. Her mousey locks were cropped too short, which Neville thought made her look butch. He also thought that she too tall. At five ten, he was no dwarf, but she was giving him at least two inches, and had twice his bulk. There was just no other way to describe her. She was a big woman. As well as her ample bosom, she had broad shoulders, huge arms, prominent hips, and sturdy legs. Even her hands were big, with long, fleshy fingers. Where Neville came from, such hands were called 'stranglers'. As for her taste in clothes, she favoured dresses that were little more than sacks, and cardigans at least a couple of sizes too small. On her feet, she wore nurse's shoes. Neville didn't like to judge, but all things considered, couldn't Joe have done better?

CHAPTER THREE

Sean was a creature of habit, a trait that he had inherited from his mother. He rose every morning at seven. After breakfast, he'd go out to the back garden and feed Major. He'd then spend a few minutes replenishing the feed on his bird tables. During the process, if he was lucky, a few of his feathered friends might swoop down and peck the seeds right out of his hand. This always gave him a real thrill, and he'd take the time to enjoy the moment. Back indoors, he'd make himself a packed lunch of cheese-and-pickle sandwiches, with an apple and a banana. He used to make a Thermos of tea, but the Bishops had persuaded him not to bother with it. He could drink all the tea he wanted at their place. Neither did he have to bring his own lunch, they said. But he was never going to agree to that.

His route to work never deviated. There were several alternatives, each one a short cut, but he preferred to stick to the main road. This took him past the local cricket field, with its sight screen, practice nets and dilapidated scoreboard. Then he'd pass the overgrown pond, beside which was a disused scout hut, and beside that a cow gate with a sign announcing access for ramblers. Next came the boarding school, set in acres of undulating lawns. As a child Sean had dreamed of going there, and was envious of the pupils who did. Beyond the school, he'd walk for a while along a grassy verge, mindful of passing vehicles. This particular stretch of road was notoriously dangerous for pedestrians, especially in wintry conditions.

By now he could see the Bishops' place, perched on a hill.

But there was still some walking to be done before he reached it. He had to pass all those mock-Tudor mansions, some of which were screened from the road by tall box hedges, others by rows of silver birch. Every one of them had a name, usually referring to an animal. The Warren, for example, or Badgers' Lodge. Each had its own grounds, and a gravelled driveway with the very latest cars parked out front. Passing by, Sean always kept his head down, for fear of being spoken to.

The Bishops lived in a daunting neoclassical stately home, with an austere stone façade and an imposing portico. The grounds were similarly spectacular. Designed in the style of an eighteenth-century French chateau, it comprised eight acres of water meadows and picturesque gardens, which included a formal parterre, a marble fountain and an orangery.

Most of Sean's work took place outdoors. He was essentially a handyman, but the Bishops never used that term to describe him. His working for them had never been intended as a permanent arrangement. Dilys had only agreed to his helping them out occasionally as a means of getting him out of the house. But she soon discovered that there was no end to the number of 'little jobs' requiring his attention on their sprawling estate. She felt that he was being exploited, and would have put a stop to it but for the fact that having him occupied during the day made her life easier.

His tasks varied from day to day, and might include any-thing from cutting grass to painting to unclogging drainpipes. There was usually something for him to do, and if not, the Bishops liked to have him about the place just in case. At these times, he was free to do as he pleased, and would wander the estate lost in his own world. Often he'd end up in the woods, armed with an old pair of binoculars that the Bishops had given him. He'd find himself a comfortable spot, usually at the base of a tree, and while away the time watching birds: song thrushes, linnets, bullfinches. This was how he had found the injured chaffinch, its wing snapped almost at a right angle.

Alerted by its distressed call, he discovered it lying under a pile of leaves, belly up. With extensive knowledge of the species, he could tell immediately that it was a young female. Very gently, he scooped it up in his palm and headed back to the house. In the old servants' quarters, he set about constructing a splint. It was a fiddly job, one requiring intense concentration. Attaching it to the bird's wing was slightly easier. The little thing seemed to know it was being looked after, and didn't put up a struggle. Later, on his way home, Sean had made a detour into town and bought a small cage from the local pet store. When he had got in, Dilys said: 'Who's this, then?' He smiled and replied: 'Lucky.'

Neville woke with a start, roused by Dilys knocking on his door. He had asked her to, the night before, but her shouting 'Wakey, wakey' he thought was completely unnecessary.

The factory was farther away than he'd imagined, only just within walking distance. It was on the northern edge of the town centre, part of a mini-industrial estate. Next to it was a low-rise housing estate, called Gorswood Close. It consisted of four blocks of flats, which had been erected around a concrete courtyard, in the middle of which was a children's play area: swings, a slide, a sandpit, a roundabout, a six-seater rocking horse. A few mothers and toddlers were making use of the facilities. Neville could tell right away that this was the poor part of town.

He walked into the factory, accosted the first person he saw, and was hastily directed to the manager's office. He had to cross the factory floor to get to it. Heads turned, as they had when he and Dilys had walked through the town centre that morning. It was something he could never get used to, and he wondered if Joe had. Now he knew how Pinkie, the albino from his village, felt.

The manager, busy fielding a call, couldn't help him. He

was new in his job. The supervisor, two doors along, was the person he should speak to.

'Joe! Oh my God!'

Neville wasn't expecting a woman, and such a young, pretty one at that: blonde, cherubic, twinkling eyes. 'No,' he said. 'Him twin.'

The supervisor widened her eyes. 'Oh, yes. Yes, of course. I remember him mentioning you a couple of times. My goodness, you look so much alike.'

Neville wasn't listening. He'd noticed something stuck to the phone on the desk, perched atop the receiver. It was some kind of furry creature, a squirrel perhaps. It was buck-toothed, had two black beads for its eyes, another for its nose, and claws made out of green felt. In fact it was green all over.

'Please,' said the supervisor. 'Take a seat.' Neville sat down. 'Christina Moyles. Pleased to meet you.' She reached her hand across her untidy desk. Neville shook it, his grip loose, unaccustomed to shaking hands with women.

'Neville Forbes,' he said. Christina pointed out that she already knew his surname. He smiled.

'So. How is Joe? More importantly, *where* is he?'

'Dat's wha' me come about.'

He watched her closely for a reaction. Nothing, except a genuine look of confusion.

'I'm sorry, I don't understand.'

Neville told her. When he'd finished she leaned back in her chair and said: 'So that's what happened.'

A young woman entered the office, waving some papers. She was evidently surprised to see Neville, but did her best to conceal it.

'Sorry, Chris,' she said. 'I didn't know . . .' She looked round at Neville. 'All right, Joe?'

'This is Neville,' said Christina. 'Joe's twin.'

'Really? I didn't know Joe had a twin. Well, well. They don't half look alike. Don't you think, Chris?'

Neville smiled. He'd forgotten what a fuss people made over twins.

'Is there something you wanted, Dawn?' said Christina.

'Huh? Oh, sorry, no, it can wait. Nice to meet you, erm . . .'

'Neville.'

Dawn smiled at him and left.

'Sorry about that,' said Christina. 'Now where were we?'

'You nevva bodder try an' fin' out wha' 'appen to Joe?'

'Actually I did. I called his house a few times, and left messages. His wife finally called back and said that he was no longer living there.'

'Da's all she say?'

'Yes. And I knew better than to ask for explanations.'

'Soun' like you know ar quite well.'

Christina laughed. 'Know of her would be more accurate. This is a small town. People talk. You hear things.'

She could see that Neville wanted her to elaborate, so she obliged. She wasn't being funny, Dilys being his sister-in-law and everything, but it was common knowledge that she wasn't all there. Neville thought about it. If Christina was alluding to madness, he'd seen no evidence of it.

'Oh yes,' said Christina, warming to her theme. 'There's supposedly a long history of mental illness in that family.'

She told Neville about Dilys's parents, both dead. Apparently, the mother was a notorious occult follower whose spectral figure was often seen at night stalking the local burial ground. The father was more conventionally insane, driven mad by some terrible event in his past, the exact nature of which was never truly established. It was said that he had never left the house in more than twenty years.

Neville waited a second or so, making sure Christina had finished. Then, trying not to laugh, he said: 'You don't say?' What he'd been told seemed so fanciful as to be almost comic. The phrase 'Carry go, bring come' suddenly popped into his head. It was an old Jamaican term for gossips and rumour mongers, a breed he had no truck with, having suffered so badly at their hands. 'Ah was wondering,' he said, 'if any of Joe old colleague still working 'ere.'

'Most of them are. Why?'

Maybe they could tell him something. For example, where Joe went after work that day.

'Maybe,' said Christina. 'But it was over two years ago. I wouldn't get my hopes up, if I were you.'

Hope. It was all he had.

'Come on,' said Christina.

She led him to a production line manned by about a dozen men. As soon as they saw him they started whooping and cheering and passing remarks in pathetic Jamaican accents. He was appalled to think that Joe might actually have encouraged them to behave towards him in such an insulting fashion. During the commotion, he noticed that one of the men (youngish, ginger hair) hadn't said a word, nor had he stopped working. Christina eventually silenced the others, then proceeded to explain who Neville really was and the purpose of his visit. Sadly, none of them could help him. As far as they could remember Joe left the factory that day bound for home. They wished Neville all the best in his search, expressing their hope that he found Joe safe and well. Joe was a nice fellow, said one man. Absolute salt of the earth, said another. Neville thanked them (feeling guilty for having judged them so harshly), then he and Christina let them get back to work.

Before she said goodbye, Christina echoed the sentiments of her staff. She, too, was very fond of Joe, and she hoped nothing bad had happened to him. She'd like Neville to keep her informed of developments, and if there was anything she could do to help, anything at all . . . Neville thanked her and left.

He went straight to the police station. He'd noticed it while walking through the town centre that morning. It was a single-storey red-brick building sandwiched between an estate agent and a funeral parlour.

The young officer at the front desk took down the essentials of his business. There was a sluggishness about him that Neville found insolent. He behaved as though the job of being a police officer were beneath him. Neville couldn't understand why he'd been put out front to deal with the public when he seemed to lack basic communication skills and common courtesy. He refused to make eye contact, for example, and was clearly irritated by Neville's accent. His long neck and upturned nose only seemed to add to his air of lofty disdain. He finally finished writing and buzzed Neville through to a side room to await another officer.

Neville was soon joined by a uniformed sergeant, a short, heavy-set man in his mid-forties. He was carrying a clipboard.

'Morning, Mr Forbes,' he said, extending his hand.

Neville shook it and said: 'Good morning.'

'My name's Sergeant Pettifer. Very pleased to meet you.'

'Likewise,' said Neville. This man, he thought, should be on the front desk. The officer drew up a chair, invited Neville to do the same. They sat opposite each other, separated by a small Formica table, beneath which their knees were almost touching. A barred window, set high in the wall, afforded a modicum of light.

Sergeant Pettifer rested the clipboard on the table and said: 'First of all, let me take this opportunity to welcome you to our little town.'

'T'ank you very much,' said Neville.

'I also understand it's your first visit to this country.' Neville nodded. He liked the way the sergeant was conducting the proceedings. Here was a man, he thought, who clearly placed great store in doing things properly. 'Well, I hope you enjoy your stay,' said the sergeant, diffidently, and he lowered his voice before adding, 'despite the circumstances of it.' He paused, then said: 'Now, before we proceed, is there anything

I can get you – a cup of tea, maybe?' So it was true, after all. The English really were obsessed with tea.

'No t'anks,' said Neville. 'If it all right wid you, Sergeant, ah would like to get on.'

'My thoughts exactly.'

Sergeant Pettifer removed a pen from his breast pocket in readiness to record Neville's statement. 'Now then, Mr Forbes . . .'

'Please. Call me Neville.'

Sergeant Pettifer smiled. 'OK, Neville, tell me everything, from the start.'

Neville cleared his throat and began. There wasn't much to tell. He and Joe had been writing to each other fairly regularly over the years, but in the last couple of years Joe's letters had dried up. He thought something must be wrong, hence his visit.

'I see,' said Sergeant Pettifer. He quickly wrote something down. 'What made you so sure something was wrong?'

'Joe is me twin brodder.'

'Oh. I didn't . . . Identical?' Neville nodded. 'Good. That takes care of the description.' The sergeant made some notes, then said: 'So what have you discovered since you arrived?'

'Nutten, except dat Joe wasn't getting on with him wife.'

'How do you know that?'

'She arself tell me. Ah staying wid her at de moment.'

'Your sister-in-law?'

Neville nodded.

'And her name, please?'

Neville told him and said: 'Me surprise you don' know ar.'

'Why, is she famous?' asked the sergeant. He was being serious, and when he noticed Neville smiling he said: 'I've only been stationed here a couple of months.' Neville thought that he sounded offended; either that or he had no sense of humour. 'OK. Let's establish the facts. Do we know when your brother was last seen?'

At approximately 6.15 p.m. on 27 January 1999.

'Where was he last seen?'

Leaving the factory where he worked.

'And who last saw him?'

A group of his colleagues.

The sergeant wrote everything down, then said: 'All that will have to be checked. So why didn't –' He peered at his notes 'Dilys come to us before?'

'She say she don' want to fin' him.'

'Things were that bad, eh? Ah well, we won't dwell on it. You're here now. Better late than never. Are you sure I can't get you something?'

'No, t'ank you.'

'Right, then. Let's change tack slightly. What about relatives?'

'What about dem?'

'Might he have gone to stay with any?'

Neville thought for a while. It seemed a really obvious thing to consider, and yet it hadn't even crossed his mind. It was a possible explanation for Joe's disappearance, but not a probable one. Yes there were relatives dotted about the country, but they were such distant ones . . .

'No, Sergeant, dere's no relatives.'

Sergeant Pettifer wrote down his answer.

'How close would you say you and your brother were, Neville?'

'Quite close. Why you ask?'

'Do you think he'd tell you if he had a mistress?'

'Wha'? You not suggesting . . .'

'Please don't take offence. We have to explore every possibility. So, tell me, did he ever mention anything like that in his letters?'

'No,' said Neville, emphatically, resenting the insinuation.

'In his letters, did your brother ever mention being in dispute with anyone?'

'No.'

'And you don't know of any person or persons who might want to do your brother harm?'

Neville shook his head. Sergeant Pettifer noted his response, then said: 'Right, then. That's it. We're done. For now. If you'd like to sign your statement for me . . . just there.' He handed Neville the pen and clipboard. Neville scribbled his signature in the designated space. 'Have you got a photograph of your brother?'

'No, but Dilys might.'

'Find out, please. It would help a lot.'

The sergeant stood up, prompting Neville to do likewise.

'So wha' 'appen now?'

'Procedural stuff. I'll fill out an official Missing Persons report, which will then be entered on to our computer database and circulated to all the police forces in the country. It'll contain a detailed description of your brother, including photograph – if you can let us have one – as well as his last known movements. In the meantime, we'll start making one or two enquiries. In as much as we can, we'll try to keep you informed of the progress we're making. But it's my duty to tell you, Neville, that these things have a habit of dragging on, sometimes for years, and when they are finally concluded, if they are, then the outcome is not always a happy one. I'm sure I don't need to spell out to you exactly what I mean.' Neville smiled grimly. 'Here's my card. You can reach me on that number most days. If for some reason you can't, I'll get any message you leave. How long are you planning on being in the country?'

'Me have a t'ree munt' visa.'

'Oh, so you'll be around for a little while at least. What's the number where you're staying?' Neville told him and he wrote it on his clipboard. 'OK, now don't forget. Ring me if you have any information.'

'Don' worry, ah will ring.'

'Well, goodbye, Neville. I hope everything works out the way you want it to. Stay here for a second. I'll go through and buzz you out. See you.' Neville waved him goodbye.

Seconds later he heard the door buzz and he pushed it open and walked through to the front desk. The young officer was still there, pretending to read an official-looking document. ''Bye, then,' he said, looking up briefly. Neville kissed his teeth as loudly as possible and walked out.

When he got outside he stood for a moment on the steps, examining the sergeant's card. Sergeant David Pettifer. He tucked it away in his pocket and looked out across the town square. Once he'd spotted the launderette, he relaxed and took in some of the other sites.

In terms of size, the town centre wasn't much bigger than Mount Moriah. But there were certainly more people, and many more shops. Neville read some of the names. Somerfield's. Wine Rack. Blockbuster Video. Dominating the square was a huge stone monument, a memorial to the fallen of both world wars. Next to it was a clock tower, surrounded by a circular flower-bed. Dustbins, benches and period streetlamps completed the picture.

Neville saw a couple of tiny old ladies walking towards him, arm in arm. They slowed as they approached the station. Neville noticed that they had blue hair. They gave him the once-over then walked on, whispering to each other. And that's when it suddenly hit him, the unrealness of his situation. There he was, thousands of miles from home, in a foreign country, all alone, being gawped at everywhere he went as though he had four heads. Perhaps Joe really had run off, he thought, fed up with being constantly stared at.

He walked across the square to the launderette, and found Dilys embroiled in an argument with another woman. They seemed to be on the verge of swapping blows, so he hung back, watched and listened. Like most men in that situation, there was a part of him that wished they would just get it on. It would have been a fair old scrap. They were a good match, roughly the same age, height and build. Dilys had a slight advantage in that her arms were bigger. There was obviously a history of bad feeling between them, for they kept bringing up old disputes. Neville soon learned the cause of the present one. The woman was accusing Dilys of deliberately ruining her mother's clothes. She was threatening to get the authorities involved if Dilys didn't a) accept liability, and b) agree to compensation. Dilys told her 'hell would freeze over' before she did either thing, at which point the woman turned to leave and bumped into Neville. She looked him up and down, then breezed out. Dilys explained who she was. Her name was Becky Marshall, and they'd been enemies since school.

'She did look really vex,' said Neville.

'Like I care. What're you doing right now?'

'Nutting.'

'Fancy a liquid lunch?'

'A wha' kin' a lunch?'

'Come on.'

At that precise moment, Sean was getting ready to have his own lunch. The Bishops had invited him to join them in the house, but he wanted to eat his sandwiches outside. He'd spent the morning cleaning out the coal cellar, and craved fresh air. So he went and sat on a bench overlooking the croquet field, which down the years had gone to seed. There he could watch the many furry creatures scurrying about in the tall grass. They no longer hid when they saw him, so frequently did he use that spot. The squirrels were especially bold, and would often walk right up to him begging for food. Sometimes he'd bring nuts for them specially.

Mrs Bishop, walking with a stoop, brought him out a glass of squash. 'Is everything all right, Sean?'

'Yes,' he replied.

'Are you sure?'

'Yes.'

'Things all right at home?'

'Yes.' He sipped his squash.

'OK, then. If you're sure. But just remember, you can talk to either one of us about anything that might be bothering you. Anything at all. Understand?'

He nodded, and Mrs Bishop went back inside.

He felt guilty. He hadn't told the truth. Things were not all right at home. His father had come back, but was pretending to be someone else. He didn't understand, even though his mother had tried to explain. She'd lied to him. She'd told him that his father was never coming back. But he had, and now everything was ruined.

'God,' said Dilys, looking around. 'The Crown. Can't remember the last time I was in here. It's where me and Joe used to . . .' She caught herself, looked at Neville. Taking in the décor he seemed oblivious.

'So dis is de famous English pub?' he said.

'What d'you think?'

'It not so great.'

Dilys laughed.

'No,' she said. 'This one could do with brightening up. There's more dust in this carpet than on a building site.' She demonstrated by stamping her foot into the brown carpet, sending a plume of dust rising into the air, which made Neville sneeze. 'But it's always quiet, and the beer's good. Cheers!' She and Neville touched glasses.

'How she jus' a look 'pon you like dat?' asked Neville. He was referring to the middle-aged barmaid. She was supposed to be pulling a pint for the old man in the granddad cap who was sitting on a stool in front of her, but she seemed more interested in Dilys.

'Madge Winters. Mutton dressed up as lamb. Just look at her, showing off her boobs like that. At her age.'

'She really a look 'pon you 'ard.'

'Let her look. She probably thinks you're Joe. I know she always had a thing for him, the cow. I've had some battles with that woman, I can tell you, especially over Sean. When I think what her son did to him it makes my blood boil.' She shook her head at the memory. 'I feel so guilty that I wasn't able to protect him more.'

She told Neville about Sean's brief period in school, about how the other children had made his life a misery. They'd teased him mercilessly, calling him 'half-breed' and making fun of his epilepsy. Dilys said she had gone berserk when she had found out. She had visited the parents of each child and engaged them in slanging matches. One of them was Madge Winters, whose son, Billy, had been Sean's tormentor-in-chief. However, despite all her efforts, and perhaps because of them, Sean's ordeal had continued unabated. In the end she'd made the decision to keep him at home.

Dilys finished speaking and sipped her pint. Neville felt the pressure to respond, but couldn't think of anything to say. There was a long, uncomfortable silence, which Dilys finally broke. 'So, tell me, how did it go this morning?'

'So, so,' he replied, and he sipped his beer. She realised he wasn't going to elaborate.

'Is that it?' she asked.

Perfunctorily, he explained how he'd come away from the factory feeling a bit downhearted. But after speaking to the police his spirits had been revived a little.

'You went to the police?' She made it sound like a betrayal. He almost apologised.

'Yes,' he said. 'Jus' before me come to see you. Ah taak wid a very nice sergeant.'

'Did you, now. About what exactly?'

He paused before answering. He didn't like the way the conversation was going. It was starting to feel more like an interrogation. His. 'Me had to ansa a whole loada question.'

It was the biggest hint he could have dropped, but it went over her head.

'My name come up?'

'One or two time.'

'Why?'

'Dem need a photo of Joe. Me tell dem you might 'ave one.' Her unflinching gaze unnerved him. 'You 'ave any?'

'What?'

'Photo?'

'Somewhere.'

Now that he'd gained the upper hand he sought to press home his advantage. 'Any of Joe ol' clothes at de house?'

'Why?'

No, no, no. He was doing the questioning, damn it. 'A yes or no will do.' He smiled, not wishing to appear confrontational.

'There's some stuff in the attic, I think.'

'Min' if me look t'rough dem?'

''Course not. What're you looking for?'

'Ah see dat it starting to get col', an' ah don' bring no warm clothes wid me.'

Dilys studied him. He was a funny one, not at all like his brother in many ways, but so like him in others. Certainly they shared the same fondness for drink. But where it made Joe aggressive, Neville simply became talkative. His tongue loosened by the beer, he was soon rambling on and on about the most intimate details of his life.

He spoke of his parents, and said he missed them dreadfully. He said he also missed his wife, and expressed regret that they hadn't been able to have children. Dilys was tempted to ask the reason, but suspected that any revelation would be later regretted. He talked about his friends, about Sam and Freddie in particular. They were the two best friends a man could have, he said. He talked about Adlyn, saying that she was as much a mother to him as his own departed one. If only she would learn to relax, control that tongue of hers, they might actually get on. He talked about Joyce, about how close he'd come to marrying her and how he often wondered what things might have been like had he done so. He talked about Joe, at which point Dilys pricked up her ears. He said that as children he and Joe had been practically inseparable. When Joe went away, first to Kingston and then abroad . . . . 'Excuse me,' he said, dabbing his eyes.

'You all right?' asked Dilys.

Close to tears he couldn't go on. Dilys was embarrassed and touched all at once. She watched him trying to recover his dignity, and was forced to revise her earlier judgment.

'You're not like Joe at all,' she said, then elaborated. In all the years that they were together, she had never once heard Joe speak with such openness, such passion. And as for all the people Neville had just mentioned, she hadn't heard of a single one of them. Joe never talked about his life in Jamaica, as though he were ashamed of it. She'd ask, but he was always vague, evasive. Soon she learned not to pry. After all, it was his life.

'But him did mention me, right?'

Although he knew the answer, he needed to hear it again.

'Yes. He mentioned you.' She thought for a while, then said: 'Often.'

'You don' 'ave to say dat.'

She smiled. 'And what about me? Mention me in his letters, did he?'

'You mean you nevva get a chance to see dem?'

'Told you. It wasn't my place to pry.'

Neville sipped his beer. 'Him mention you, of course. And Sean.'

'Saying what?'

Neville had to think about it. Over the years the letters had painted conflicting pictures. There was an old Jamaican saying that best described it: sometimes coffee, sometimes tea.

In other words, things were fine one minute, horrible the next. But the overall message seemed to be one of contentment.

'When you say horrible, you mean he told you about our marriage problems?'

'Good God, no. You youself say how vague him was. No, ah mean in general terms. Life in England, dat kin'a t'ing.'

'But you said he wrote to you about us.'

'Da's right.'

'Well, what did he say exactly?'

'Put it dis way, it was quite clear to me dat he was devoted to you and Sean.'

'Ha! Devoted? Don't make me laugh.'

Neville waited a moment, then said: 'Ah can see now that him mislead me.'

Dilys didn't respond. She was elsewhere; sitting with Neville, even looking at him, but elsewhere.

They didn't realise how tipsy they were until they got outside. Hit by the fresh air, they had to grab on to each other lest they topple over like a couple of bowling pins. Neville couldn't believe Dilys was even thinking about returning to the launderette. She should stop her 'foolishness' and come home with him. Dilys laughed, partly because of the ludicrous suggestion that she should take the rest of the day off, and partly because of the unwitting double entendre.

'But you not in a fit state to work,' Neville protested.

'I'll be all right.'

'You sure?'

'Yes. I'm more worried about you. Think you can make it back to the house?'

'No problem,' he said, and his legs wobbled slightly.

'OK, then. I'd best be getting back. See you shortly. And mind how you go.'

'You too. And t'anks for de . . . wha' you call it again? . . . liquid lunch?'

They giggled, then went their separate ways.

Neville decided to take the scenic route, which Dilys had pointed out to him that morning. 'You can't get lost,' she'd said. 'All you have to do is follow the road.'

He had no burning desire to see the narrow-boats on the canal, or the Roman footbridge, or the golf course with the rolling greens, or the heritage guest houses, or any of the other sights that Dilys had told him to look out for. His intention was to try to walk off the effects of four pints of lager, for the route was not only scenic, but long. Dilys had warned him about this. To attempt the walk, she'd said, one had to be in the right frame of mind, not to mention a reasonably good state of health. Forty-five minutes into the journey and Neville was beginning to understand what she meant, for he was dismayed to find himself meandering along a narrow, seemingly unending country lane whose tall hedges not only dwarfed him but also had the unsettling effect of appearing to be closing in on him. Only after he'd cleared them was he able to take in the panoramic views, and then he wasn't that impressed. He found the landscape too flat and the sky lacking in drama. Still, he was glad he'd gone that way, for although he reached the house exhausted and struggling for breath, at least he'd sobered up.

The attic was packed to the rafters. Neville could barely move for stuff. He couldn't even begin to imagine where amongst it all Joe's clothes might be. If only he'd remembered to ask Dilys. That's what drink does to you, he thought. He stood there bemused, wondering where to begin, the skylight throwing a spot over him, as though he were on-stage. He noticed a stack of cardboard boxes almost as tall as himself. As good a place as any, he thought, and took the plunge.

As luck would have it, the very first box he opened contained some of Joe's old shirts and trousers. Every item was musty and mildewed, and would need several washes before it could be safely worn again. One by one Neville removed them from the box, lifting them scornfully with his thumb and forefinger.

He lingered over a pair of thick brown corduroys. Perfect, he thought, except for the blasted turn-ups. He suddenly remembered that it was a style Joe loved, even as a boy. He, on the other hand, saw it as a waste of material, useful only for gathering dirt. It was just one of the many things over which he and Joe had differed, over which, as children, they had secretly argued. It had to be in secret because of the constant pressure on them to agree on everything, to be alike in every conceivable way, to be, in effect, one person. It was a myth that their parents worked extremely hard to promote. They dressed them in matching clothes, insisted that they went everywhere together and put up a united front, and invariably referred to them not by their names, but as 'the twins'. Yet it had been obvious to most people how different they were. Joe was the naughty one – manipulative, prone to tantrums when he failed to get his own way. Neville was much the quieter of the two, so introspective in fact that his parents had suspected abnormality. They had him examined, first by the local bush doctor, who made him drink an infusion of foul-tasting herb tea, and then by the local GP, who tapped his chest a few times and got him to say 'aaaah'. Neither had found anything wrong with him, leading his parents to the comforting conclusion that he was quiet not through any mental deficiency, but because 'him waters run deep'.

Neville had doted on his 'big' brother, who was older than him by ten minutes. Joe, for his part, couldn't stand Neville's puppy-dog devotion, hated the way Neville was always under his feet. He found the attention both a burden and an obstacle to his freedom, and longed for some time alone. He had finally got it at school.

That was when they began to drift apart. For the first time they had separate friends, pursued separate interests, led separate lives. Indeed there was a period when they didn't see each other at all. When the time came for them to go to high school, Joe got invited by his aunt to go and live with her in

Kingston. He readily accepted, and his parents were happy for him to have a different experience. They weren't to know that he had an ulterior motive for wanting to go, but the truth was that he'd tasted freedom from Neville and wanted more. It was this same desire to put distance between himself and Neville that eventually took him abroad. Neville had been devastated, almost bereft. He felt abandoned, rejected, and resented Joe for years. After a while, though, that resentment had given way to nostalgia, and he began to wonder if they'd ever be reunited. Now here he was, actually staying with Joe's family, yet wondering the same thing.

The turn-ups would have to go, he decided. He began inspecting them to see whether they'd been stitched into place or were the type that could simply be turned down and ironed. As he ran his finger along the inside of the left fold, he discovered a scrap of paper with a telephone number on it.

The phone rang three times before the answerphone came on. He listened to the message, then hung up.

If he hadn't been so tired he would have gone straight back to the factory. Instead, he went up to his room, stretched out on his bed, and allowed himself to succumb. The plan was to take a short nap, half an hour at the most. He was out for two hours and woke up feeling even more tired. He swung his legs over the side of the bed and sat up, groggy with sleep. The sunlight poured in through the window. He closed his eyes for a second, protecting them from the glare. When he opened them again he heard a strange squawking sound, and a sort of light tapping, as though someone were knocking on the window. Funny, he thought. He went to investigate, and got the fright of his life. Crows: at least half a dozen, perched on the windowsill, pecking at the glass with their long bills. Horror-struck, Neville backed away from the window, and as he did so he noticed that there were spots of blood forming a trail on the carpet, leading from the window to where he currently stood. To stifle a scream, he put his hand over his mouth, and discovered that he had a nosebleed, his first ever. Cupping his palm under the flow, he fled to the bathroom.

Washing his face, he reflected on how his superstitious nature had again got the better of him. As a boy he'd been obsessed with portents and omens. Birds getting into the house was one of the more terrifying. It meant that there'd been a death in the family. He blamed his parents, of course. Time and again they would threaten to set the 'duppie man' on him if he didn't carry out his chores, or behave, or do well in school. Did they know that at age forty-eight he'd still be jumping at his own shadow?

While he was in the bathroom, the doorbell rang. This time he didn't have to guess who it was.

When he opened the door Valerie took one look at him and started sniggering. Only then did he remember that he had bits of tissue stuffed up his nostrils. He quickly removed them, relieved to see that the worst of the bleeding was over. 'Excuse me,' he said, then disappeared inside to dispose of the bloodied tissue. When he returned, he said: 'Sorry 'bout dat. Had a likkle accident.'

'Oh? Nothing serious, I hope.'

'No, no.'

An awkward silence, quickly broken by Valerie. 'Thought you might have popped by the other day.'

'Erm . . . yes.' He suddenly remembered his manners. 'Look. You want to come inside?'

Valerie shook her head vigorously. 'I don't think that's a good idea. You see, the thing is . . .' and she proceeded to explain why Dilys wouldn't appreciate it. As she spoke, Neville looked her over. She had dark brown hair, streaked with grey. The last time he saw her, she'd been wearing it down. Today it was up, and it drew attention to her slightly long face, which was subtly painted. She was wearing a red tartan sweater and a brown, pleated, A-line skirt. Below, she had on a pair of brown tights, and some sensible black shoes with a gold buckle and flat heels. 'Much better if you came to mine.'

'Huh? Erm . . .'

'Of course, if you're busy . . .'

He looked at her. She shuffled her feet, arms folded: waiting. 'Two second while ah get me shoes.'

Entering the house, he was immediately struck by how little clutter there was in the hallway. There was nothing except a few pictures on the wall and a table with some fake flowers. No shoes, no mountain of junk mail, no broken-down coatstand, no mildewed umbrellas, no bric-à-brac, and definitely no dirt, all of which could be found next door in Dilys's hallway.

They walked through to the lounge, which had a white shag-pile carpet. Neville was asked to remove his shoes, and he realised that he was dealing with one very fussy woman. When Valerie left to make tea, he quickly sat in an armchair, for fear of disturbing anything. Looking around, it was difficult for him to imagine a more ordered room.

The fireplace had all the necessary accoutrements: a basket full of logs, a scuttle full of coal, two pokers, a shovel, a pair of tongs, and a bellows. Above the mantelpiece, there was an oval mirror with a gilt frame, with not a fingerprint in sight, while the mantelpiece itself was lined with ornaments: glass cats, china dogs, mounted plates. There were mass-produced watercolours on the walls, depicting various aspects of rural life, each with the same coloured frame. The matching three-piece suite was upholstered in blue and white checks, and was stainless. Similarly, the white wallpaper, with its blue fleur-de-lys motif, looked as though it had just been hung. There were standard lamps in the corners, with blue velvet shades fringed with gold tassels. The windows were framed by floor-to-ceiling drapes, made from a heavy blue material. A TV and video sat snugly in a corner, next to a magazine rack, which was stuffed with copies of the *Radio Times*. On the smoked-glass coffee table was a copy of the *Daily Mail*, and a bowl of potpourri.

Valerie came back, carrying a china tea set on a wooden tray. As she began to pour, Neville asked: 'What's dat t'ing?'

Valerie smiled. 'It's called a tea cosy. Keeps the pot warm. Milk and sugar?'

'Yes, t'ank you.'

'How many sugars?'

Neville looked at the dainty cups, which had gold rims. 'Three.'

'My goodness. We have got a sweet tooth.'

Valerie served him his tea, poured herself a cup, then sat down. 'Help yourself to biscuits, by the way.'

Neville grabbed a couple of Jaffa cakes, which were on a plate in a neat ring. Valerie sipped her tea and said: 'So. Just visiting, are we?'

'Yes. Ah come to see Joe, but . . .' He nibbled at his biscuit. '. . . well, ah s'pose you mus' know all about it.'

Valerie shook her head.

'Wha', you mean to say you haven' notice dat Joe not aroun' any more?'

'Of course I have. But as to the reason . . .' She trailed off.

Neville explained. In the middle of it, he noticed how calm Valerie seemed, as though she were not really listening. When he'd finished, she waited a moment, then said: 'I see. So that's it.' Neville instantly regretted telling her. 'I'd just assumed they were . . .' She groped after the right word '. . . separated.' She sipped her tea. 'And her theory's that he ran off?'

'Yes,' said Neville, reaching for another biscuit.

'But you don't believe that, right?'

'No.'

Valerie waited to see if he would elaborate, but he seemed more taken with the biscuits.

He was savouring each mouthful, as though trying to decipher the ingredients.

'Where do *you* think Joe is?'

Neville shrugged. He was tempted to have another biscuit, but didn't want to appear greedy.

'I'm sure you'll find him,' said Valerie, and she paused before adding, 'eventually.'

After that the conversation all but dried up. Neither knew what to say to the other. They made attempts – Neville praised the house, and Valerie expressed a desire to visit Jamaica – but mostly they sat smiling at each other. When he could stand it no more, Neville made his excuses and left. Before he went, Valerie made him promise to visit again soon.

Dilys came home and found him in the living room watching the early evening news, his nostrils stuffed with tissue. After he'd left Valerie, the bleeding had started again. Could it have been connected to Dilys's house? he'd wondered, superstitiously.

'Oh my God! What happened?'

'It dus' start bleed for doh reason,' said Neville, nasally.

'Dear oh dear.' Dilys shook her head. 'Can't leave you alone for a second, can I? Here, let's have a look at that.'

Holding him by the forehead with one hand, she tilted his head backward, then, using her other hand, she removed the bloodied tissue. She peered into his nostrils.

'Well, it looks as if the bleeding's stopped.'

'Me really sorry,' said Neville, 'but me get a likkle blood on you carpet upstairs. Ah wash out most of it, but . . .'

'Don't worry. Cuppa tea?'

'Dat would be nice,' he said. Dilys left him and went out to the kitchen.

Sean had just left the Bishops', looking like a chimney sweep. The dirt from the coal cellar was in his hair and all over his face. The Bishops had advised him to have a wash, but he'd told them that he preferred to save it for his bath. They were worried about him. It wasn't so much his quietness, or his need to be alone. That they were used to. What concerned them was his recent tendency to linger after hours, as though he didn't want to go home. Now they were having to coax him.

Edward: 'Off you go, then, Sean. There's a good chap.'

Margaret: 'Yes, run along now. You know how your mother worries.'

And off he went, reluctantly, his Tupperware sandwich box tucked under his arm.

He idled as he walked, stopping on occasion to watch birds as they flew by overhead. He saw some wagtails soaring on an air current. There must have been two dozen, flying in a Y formation. He tried to count them, but they were gone before he got to ten. He loved wagtails, and became really excited whenever they showed up at his feeding tables. He really enjoyed watching them, and could do so almost indefinitely. Of all his visitors, he thought that they had the most character: black and white feathers, bobbing heads, endlessly wagging tails, hence the name.

He passed the last mock-Tudor mansion and saw a car coming towards him. He recognised it, and became immediately nervous. It was an old Ford Capri, haring along at nearly twice the forty-mile-an-hour speed limit. As it raced past him, he caught sight of the driver: Billy Winters. He prayed that he wouldn't stop, but at the crest of the hill, a few yards shy of the Bishops' place, the car screeched to a halt. Refusing to look round, Neville heard Billy fighting with the gears, and then the unmistakable sound of a car travelling in reverse. When it pulled up alongside him, he quickened his step. The insults came thick and fast. Nig-nog. Half-breed. Spastic. He did his best to ignore them, but when Billy said something about his mother he turned and began to approach the car. As always, Billy waited till he was near, then sped away, laughing. Sean stood in the middle of the road and watched the Capri disappear over the crest of the hill. Seconds later he was beeped by another car, approaching from behind. He didn't hear it and the driver was forced to swerve. 'Get out of the road, moron!' Only then did he come to his senses. Hugging the verge, he continued on his way.

Soon he was home. Tentatively, he poked his head into the front room. He saw Neville and was about to escape when, in a voice full of authority, Neville said: 'Come 'ere to me, bwoy.' Sean obeyed. He walked slowly across the room and stood before Neville, his head bowed, as though he were about to receive communion. Neville studied him closely, looking for resemblances to Joe. The nose, perhaps, and possibly the chin, but other than that . . . In fact, seeing him up close this way, Neville realised that he was quite odd looking. His hair, for instance, was a strange hybrid of straight and curly, with a peculiar orange tint to it, while his complexion was a pallid shade of green. And how big he was! Six feet at least, with his mother's wide arms and broad shoulders. 'You nuh 'fraida you uncle, is it?'

Sean shuffled his size-ten feet.

'Siddown yasso,' said Neville, patting the space next to him on the sofa, 'mek you and me 'ave a taak.'

Sean shook his head. Neville raised his brows, surprised. He hadn't expected defiance.

'You nuh wan' taak to me?'

Again Sean shook his head. Neville lost his temper.

'Away wid you, den, bwoy. Don' mek me keep you from you madder skirt tail. Go on. Go!'

Sean turned and ran straight past Dilys, who'd been standing by the door, tea tray in hand, observing the whole scene. Neville caught her accusatory stare.

'Remember,' she said. 'Patience.'

Sean ran up to his room and flung himself on his bed, soiling the covers and the pillows. For a moment he lay staring up at the ceiling, his mind going in all directions at once. He was brought back to earth by Lucky's cheeping. Poor thing, he thought. She was probably hungry. And her cage could do with a clean, too. Her pleas became shrill, so he went and saw to her.

Meanwhile, downstairs, Neville was feeling ashamed. He apologised to Dilys.

'I'm not the one you should be saying sorry to.'

'Yes, well, me sorry anyway.'

And he was. His nephew was a pitiable boy. What a lot of weight he was carrying on his young shoulders. He'd clearly been affected by all the problems between his parents, not to mention all the stuff at school, all the bullying. If only he'd had the courage to stand up for himself, to fight back. Neville knew from bitter experience that it was the only way to deal with bullies.

He recalled the time when Bunny had been harassing him for months. If Joe had been around, things would never have reached that stage. But he was in Kingston at the time, running rings around his poor aunt. So this had been one battle Neville had to fight on his own. As it turned out, he was more than up to the task.

One day his patience had snapped and he told Bunny to name the time and place. They agreed to get it on that very day after school.

The bell rang. The pupils immediately deserted the schoolhouse and rushed up to the gate, all trying to squeeze through at the same time, causing a log-jam. Bunny and his cronies were at the head of the throng, with Neville and his supporters (including Sam and Freddie) bringing up the rear. They finally left the grounds and walked a few yards along the main road, before turning down a dust track that opened on to an overgrown cricket field. The noise they were making could be heard for miles.

A ring of spectators was quickly formed, with a lot of jostling for the best vantage points. Bunny looked relaxed, confident, a scornful smirk on his face. He and Neville squared up.

'Well,' said Bunny. 'Do suppen, den.'

'You fus',' said Neville.

'No, you fus'.'

'You.'

The spectators had had enough.

'But is wha' dis, a conversation or a fight?' said one.

'Yeah, ease up 'pon de gums and mek we see some fis',' said another.

Bunny and Neville were losing face, knew they had to act. They edged close to each other, closer still. Then, quick as anything, Bunny punched Neville in the eye. Neville reeled backwards, temporarily blinded. The spectators cheered. Bunny looked triumphant. His seconds were urging him in for the kill. Neville heard them. Still rubbing his eye, he threw himself at Bunny's knees, felling him instantly. It was time for *his* seconds to cheer, led by Sam and Freddie. Alas, the spectators wanted to see boxing, not wrestling, and they began to boo and hiss. They closed in on the combatants and Neville felt one or two biased kicks to his ribcage.

He and Bunny wrestled and rolled, rolled and wrestled, trying to throw punches from impossible angles. Bunny aimed one at Neville's face, but Neville just managed to get his head out of the way. Bunny's fist hit the ground, and Neville saw his lips form the letter 'o'. The spectators winced. This was the turning point in the fight. Neville seized the initiative. In one swift manoeuvre he rolled himself on top of Bunny, to the delight of the few girls watching.

'Fight him, Neville,' said one of them, 'don' kiss him.'

She and her friends giggled. Neville was oblivious. He was concentrating intensely, refusing to let his slight advantage slip. He now had his knees pressed firmly on Bunny's arms, crushing them, draining them of any remaining strength. Yet he knew he couldn't contain Bunny in that position indefinitely, so he head-butted him. Ironically, it was he who acquired the 'coco', a massive lump on his forehead. Still, the swelling was nothing compared to the state of Bunny, who was out cold. The spectators fell silent, sensing a major upset. Neville was shocked. Briefly, he thought he might have killed Bunny. He looked up to see a ring of grave faces. Bunny's cronies shuffled about, uncertain how to react.

Neville eventually rolled off his opponent, exhaustion quickly setting in. That was the signal for Bunny's cronies. They crouched around their man, began to nurse him. He quickly responded to their ministrations, opened his eyes. They were vacant, glassy. Neville, relieved to see he was alive, turned to Sam and Freddie, who started straightening his clothes and dusting him down. They then turned to leave, but after only a few steps they heard: 'Neville! You dead!'

Neville spun round. Bunny, barely able to stand up, was clutching a huge rock in his hand. Neville sighed wearily. He felt tired. The lump on his forehead was impairing his vision. He wanted to go home. He was about to suggest a truce when Bunny, egged on by his cronies, hurled the rock at him. It hit him on the forehead, opposite his lump, creating an identical one. He leaned forward and buried his face in his hands, trying in vain to massage away the pain. The spectators, already subdued, were now positively solemn.

Neville finally uncovered his face, which was soaked in tears. Tears of rage. He stared maniacally at Bunny, then rushed at him. Uncertain of their own safety, Bunny's cronies scarpered. He glanced round to see them scattering every which way, and decided to follow suit. Neville chased him round and round the field, but Bunny, propelled by fright, was just too quick and he eventually escaped through a clearing in the surrounding shrubbery and sped off down the road. Neville stood in the middle of the road shouting threats after him, until Sam and Freddie came and led him away.

The following day Neville showed up for school looking as if he'd walked into a wall. But at least he'd showed up, which was more than could be said for Bunny and a good number of his cronies.

Bunny never got over the incident, and had hated Neville ever since.

CHAPTER FOUR

On her way to work the following morning, Dilys found Neville asleep on the sofa, looking so much like Joe it made her gasp. What exactly was she doing? Where was her mind? Why had she even let this man into her house, a living, breathing, daily reminder of someone she'd much rather forget? He'd have to go – soon. In the meantime, she eased a cushion under his head, so that he wouldn't wake up with a cricked neck, and left beside him a photograph of Joe, and an affectionate note which read: *Didn't want to wake you. Not sure what your plans are for today, but if you get a chance, you know where I am. D.* She also left him a spare front door key.

It was gone four in the afternoon when he finally woke up. He swore when he realised the time, cursed Dilys for not rousing him before she left. But all was not lost, he thought. If he could shower and change quickly enough then he could still get to the factory before it closed at five-thirty. And since police stations never closed, there was no real urgency regarding the photograph.

He was about to step into the bathroom, dressed only in a towel, when he decided that there was something he had to do first. It would only take a couple of minutes and his curiosity would be satisfied once and for all.

He opened the trunk and was severely disappointed with what he found. Old frocks, obviously from a bygone age. He decided that they must have belonged to Dilys's mother, and that she must be the bloodless woman in the photograph on the bedside cabinet. Feeling cheated, he began to rummage, and discovered a metal cash-box with a broken lock, as well as an A4-size writing pad covered in doodles. He opened it and saw that it was a diary. Sitting with his back against the wardrobe, he began to read.

15. 3. 63

FORTY WINKS

Woke this morning at eight. Quite late, for me. Didn't go down immediately. Couldn't face them straight off. Sat staring out the window. Dreaming of escape, of freedom. Could run away. Could just up and run away. That'd show them. They'd be sorry then. Or would they? Would they even notice I was gone? 'Course they would. Him especially. Needs me, he does, the hopeless bugger. Which is more than she can say. She doesn't need anybody. She has Al. Lucky her. Who've I got?

Went down eventually. Found them in their usual place. At the kitchen table. Waiting. Waiting to be waited on. She had a sore head. Natch. He was spoiling for a row. Obviously. Cooked them breakfast then split. Left the house thinking: goodbye, loving parents, see you in thirty years. If you're lucky.

Typical day at school. Kept my own company. Daydreamed through my lessons. Got picked on. Had a fight. Tried not to bite, like a girl. Kicked and punched instead, aimed for the head. Got sent home early.

Had another fight when I got in.

Found the house in a mess. Breakfast stuff cluttering up the sink. Went looking for the culprits, mad as hell. Couldn't find them downstairs. Stood at the foot of the stairs, called up. No answer. Called again. Still nothing. Became slightly concerned, wondering where they could be. They never left the house. Ran upstairs in a panic. Stumbled across her on the landing. Passed out. Face down in a pool of vomit. Had to cover my nose against the stench. Immediately feared the worst. Then I saw it. The note. Wedged under her head. It read: *Do something for your mother. I'm having forty winks.*

Forty . . . Went bursting in on the bastard. Jumped on him, rained blows down on him. He woke up, grabbed my wrists. We struggled. He slapped me hard across the face, sent me sprawling across the room. He came at me, fists doubled. The scream was so loud it didn't seem to come from me. It froze him. For a moment he didn't know what to do, just stood there glowering at me, fists clenched, eyes red with sleep, with rage. 'Get out!' he shouted. Didn't move, couldn't. 'GET OUT!!!' he bellowed, coming at me once more. Ran for my life.

Came out to find her gone. Heard water running in the bathroom. Pressed my head against the door, listened. Called her name. No answer. Tried the door. Locked. About to barge it down when I heard her voice. Faint. Like a child's.'Don't you have homework, Dilys?' Help!

24. 3. 63

GRAVE RUMOURS

Got a crush on someone. Someone at school. A new music teacher. Big news, this. Never get crushes, me. Even hate The Beatles. Must be the only fourteen-year-old girl. In the world. Who does. What a fab (four) thought.

Doesn't know I exist, this teacher. Not surprised. Don't push myself on him like Becky Marshall and all those other sluts. Always flirting with him, they are. Always lifting their skirts and. He doesn't seem to mind. Clearly likes young girls. Got an eye for 'em, as they say. If only he'd cast it in my direction now and then. Maybe he's deliberately ignoring me. Wouldn't be the first teacher. Maybe he's heard things. Already. Things about me, about Mum and Dad. Rumours. Wonder which ones have so far reached his ears. They're so far fetched, surely he wouldn't believe them. He's an intelligent man – can, I'm sure, recognise hogwash when he hears it. Even so, true or no, hope he hasn't heard the one about Mum and her trips to the graveyard. If he has, he'll never speak to me.

25. 3. 63

BARRIERS

Just had Mum in my room. Came in for one of our 'chats'. Half cut, of course. Eyes glassy as hell. Reeking of Al. Speech slurred. Had to listen keenly, to every word. Don't know why I bothered. Was the usual spiel. I shouldn't hate Dad. He meant well. Had both our interests at heart. Was a good man. Confused, yes. Frustrated, certainly. Got angry from time to time, but then who didn't? I should try not to be so hard on him. Should remember he'd had a troubled past. Had affected him. Would affect anyone, that kind of thing.

Finally held my hand up, silenced her. No more, I said. Time she stopped making excuses for Dad, time she stopped worrying about him and started worrying about herself. In case she hadn't noticed, she had problems of her own. There were people who could help, if only she'd

Could see I wasn't reaching her. The barriers were up. She sat hunched at the foot of my bed, her mind far away. She looked tired, weary. Thirty-five in years, middle-aged in appearance. Eased forward and put my arms around her. Put hers around me. Sobbed on each other's shoulders for a while. Then, with a pained smile, she started tucking me in. Like the good old days. Before she went, she told me everything would be all right. Her voice was soft, soothing. Almost believed her.

2. 4. 63

SPAM SANDWICHES

I'm the happiest girl alive. He spoke to me today. Walked right up and said, 'Hey.' Spooked me, actually. Was eating my lunch, alone, in the farthest corner of the playground. Trying to ignore the idiots shouting abuse at me. Becky Marshall and that lot. Big Arms! Thunder Thighs! Water off a duck's back. Suddenly felt this hand on my shoulder. Swivelled instantly, ready to draw blood. There he was, my reason for being. Smiling. Smiling at me. At me! Thought to myself: this is bliss, this. He asked how I was doing. Could barely put together an intelligible response. Went all goo-goo, ga-ga. Stalled for time. Brushed crumbs from my mouth, off my uniform. Put my half-eaten sandwich away. Finally managed to say: 'OK, sir. You?' He thought for a while, said: 'OK, but a bit puzzled.' 'Puzzled, sir?' 'Yes, puzzled.' He sat down next to me. Instinctively I shoved up. Because of my size, I need space. His face changed. Asked me the weirdest question. Wanted to know what my sandwich filling was. I told him. Asked whether he could try a bit, said he loved Spam. Handed him a limp sandwich. He examined it for a second, looked at me. Obviously thought I thought he was having second thoughts. So, just to show me, he bit into the sandwich. 'Yes,' he said, chewing. 'I'm puzzled. Puzzled as to why a beautiful young girl like you is having lunch all alone.' I looked away, could think of nothing to say. Felt his eyes on me. 'Don't worry,' he said. 'We don't have to talk if you don't want to. Let's eat instead.' And that's what we did. We ate. My sandwiches. Together.

Later, on my way home, it occurred to me: no one had ever called me beautiful before.

19. 5. 63

I WISH

My name's Ziggy, short for Zigani. Funny name, I know. Like it, though. Eastern European, I think. Mother gave it to me. Means – something. Father was opposed to it, apparently. Bless him. Bit stiff, Pops. Don't get me wrong, I love him dearly. He's soooooo handsome, soooooo charming. All his patients are soooooo in love with him. Gynaecologist. That's how he met Mother, in his surgery. They're divorced now. Amicable split. Seeing other people. I'm comfortable with it. Father is, too. Not so sure about mother. Famous actress, you see. To her, image is everything. Ah, Mother. Mother, Mother, Mother. Hates it when I call her that. Particularly when she's 'entertaining'. Insists I call her Rebecca. Makes her look modern, liberal. Which of course she is. Everyone says so. The papers. Her fans. Her lover, Franz.

We live an idyllic life, Mother and me. Flat in the city, house in the country. We go abroad lots. She sunbathes, I swim. Often we're joined by Franz, who'll fly out on a whim. But it's not all play. Mother has 'commitments'. I've got school. Which I love. Hate to sound smug, but I'm quite the Miss Popular. Got friends coming out of my ears. Don't even mention boyfriends. Phew! Talented, too. Musical. Hope to be a famous cellist one day, like Jacqueline Du Pré. Taking lessons at the moment. Tutor says I hardly need them, that he can't teach me anything. Calls me a prodigy. Imagine that. Me. A prod. Says the nicest things, my music tutor. I've fallen for him in a big way. We flirt. Would do it with him. But for the hurt. It might cause. Mother. Oh, Franz!

I wish

22. 7. 63

LOVER'S TIFF

They've arrived. They're here. The summer holidays. Oh dear, oh dear. Six whole weeks cooped up with those two.

Six long weeks. I'm all in a spin. Can I go that long? Without seeing him? Wonder who he'll spend the holidays with. Know practically nothing about the man. Is he hitched? Are there sprogs? A house with a fence? Dogs? Bloody hope not. Anyway, kiss, kiss, my darling. Have a good summer. Wherever you are. And remember, thou art in my heart, always.

10. 8. 63

SIBLING RIVALRY

My sister's birthday today. Get on we don't. Mum will go and see her. Dad and me won't. Though for very different reasons.

17. 8. 63

BACK TO MY ROOTS

I'm up north. My first trip. It's not Corfu, but it'll do. Just nice to get away for a change. Grim place, though. Had no idea how grim. Row after row of terraced houses, all backing on to each other. Could be the set of *Saturday Night, Sunday Morning.*

Visiting my Uncle Stan (Mum's brother) and his wife Elsie. Mum's with me. Dad stayed home. Cried off at the last minute.

Sick, he claimed. Dicky tummy. Dicky head, more like. Poor Uncle Stan. He'd bought beers and everything.

Dinner tonight was a tense occasion. Aunt Elsie put her foot right in it. Said she couldn't abide excess of any kind, especially drinking. Mum squirmed, sipped her water. Uncle Stan glowered at his wife. She twigged, flushed red, muttered an apology. Mum waved it aside. Could see she wanted to run off and hide. She smiled, crookedly. I felt for her. Wanted to gather her up in my arms and comfort her. Uncle Stan tried to lighten the mood. Asked how things were with me, for the umpteenth time. 'Fine, Uncle,' I said. Wanted to say: Well, actually, Uncle, I'm the most hated girl in my school; I've got no friends whatsoever; I never go anywhere or do anything; my mum's an alcoholic and my dad's a violent agoraphobic; but apart from that

Relaxed a bit after dinner. Watched some TV. Played some cards. Went for a walk. Back for charades. It got late, they ordered me to bed. Put my foot down, won another hour instead. Told them they were treating me like a child. I was a child, they chorused, like children. In the eyes of the law, I replied. Only in the eyes of the law. Cue reminiscences. When they were my age this, when they were my age that. Yawn. Actually their talk wasn't all dull. Found it interesting to hear about Mum's childhood. Uncle Stan painted quite a detailed picture, making Mum blush. Apparently as a kid she was rascally but lovable. Got into countless scrapes, but always managed to charm her way out of punishment. Couldn't believe what I was hearing. Mum? Getting into scrapes? Never. A few toe-curling anecdotes later and my doubts were banished. Well, well, I thought. It's always the quiet ones.

Leaving in the morning. Wish we were staying longer. Mum needs to get back. If only she were stronger. Dad and Al. They've got her all in a bother. Frightened of the one. Dependent on the other.

21. 8. 63

WITH THIS RING I THEE WED

Mum wants me to leave home. Said I should go and live with Uncle Stan. Could no longer live with the fear, she said, of what Dad might do to me. Could no longer shoulder the responsibility of trying to look out for me. I had to move. For my own safety. Uncle Stan would have me any day. He'd been saying so for years. I should go to him, run to him, not look back. There was desperation in her voice. Told her not to be silly. Go? And leave her at Dad's mercy? No. I had a better idea. We should leave together. Me and her. Get a place of our own. Start afresh. Started shaking her head. My plan just wasn't practical, realistic. Where would we go? What would we live on? She couldn't hold down a job, not in her state. I could work, I said. Leave school and get a job. Support us both. She wasn't having it. I shouldn't even think of leaving school. I'd regret it later. In any case, her place was at Dad's side. She had a duty to him, had pledged herself to him. For richer, for poorer, in sickness and in Heard footfalls outside my door. Dad. Earwigging.

30. 8. 63

THE GOOD NEWS

Had a visitor today. Jehovah's Witness. Mum answered the door to her. Dad, the coward, hid himself in the living room. I stood at the top of the stairs and watched. Was amazed at how dowdy the woman looked. Expected Mum to send her away. Instead they had a frank exchange of views, after which Mum received a copy of the Bible. The Good News.

2. 9. 63

DOCTOR'S ORDERS

Went to see Dr Smith today. Surprised by how excited he was to see me. Didn't even think he'd remember me. He couldn't get over how I'd grown. Came from behind his desk and held me at arm's length. Looked me up and down. Spun me around. Said last time he saw me I was so high. Treated me for mumps, if memory served him right. I smiled. Embarrassed. He opened the door and looked out into the waiting room. Closed it again then looked at me quizzically. Had I come alone? Yes, I replied. Oh, he said. I see, he said. Went back behind his desk. Put on his serious face and his glasses.

What could he do for me? he asked, clearly expecting me to confess some secret. Pregnancy, perhaps. Or the clap. Come about Mum, I said. He relaxed. Could see his brain working, his thoughts writ large across his forehead. What about her? he asked. It's her drinking, I said. It was getting worse and it was up to me and him to do something about it. Started crying. He came from behind his desk again, rested his hand on my shoulder. Come now, he said, no need for that. I blubbed on. Look, he said, do you think you could get Kath to come and see me? Shook my head. What about John? He doesn't bloody well care, I croaked, between sobs. He thought about it, then said: all right, tell you what; why don't I pay you all a visit, make it look all casual like? Stopped crying instantly. Oh, would you, Dr Smith? Would you really? Yes, yes, he replied. But, he warned, if Kath refused to be helped then there was little he or anyone could do for her. I didn't want to think about that.

5. 9. 63

BETRAYAL

Dr Smith kept his word. Popped by this afternoon. Took Mum and Dad completely by surprise. No prizes for guessing that Mum was already wasted. Sounds bad but I was glad. Dr Smith could assess her condition for himself. Never seen Dad so hospitable. Half expected him to go and put on his Sunday best. What is it about doctors?

Lunch. Tea and tuna sandwiches. Prepared by moi, natch. While they ate, the men made small talk. Mum, wanting to join in, rambled nonsensically. Tried to keep her occupied, but she was determined to talk to Dr Smith. Dad kept apologising to our guest for his 'wife's' behaviour. Dr Smith, debonair, seemed to take the whole thing in his stride. Even found time to give me a reassuring wink. Don't think Dad noticed. Know Mum hadn't. She'd passed out. Banged her head against the table. Dr Smith gave her the once-over, satisfied himself that she was only drunk. He and Dad then took her upstairs to bed.

A few minutes later they returned, laughing and joking. Dad told me that they wished to be left alone, to talk. I should make a fresh pot of tea then make myself scarce.

An hour later they emerged from the living room, laughing and slapping each other's back. Didn't know what to make of it. Had they discussed Mum at all? Evidently not. Men, I thought. Leave them alone for a second and . . .

They swapped goodbyes at the front door. Dad went back to the living room. I waited for a moment then ran downstairs and out into the street. Caught up with Dr Smith.

Well?

Ah, Dilys, the girl with the vivid imagination.

What?

Everything is going to be just fine. Your father and I have spoken. According to him, you like to make up stories.

You told him about our meeting!?

Of course.

And what did he say?

Never you mind about that, young lady.

Doesn't matter, anyway, you saw Mum for yourself.

I did, and she was undoubtedly drunk. But that doesn't make her an alcoholic. Why, even I get tipsy on occasion. Especially when I've something to celebrate.

Celebrate?

You mean to tell me you didn't know it was your parents' wedding anniversary today?

(Did a quick memory recall. Shit! Was as well.)

But, but, but

Must dash, Dilys. I've another, slightly more urgent call to make.

But what about Mum?

(He didn't answer. Or look back.)

Went back indoors. Dad was waiting for me. Had a murderous look in his eye. Expected him to hit me. Instead he lifted me up. Literally scooped me up in one of his giant's arms. Carried me upstairs and locked me in my room. Been here since four this afternoon. It's now eleven.

7. 9. 63

FOR WHAT WE'RE ABOUT TO RECEIVE

Before dinner this evening a first took place. Dad and I were shocked to hear Mum say grace.

9. 9. 63

BOY RACER

First day of term today. Felt good to be back. Never thought
I'd hear myself say that. He was there. My knight. Went out
of his way to greet me before assembly. Made Becky Marshall
green with envy. Expected her to start slagging me when he'd
gone. But *au contraire*. She actually said hello. Managing to
sound sincere.

Didn't end there, this new friendliness. Carried over into
break time. Nothing excessive, mind. A smile, an offer of gum,
peace for a change. Did my best not to appear suspicious.

Didn't have him at all today. Went from lesson to lesson
hoping to bump into him. Saw him a few times, from a
distance, talking to other teachers. But he didn't see me. Every
time I thought I'd caught his eye, he'd look away. It was agony.
Wasn't till after school that we spoke again. Gave me a lift
home. Which was nice. If a little weird. Didn't let on, but I
was really scared. Was my first time in a car. Mightn't have
been so bad if his had a roof, four doors instead of two, and a
much quieter engine. As we drove, could barely hear what he
was saying. And he was shouting. Had to lip-read him most
of the time. Must say, though: was good to feel the wind in my
hair. He beeped me as he reversed out of our street. The sight
of twitching curtains sent me scurrying indoors. Giggling.

18. 9. 63

OVER THE THRESHOLD

Went round to his place this afternoon. Was giving me a lift home when he suddenly announced he was taking me there. Said it was only fair. He'd been to my house, after all. He might as well have proposed, I was so dumbfounded.

Lives in a rented cottage, on a windy hill. Quite a few miles outside town. Cramped. Cluttered. Books scattered hither and thither. Cello in the corner. Sheet music everywhere.

Played Truth or Dare. Both opted for truth. Asked him if he had a girlfriend. He doesn't. Asked me if there was anything I would change about my appearance, given the chance. My wrestler's arms. He laughed, said my arms were perfectly normal.

Asked me what my plans were for the future. Told him I hoped to go to university, to study literature. He was surprised, said I didn't strike him as the bookish type. I was offended, forced to put him straight. I might not have the same number of books as him, but I read avidly. Thank God for libraries, I told him. He asked me who my favourite writer was. Didn't have to think: Emily Dickinson. Been reading her poetry since I was eight. He said he knew of her, but was 'unfamiliar' with her work. Could I recite him something of hers? Went for one of the shorter ones, called 'Love Is'.

> Love is . . .
> Anterior to Life
> Posterior to Death
> Initial of Creation
> And the exponent of Breath

That's beautiful, he said, then drove me home.

25. 9. 63

SEA CHANGE

Smell a rat. Something's definitely up. How else can I account for the change in Miss Marshall? This past week she's been

94

a model of consideration, which basically means she's hasn't called me any names. Finding it a bit disorienting. Feel like screaming at her: what the bloody hell are you playing at?

Mum came down just now. To say goodnight. Said a prayer first. Asked God, through Jesus, to look after me and keep me safe from harm now and forever more, amen.

8. 10. 63

ST MICHAEL

Been avoiding each other the last couple of days. Cracked today, though, after school. Was walking along when I heard his melodic car horn behind me. Room for one, he said.

We went to his place. This time at my request. Told him I didn't want to go home. Not just yet. He said my wish was his command.

HIM: So I see you're getting on better with your fellow pupils.

ME: Wouldn't say that, sir. They're not calling me names any more, but we're hardly getting on. Still . . . (noticed him smiling) What? (shook his head quickly, still smiling) What, sir? (wouldn't be drawn, then it dawned) You've got something to do with it, haven't you? Of course.

HIM: My secret's out.

ME: You didn't speak to them, did you, sir? Tell me you didn't. (he nodded) Oh no! How embarrassing. I don't believe it. I can never show my face in that school again. Oh no. What did you say, sir?

HIM: You're not upset, are you? We were only trying to help.

ME: We?

HIM: My colleagues and I.

ME: Your . . . Hold on. No, wait. Your colleagues?

HIM: OK, look. If I tell you, do you promise to keep it to yourself?

ME: 'Course I do.

HIM: I mean it, Dilys. I could get into a lot of trouble over this.

ME: Sir!

HIM: OK, OK. And remember, whatever we did, we did in your best interests. Right, then. Remember the day I saw you having lunch in the playground? (I nodded) I couldn't help thinking how sad you looked. How utterly lonely. I felt so sorry for you.

ME: Sorry for me?

HIM: Yes. Is that such a crime? (I shrugged) Anyway, after speaking to you that day, and remember you didn't say much, I decided to make a few discreet enquiries. I had to find out if your having lunch alone was a regular occurrence or an isolated incident. I don't need to tell you what I discovered. I was furious. Less with those pupils making your life a misery, and more with my colleagues for standing idly by while it happened.

ME: My life wasn't such hell, you know, sir.

HIM: Yes it was. Now you've distracted me. Where was I?

ME: Furious with your colleagues.

HIM: That's right. Furious. I told them that the situation, in all conscience, could not be allowed to continue. I told them that as teachers we had a duty to try to foster a spirit of friendliness among the pupils. Failure to do so, I told them, amounted to a dereliction of that duty. According to them I was like every new teacher, full of reforming zeal. It would wear off, they said. But I wasn't going to be fobbed off that easily. I hounded them and hounded them. In the end, simply to shut me up, I suspect, they agreed to support any initiative I cared to implement.

ME: And what was that?

HIM: Nothing radical. I made a speech at one of the parents–teachers meetings.

ME: You didn't mention my name, did you, sir?

HIM: I'm afraid I did. (I groaned) With hindsight, I can see that was a mistake. But at the time . . . Anyway, I only mentioned your name as part of a more general point about the need for pupils to respect each other. I urged those present to take the message back that we as teachers and parents could not and would not tolerate bullying in our school. There was no place for it, and anyone found guilty of it would be severely punished. From what I've seen so far this term, the message seems to have got through.

A long silence. Didn't really know what to think. He'd made me sound like such a victim. Yet I was impressed by the passion he'd shown on my behalf.

ME: You did all that for me, sir?

HIM: (smiling) Just doing my job, Dilys. (looked at his watch) Is that the time? Come, let's get you home, young lady.

He drove me home. Before I got out of the car I leaned across and kissed him on the cheek.

ME: Thanks, sir.

HIM: Michael. Call me Michael. (I blushed) But only when we're alone, mind. Now go on, shoo. And don't be late for school tomorrow. (I started walking away) And Dilys. (I stopped) You're welcome.

Waved him goodbye and went indoors thinking: it can't get any better.

12. 10. 63

WHAT A WASTE

Mum's dead. Murdered. Poisoned by Al.

Funeral was well attended. Me, Dad, Uncle Stan and Aunt Elsie. Oh, and Rev. Patterson, though he doesn't really count. He said a few words. Thanked the Lord for entering Mum's life in her final days. Uncle Stan was inconsolable, kept repeating to himself, 'What a waste, what a waste.' Threw gravel on to the coffin then came back here for tea and biscuits. Uncle Stan and Aunt Elsie stayed a couple of hours then left. Dad went to his room. I went to mine. Cried all night.

2. 11. 63

BIG BROTHER

He's been ever so good since . . . Told me I could visit him any time. There for me, he said. Round his every chance I get. Funny, don't see him in that way any more. Romantically, I mean. Don't think I ever did, really. Know if he was to make a pass I'd run a mile. Wouldn't, of course. Too much of a gentleman.

Told him this would be my final term. Was quitting school to look after Dad.

HIM: Why, what's wrong with him?

ME: Hasn't left his room since . . . Hasn't spoken, either. Hardly eats. I feel guilty leaving him alone. He's not been the best father to me but I'm all he's got.

He thought a while.

HIM: You know what you're taking on, don't you? Your father sounds like a very sick man. You could be looking after him for years to come.

ME: I know. My Uncle Stan says there are places, institutions, but . . . well, let's just say I can't do that to him.

HIM: I understand.

ME: I know you do.

HIM: Come here.

We hugged. It became awkward. We broke.

ME: You know, sir . . .

HIM: Michael. How many more times? I feel so old when you call me sir.

ME: (bashful) If I had a big brother, I'd . . . I'd want him to be like you.

He smiled, and for a moment the future didn't seem so bleak.

Neville eagerly turned the page, and was crestfallen to see that there were no more entries. He closed the pad, lingered over the doodles for a while, then put it and the cash-box back where he'd found them. He remained on the floor – cold feet, numb bottom – and thought about what he'd read. He could think of only one word to describe it – grim. How Dilys had escaped the madhouse was beyond him. The rumours about her parents were now cast in a new light. Her mother sounded pathetic, her father like the Devil himself. Neville glanced at the photograph of them on the bedside cabinet, paying extra attention to the father. How Dilys must have suffered at his hands. No wonder she was so angry, so distrustful, so bitter. He tried to banish the thought. It wasn't his place to judge. He'd intruded upon something private, glimpsed something not intended for his eyes. Now he must forget about it, put if from his mind – which was easier said than done. He wondered how Joe had coped with the knowledge, or whether he'd even been aware of it. Perhaps Dilys hadn't told him. And why would she? Neville had found the events of her past so harrowing that he couldn't imagine Dilys revealing them to another person, not even to her husband. They had about them the quality of secrets, of the sort that she might want to take to her grave. If that were the case, then by reading her diary had he not committed a sinful act?

With these thoughts running through his mind, Neville noticed that the carriage clock was showing a quarter to six. So much for his trip to the factory, he thought. He laboured to his feet and went to have his shower. Dilys and Sean were home before he'd finished. Later, after dinner, he invited Dilys to the Crown. He felt a strong desire to be alone with her, to get her out of the house. *I never go anywhere or do anything.* Dilys declined his offer, pleading tiredness.

That night, after Dilys and Sean had gone bed, Neville stayed up to watch TV. He sat through a rerun episode of an eighties sitcom, and laughed not once. It featured a family of couch potatoes, and he wondered whether it reflected English life. If it did, then what a sad reflection. Perhaps it was the weather, but these people really needed to get out more. As children, he and Joe had always been out and about doing something; something physical, active, which made them as strong as horses. Swimming had been one of their favourite pastimes. There was a large, secluded lagoon set in the upper regions of the hills around their village, and they'd escape to it whenever they could, sometimes spending the whole day there. They'd swim, get out, sun themselves on the surrounding boulders, then dive back in, doggy-paddling in lieu of any of the more efficient strokes. To break the monotony of going from end to end, or rotating in circles, they'd diversify into water games: who could hold their breath the longest, float the longest, tread water the longest; who could dive the deepest, swim the fastest, cause the biggest splash. By now they'd be ravenous, and would set off in search of something to eat. They'd stroll about the countryside picking and devouring anything they could find – guavas, jackfruits, rose-apples – causing mayhem wherever they went. Birds, lizards, goats – all were pelted with stones. Whole colonies of ants were ruthlessly trampled underfoot. Private property was trespassed, looted and vandalised. Freshwater streams were sullied with urine. Animal traps were sprung, their bait scattered. Their rampage normally came to end when they were recognised by a scandalised adult, who, calling on God to bear witness, would promise to report them to their 'people'. They'd run home, praying that the would-be informant had only meant to scare them, which was invariably the case.

He switched the TV off and thought for a while. He really should call Joyce, soon, for she was not the type to let such an obvious snub go unremarked. And yet, as much as he wanted to, there was something holding him back. The truth was, he didn't like the idea of her husband. Yes, Joyce was separated from him, and he'd long since moved out, but his presence in her life would linger for some time to come. Neville was confused. On the one hand he was keen to revive what had once existed between himself and Joyce, yet on the other he didn't wish to become entangled in her life. But wasn't he doing exactly the same thing with Dilys? If he was, then it didn't feel that way. After all, she was a stranger, and despite her being married to his brother, theirs was a tenuous link. By contrast, he and Joyce were bound up in each other's lives, and had been since they were children. When she left for England, he'd felt hurt and rejected, and had never really got over it. Now that they were single again, old feelings had begun to stir, certainly on his side. But he didn't know what Joyce was up to, couldn't read her. Her visits to Jamaica were becoming more frequent (at one point she hadn't been seen over for a decade), but he didn't know what, if anything, they signified. Perhaps she just missed the place, though he doubted it. Perhaps she missed Adlyn, and wanted to spend more time with her. The old girl didn't have long left, and was now simply going through the motions. Would Joyce come home and take care of her? That remained to be seen. Of course, if it came to it, he'd have no qualms about stepping into the breach himself. But if Joyce was expecting it, taking it for granted, then they would need to talk.

CHAPTER FIVE

At four o'clock the following afternoon he walked into the factory. This time he ignored the stares and strode up to Christina's office and knocked on the door.

'Come in.'

He entered and closed the door behind him.

'Oh. Neville. Wasn't expecting to see you again so soon. Please, sit.' Neville sat down. 'Tea?'

Neville groaned. 'No t'ank you.'

Christina leaned forward in her chair, rested her elbows on her desk and locked her fingers under her chin. 'So. How's it all going?'

Neville shoved the scrap of paper across the desk. Christina picked it up and examined it.

'What's this?'

'Is a phone number.'

'I can see that. But whose is it?'

'Phone it.'

'What?'

'Phone it.'

Intrigued, Christina dialled the number. She listened for a minute, then hung up.

'Now I'm confused. Why've you got Dawn's home number?'

'Ah fin' it in one of Joe ol' trowziz.'

Christina leaned back in her chair. 'I see.' She thought for a moment, then added: 'Could all be very innocent, of course.'

'Mek me taak to ar and fin' out.'

Christina regarded him dubiously. 'As you wish,' she said, then rose and left the room.

While she was gone, Neville studied the green creature stuck to the phone receiver. It seemed different, somehow: more hideous, more sinister.

Christina came back with Dawn. 'Should I leave you two alone?' she said.

Dawn looked worried.

'No, no,' said Neville. 'Me preffa you stay. If you don' min'.'

Christina went back and sat at her desk. Neville offered Dawn his chair. She said she'd rather stand.

'What's this about?' she asked, looking at Christina. Neville came straight out with it.

'Dere was somet'ing going on 'tween you and Joe?'

Dawn wobbled, but quickly regained her composure. 'Who told you that?' she asked.

'Yes ar no.'

'No.'

'Ah don' believe you,' said Neville.

Dawn flushed. 'I don't care what you believe. It's the truth. You've got some front coming in here . . .'

Neville handed her the scrap of paper. From her reaction, he knew it was the clincher.

'Look,' said Christina. 'Whatever you say will remain in this room. No one's here to judge you. Neville just wants to find his brother, that's all. Besides, the police are involved.'

Dawn chewed the inside of her lip. 'OK, OK,' she said, and paused before adding: 'We saw each other briefly. I'm talking really brief. Two, three times at the most. It really was no big deal.'

'You was still seeing one anodder before him go missing?'

'No,' said Dawn. 'We broke it off about a month before. Jason found out.'

'Jason knew?' asked Christina.

104

'Who's dis Jason?' asked Neville.

'My boyfriend,' said Dawn.

'Works here, too,' said Christina to Neville. 'One of those guys you met the other day.'

Neville tried to recall the faces, but only one stood out: the redhead with the sour expression. 'So when las' you see Joe?' he asked Dawn.

'Haven't seen him since the last day he was here. And that's the God's truth.'

'You believe her?' asked Sergeant Pettifer. They were sitting in the same poky side room, the sunlight shining down through the barred window, their knees brushing lightly under the table.

'Yes,' Neville replied.

'Which brings us back to square one. You brought that photograph of your brother?'

Neville handed him the photograph, taken in Great Yarmouth. In it Joe was standing on the crowded beach, his trousers rolled above his ankles, balanced on one leg. He was looking at the camera but pointing out to sea, a huge, toothy grin on his face. When Neville first saw it he imagined Dilys standing behind the camera ordering Joe to stand still, to stop larking around, to stop making a spectacle of himself.

'Hmmm,' said Sergeant Pettifer, looking at the photograph. 'This the best you can do?' Neville nodded and the sergeant slipped the photograph into his file. 'OK, then, Neville, if there's nothing else . . .'

Neville shook his head and both men rose to leave.

Over at the Bishops', Sean was daydreaming. He was meant to be cleaning windows on the mansion's east wing, but his mind was far away. Halfway up the tall ladder, with his back against the rungs, he looked out across the estate. He felt a nagging guilt at being so idle, but was unable to concentrate on the job at hand. Most days he went about his work quietly and efficiently. The Bishops gave him instructions and he carried them out to the letter. Rarely did they have cause for complaint, and often felt the need to praise him. They'd employed many people down the years, but he was by far the most conscientious. It was a stroke of luck that he'd answered their ad in the local paper, and they dreaded being deprived of his services.

But lately he'd become distracted, and his work had suffered. A certain sloppiness had crept in, which in the last few days had become pronounced. There'd been a couple of incidents only that morning. Asked to mow the lawn, he'd forgotten to pick up the cut grass. He'd washed and waxed the Range Rover, but had failed to vacuum the interior. Margaret Bishop had had a quiet word with him. Ashamed, he apologised and corrected his oversights. But he was clearly not himself, so the Bishops, worried, decided to speak to Dilys. It wasn't the type of thing they could mention on the phone, but perhaps she could come to lunch.

On his way home that evening, Sean dawdled as usual. He'd not had a good day, and he hoped that the Bishops weren't too angry with him. He'd let himself down, and would make up for it the next day by completing all his tasks. If necessary, he'd volunteer to do extra ones.

As he neared the old scout hut, he saw them coming towards him. Normally he'd have stood his ground, but, outnumbered two to one, he crossed the road. Billy and Danny did the same. Minutes later, they were blocking his path.

'Where d'you think you're going?' said Billy.

'Please move,' said Sean.

'Make us,' said Danny.

He tried to go by, but Billy stepped in front of him, shoved him. He retaliated and before long there was a scuffle. They wrestled him to the ground, kicked and punched him and called him racist names. Instinctively, he curled himself into a ball. It was the quickest way to get them to stop, something he'd remembered from his schooldays. Sure enough, they soon let up, then walked off, giving each other victory hugs. He waited a moment then got to his feet. With no serious injuries, he dusted himself down and set off home.

When he got in, his first thought was to go and find Dilys, but he chose not to, and went upstairs instead.

His anger was delayed, and only really hit him once he got to his room. Without some way to vent it, he paced to and fro, to and fro, muttering to himself. Eventually he grew tired, and went and sat on his bed. He remained there a long time, head in hands, thinking dark thoughts. Shortly afterwards, Dilys came into his room.

'Thought I heard you come in.'

He didn't respond.

'What's the matter, Sean?'

'Nothing.'

'Don't give me that. What's bothering you?'

'Nothing.'

Dilys was unconvinced, but knew not to pursue it. 'What did you do at the Bishops' today?'

Deadpan, Sean listed his jobs. Dilys hoped that he hadn't been overworked.

'Did you remember to take your pills after lunch?'

He nodded. Dilys walked over and stood beside him. She stroked his hair, which she noticed was looking a bit matted. He was due for a trim, she thought. Now where had she put those clippers? The scissors might have to do.

'Come now. Your bath's ready.'

After his bath, Sean went back to his room to await dinner. Lying on his bed, he began paging through one of his subscription magazines. It had a monthly feature on exotic birds, complete with glossy photographs. That particular issue contained a four-page spread on Ugandan 'avi-tourism', a scheme aimed at promoting the country's bird-life abroad.

The text spoke of 'avian diversity' and 'protected birding areas', but Sean was more interested in the pictures. He was amazed by some of the birds shown. They not only looked great, but had wonderful names: red-necked spurfowl, African skimmer, palm nut vulture, long-toed plover. He'd have given anything to observe them in their natural habitats. Fantasising thus, he dozed off, the magazine open on his stomach.

Neville left the police station and headed straight for the Crown.

He found it deserted, except for Madge Winters, who was twiddling her thumbs at the bar. She immediately brightened on seeing him. He headed over to her.

'Neville, is it?' she said. Neville nodded and eased himself up on to the high bar stool, ordered a pint.

'Marjorie Winters. Madge to my friends. Pleased to meet you.' She extended her hand. Neville shook it, conscious of his grip. Madge started pulling his pint. 'Heard you were looking for Joe.' She studied him. 'It's unreal. You're his spitting image.'

She handed him his beer. He took a quick sip.

'So when las' you see him?' he asked. The question was beginning to sound hollow, hopeless.

'Not for a long time. Two years? Maybe more.' She paused, then said: 'So I take it no one knows where he is.' Neville shook his head. 'Poor man. She wouldn't stop till she drove him away. Ah well, wherever he is, he's better off. When I think about what that cow put him through.'

'You and he used to taak?'

'A lot. About all sorts. He mentioned you a few times, said you were a decent bloke but . . .' She caught herself. Neville took his nose out of his pint.

'But wha'?'

'Well, I don't like to say.'

'Please.'

'He said you lacked ambition.'

'Ha! Ambition! Ambition! If dis is ambition . . .' He spread his arms, indicating the pub and beyond. '. . . den I want no part of it.'

He settled down again, stared into his pint. Madge pondered her next move.

'I'm sure he didn't mean anything by it,' she said, tentatively. Neville murmured something, but Madge didn't catch it. 'Yeah,' she said. 'Me and your brother talked, all right. How we talked, or should I say how he talked. Sometimes he'd come in here, sit right where you're sitting now, and just pour his heart out to me. He wasn't a very happy man, your brother. I really felt for him. That woman made his life a living hell. It's no wonder he started sleeping around.'

Neville looked up. 'Him taak to you about Dawn?'

'And the rest.'

'You mean dere was more?'

'Of course. That Dawn. I see her about. She's just a child. She couldn't satisfy a man like your brother. Neither could that other one . . . what's her name? . . . works with Dawn . . . .might even be her guvnor . . . erm . . . erm..'

'Christina?'

'That's it. Another child. Pah! Dunno what he saw in 'em, personally.'

Neville was lost in thought. 'Christina,' he muttered to himself, 'dat devious, conniving likkle . . . likkle . . .' He gave up, began shaking his head.

'And there was more,' said Madge.

'What! Listen here, woman. You sure you not mekking all dis up? I mean, good God in heaven . . .'

Madge narrowed her eyes, offended. 'I'm only telling you what Joe told me. I've got no reason to lie.' She hung her head, distractedly arranged a couple of beer mats.

'Look,' said Neville. 'Ah sorry, all right? Please, continue wha' you was saying.'

'I was only going to tell you about the mystery woman.'

'Who?'

Someone came into the pub, a teenage girl, dressed in a pair of baggy jeans and an outsized parka. Her hair was spiky, green.

'Yes, love,' said Madge.

'It's all right,' the girl replied, and left.

Madge sighed. 'Get some right sorts in 'ere, I tell you. See the state of her hair? Anyway, where were we?' She thought for a second. 'Oh yeah, the mystery woman. You see, the thing is, Joe liked playing games. When he started seeing someone, he wouldn't tell me who they were just straight out like that, he liked me to guess. He'd feed me clues and everything, to help me along like, but with this one woman he wasn't giving anything away. All he said was that she was from around these parts. Even in a town this small, that hardly narrows it down. I still wonder who she was.'

Neville thought he had a fair idea. He finished his pint and got Madge to pour him another. He was determined to get drunk.

'So you're staying with Dilys, right?'

Neville nodded. Madge handed him his new pint.

'That can't be easy.'

Neville shrugged.

'Well,' said Madge, 'just so you know. If things get a bit tricky over there, I've got a spare room you could have.' She smiled, thrust out her veiny cleavage. Neville recoiled.

'Dat's very kin' of you,' he said, 'but ah don' t'ink it will be necessary.'

'Whatever. The offer still stands. Who knows, eh?' She wrote down her address and phone number and gave it to Neville. He pocketed it, without so much as a glance. 'You'll be going up to London at some point, then?'

'Wasn't planning to, no.' Jesus, thought Neville. Did she ever shut up?

'But you must. If Joe's anywhere, that's where he'll be.'

'Yes, but ah hear London is a big place. Wha' you expec' me to do, go up to the firs' person and say, "Excuse me, you know where ah can fin' a fella by de name of Joe Forbes?"'

Madge flushed, embarrassed. 'There's no call for sarcasm,' she said. Neville sipped his beer, ended up with a froth moustache.

'Don' pay me no min',' he said, by way of an apology. 'Ah didn't mean to . . . ah was only trying to . . . look, you right, a trip to London might be very useful, but ah just wouldn't know where to start look.'

'I would. I told you, Joe talked to me about everything. I know about all his London haunts. I used to love hearing about them, all the things that went on, all the people. There's one particular place that he went to a lot . . . Lattie's, in Hackney . . . he was always on about it. He made it sound really exciting. I used to pester him to take me there. In fact it became a bit of a running joke. As soon as he walked in the door, even before he'd ordered his usual, I'd be at him. "Oi, you, when you taking me to Lattie's?" He'd just laugh and say: "Soon, sweetheart, soon" in that gorgeous accent of his.' She smiled at the memory.

Neville's face was beginning to slacken. He ordered another pint, even though he hadn't finished his last. Madge started pulling the new one, studying him the whole time.

'You might look like Joe, but you're not a great talker like he was. That's OK, though. Truth be known, I prefer the strong, silent type.' She flashed Neville a smile so lascivious that he almost fell off his stool.

After six pints Neville decided to leave. By this stage a few of the locals had wandered in, all men. Carefully, Neville slid down off his stool, gripping the bar for support. Madge put her hand on his shoulder, leaned forward, kissed him on the cheek and said, conspiratorially: 'Here. Listen. Word to the wise. Watch out for that Dilys. She's no good, you understand?

She tries to come across as Lady Muck, all la-di-da and that, but it's all a put-on. She's as common as the rest of us. She can read a million books, but it still don't make her any better than the likes of me. At least I'm not working in a launderette.' Neville tried to pull away, but Madge gripped him more tightly. 'Anyway, I'm not trying to blacken her name, you must treat as you find, but as your brother's friend, it's my duty to warn you not to trust that woman.' She pulled him towards her, kissed his cheek again, then added: 'Be lucky.' She released him. Neville straightened his collar, smiled lopsidedly and staggered out into the night, the other men watching him as he went.

Recklessly, he took the scenic route, and was soon lost. At one point he wandered into a field, and fell into a ditch. When he managed to find the road again, he almost got himself run over. 'Jus' falla de road,' he kept mumbling to himself as he wobbled along. 'Jus' falla de road.' Little did he know he'd turned full circle and was heading back the way he'd come. He then saw a figure emerging from the darkness. Frightened, he stopped dead in his tracks, then started back-pedalling.

'Get away!' he shouted. 'Get away from me!'

'There you are,' said Dilys. 'You had me worried sick.'

It later transpired that she'd been scouring the town, looking for him. She'd popped into the the Crown and was told by one of the men that he'd just left. When she got him home, she tried to help him up the stairs, but it was too difficult, so she dumped him in the living room. Before she went she heard him say: 'Ah going to London tomorrow.'

'Yes, yes, of course you are,' she said, and left.

He woke up around ten the next morning, badly hung over. Never again would he touch alcohol. He was so parched his tongue was stuck to the roof of his mouth. Hauling on his underpants, he staggered to the bathroom. When he saw himself in the mirror, he recoiled. Were those his bloodshot eyes? He drank from the washbasin, then stepped into the shower. When he came out he felt marginally better, well enough to contemplate a mug of instant coffee.

Down in the kitchen, he was disgusted to see that there were still dishes in the sink from the previous night. He washed them up, nauseated by the sight of all the caked-on food, by the smell. Major saw him through the kitchen window and started barking. The noise made his head pound. 'Oh shut up, eediot dawg.'

He had his coffee in the front room. At some point he'd have to eat, but the thought of food was making him retch. If he didn't feel better soon, he certainly wouldn't be going to London. He recalled the night before. What a woman that Madge was. What a chatterbox! In Jamaica they called people like her 'labba-labba'. Still, thanks to her, he now knew about Joe's philanderings. By the sounds of it, he'd slept with half the women in the town, right under Dilys's nose. While Neville couldn't condone infidelity, he felt a grudging admiration for his brother's audacity. In such a close-knit community, his bed-hopping couldn't have been easy to conceal. Which begged the obvious question: did Dilys know? Neville shuddered to think. One thing was certain: Joe hadn't changed. As a boy he'd been known as Loverman.

He decided not to bother with London. A relaxing day indoors was what he needed. But what would he do? It occurred to him that he spent a lot of time worrying about how to pass the time. It was different at home. There, his days were usually occupied: mornings at his grung, afternoons at home, evenings at Sam's. If he fancied a change, he'd go and see Adlyn, or he might take a trip to Spalding. Ostensibly he'd go there to shop, but really it was a chance for him to hang around the plazas watching the hustle and bustle of life in a big town.

Finishing his coffee, he wondered if Valerie was in, and on an impulse he went to see her.

'Oh, hello. Come in, come in.'

'Ah not interrupting?'

'Not at all. Please, come in.'

She moved aside and Neville stepped past her. In the hall-way, she said: 'Tea?'

'Actually, no. But coffee would be good.'

'Coming right up. Go through and make yourself comfort-able.'

He went into the front room and sat down, on the same armchair as before. A beam of sunlight slanted in through the window, forcing him to shield his eyes. Valerie came in with the same tea set as last time. She poured two cups of coffee then asked Neville if he wanted cream or milk. He opted for the latter. The moment she was seated, he said: 'So. How you getting on?'

'Good, thanks. You?'

Before he could answer Valerie sniffed the air and said: 'Have you been drinking?'

He remembered that the effects of alcohol could not only be seen, but smelt. 'Sorry,' he said.

'No, no. I don't mind. But it's a bit early, isn't it?'

Neville explained. When he'd finished, Valerie said: 'I see. Bet you sunk quite a few jars, didn't you?'

'Beg pardon?'

Valerie laughed. 'Like a drink, do you?'

He couldn't deny it.

'Just like my H. Whisky man, he was. Loved the stuff. What about you?'

'Dragon.'

'Come again.'

'Stout.'

'Oh.'

There was a lull. Valerie sipped her coffee. Neville glanced around the room. Everything was as he'd remembered it, except that the bowl of pot pourri had been replaced by a vase of orchids. They'd just started to open, and were giving off a heady smell.

'Bet your wife misses you.'

Neville was jolted by the statement, but quickly composed himself. 'Me wife pass away a few years ago.'

'Oh.' A pause. 'I'm sorry to hear that.' She looked at his hand. 'I see you still wear your ring.'

Neville fingered the plain gold band, and for a moment was lost in thought. He could see Charmaine's face. Not as she was during her illness, but as she was the day they had got married. Bishop Douglas had officiated. He'd commented on her radiance, and said what a fine couple they made.

'I suppose you know that I'm also a widow?'

Neville returned from his trip down memory lane. 'Yes, ah know,' he replied.

Valerie smirked and said: 'Been regaling you with all the details, has she?'

'She tell me dat you husband die of cancer. Da's all.'

It was Valerie's turn for nostalgia. She looked towards the window, lingeringly, as though expecting Harry to walk by.

After a while Neville said: 'Me wife had de same t'ing.'

Valerie looked at him. 'Sorry. Miles away. What was that?'

'Me wife. She had . . .' He didn't get a chance to finish it.

'Oh my God. Really? Where?'

'Breas'.'

'Oh, terrible, terrible. Did she lose either of them?'

Neville shook his head.

Valerie was silent for a while, then said: 'It's a dreadful disease, isn't it?'

'You can say dat again.'

'With H, it was his prostate.'

'Yes. Wha's dat exac'ly?'

Valerie explained, quite matter-of-fact, and was relieved to see that Neville didn't so much as flinch. She went on to talk about Harry's illness, describing in minute detail its various stages; all the false dawns, all the pain, all the treatments. With each new disclosure, Neville would interject with: 'Ah know exac'ly wha' you mean,' then follow it up with a few recollections of his own. How unburdening it was to talk to someone, finally, about his ordeal. He'd never had the chance, neither during, nor afterwards. There'd been no one with whom he had thought he had thought he could even broach the subject. Whenever he tried – usually with Sam or Freddie – he was told not to be morbid. Yes, he'd received a lot of sympathy, and no little support, but he wanted to talk, wanted to convey what it was like for him to watch his wife slowly disintegrate before his eyes. Judging from her candidness, perhaps the same was true for Valerie.

At the next natural pause, she said: 'Got any kids, Neville?'

'No.'

'Why, you and your wife didn't want any?'

Neville smiled. Of course, there couldn't possibly be any other explanation. 'We wanted them all right. But . . .' He paused before continuing. '. . . we wasn't up to it. *I* wasn't.'

If the ground could open up, thought Valerie. 'Sorry. Hope I wasn't prying.'

'Is all right,' said Neville. 'Ah can laugh 'bout it now. Me frien' dem always teasing me 'bout it. Blankshot is jus' one of de names dey call me.'

Valerie giggled.

'*You* have any children?'

She did. Two sons, both married and living in London. They visited as often as they could, which wasn't often enough. She tried not to pester them. They had their own lives to lead, and she didn't want to appear intrusive. Harry's death had been a real blow to them, but in a way the length of his illness had prepared them for it. Five years on, they were doing all right.

Neville thought for a second, then said: 'And you?'

'I'm sorry?'

'You doing all right?'

'Most of the time, yes. But of course Harry was so much a part of me. Before him there was no one. We met at school. He was my first and only love. I miss him every day.' She paused. 'Can you understand that?'

Neville most certainly could. Briefly, he and Valerie discussed the bereavement process, and agreed that it was an on-going thing. Daily they thought about their lost ones, and not always in a loving way. Often they felt anger, anger at being left behind. Then there was the impatience to join them, which had to be fought like the Devil. But mostly there was an emptiness, which nothing on earth could fill.

On that note, Neville began to stir. 'Well, ah suppose ah should get going.'

'No. So soon?'

'Yes, ah mus'. Ah going to London today.'

'Oooh, sightseeing. I envy you.'

Neville smiled, stood up. 'Well, it was very nice taaking wid you, Valerie.'

'Likewise. Let's do it again soon.'

'Ah would like dat very much.'

Valerie escorted him to the front door. On the doorstep they had a final exchange.

'Any news on your brother?'

He thought about it. The vague possibility of Joe being in London was hardly news. 'No. Not yet.'

'Oh. Well, good luck with it, anyway. And remember, pop by any time.'

'T'ank you.'

They said their goodbyes and Neville went next door.

It was an old, crumbly station, with rusty tracks and exposed platforms. The ticket attendant tapped out his Super Saver Return, stealing glances at him. He didn't notice, too busy studying the electronic timetable. The train was due in fifteen minutes. It arrived on time. Neville was relieved to see that there were few passengers on board. He got on and went and sat by a window. Opposite was a young couple, kissing.

They didn't seem to notice him. Erm . . . would they mind if he opened the window? They gave him a queer look, as though he were a pervert. He apologised. They moved across the aisle to the adjacent seat and carried on kissing. Neville sniffed and hauled the window down.

During the short train ride, he found himself thinking about Valerie. Her love for Harry had been evident in everything she'd said. Neville didn't find it surprising that they'd been together so long. There'd been a girl at school (before Joyce) with whom he had thought he might easily have spent the rest of his life.

Her name was Brenda, and they'd been dancing around each other for over a year. He'd been too shy to act, but, egged on by Sam and Freddie, had decided to go for it.

He'd just left the school grounds when he noticed her sitting on a grass verge a little away from the school gate. She was sitting with her knees up to her stomach, with her blue pleated skirt covering them. Beside her, on the grass, lay her leather satchel. She noticed Neville coming towards her and smiled at him. Neville blushed, his heart skipping several beats. What was she doing there? he wondered. Surely not waiting for him.

'*Hola*,' she said as he came up alongside her. They'd had Spanish together that afternoon.

'*Hola*,' he answered. 'Wha' mek you a siddung desso?'

'Me faader picking me up. In fact, see him deh.'

Neville looked round to see a gleaming white Mercedes pull up on the opposite side of the road. Though he tried to disguise it, he was impressed.

'Me see you tomorrow,' said Brenda, jauntily walking towards the car. Neville watched as she skipped across the road and got into the back seat. Just then the electric window in the driver's door rolled slowly down.

'Hello, young man,' Brenda's father shouted. 'Come 'ere a secon', please.' Neville approached the car tentatively. He was intimidated by Brenda father's, who was well known in those parts; or at least his shops were. He leaned out of his window and said: 'So. Brenda tell me you is ar new boyfriend.'

Neville sputtered. Brenda smiled, enjoying his discomfort.

'You mus' come to dinner some time,' said Brenda's father. 'As a matter of fact, why you nuh come tomorrow?'

'Erm . . . erm . . .'

Brenda giggled, pleased to see him so tongue-tied.

'Erm? Erm nutten,' said Brenda's father. 'It sekkle. You coming to dinner tomorrah and dat's dat. Pick you up right yasso after school.'

'Pardon me, sar,' said Neville. 'Me would 'ave to tell me people dem first. Me couldn't come jus' so, not widout tell dem, sar.'

The man smiled and said: 'You know who me is, young man?'

'Yes, sar. Skipper Emmanuel, sar.'

'All right, den. You jus' tell you people dem dat I invite you to dinner. Ah feel sure dey won't min'. See you tomorrah.'

''Bye, Neville,' said Brenda from the passenger seat. She blew him a kiss, then she and her father were gone, the Mercedes stirring up a huge quantity of gravel as it went.

'De arrogance of de man,' said Granville. 'Jus' who him t'ink him is?'

'Skipper Emmanuel,' said Neville. 'You know who him is, Papa. De Skipper chain?'

'Ah know who him is,' said Granville. 'Wha' me ask was, who him t'ink him is.'

The rest of the family laughed. They were sitting around a fold-back dining table eating salt mackerels and green bananas.

'Well,' said Bunty. 'Me can't see what 'arm it gwine cause. Is only dinner.'

'An' anodder t'ing,' said Joe. 'Neville have him eye 'pon de daughter. So, you never know, Papa, a few years from now we might be rich.'

Granville waved away the suggestion. He swallowed a mouthful of food, then said: 'So when him picking you up?' The others tried to stifle their giggles.

On the way to the Emmanuels' the following evening, nestled into the back seat of the Mercedes, Neville stared out of the window at the scenery drifting by: now a goat-speckled hill, now an aromatic orange grove, now a roadside shack selling sugar cane. Up front, sitting next to her father, Brenda was showing off. She fiddled with the glove compartment, pulled down the sun visor, depressed the cigarette lighter. Mr Emmanuel finally lost patience with her. He told her, very firmly, that the road was tricky and if he were to negotiate it successfully then he could ill afford any distractions. And as if to illustrate the point, he carefully rounded a hair pin bend in the road. By the time he'd straightened up, Brenda was in a sulk. Neville continued to study the landscape. He hardly ventured outside his village, and was excited by the change in scenery. Even the soil looked different to him – redder, somehow. To his left, spread away into the distance, were beautifully configured yam hills; to his right was a frog-infested, reed-clogged swamp which at night became illuminated by 'peenie-waalies', or fireflies. Ahead, the road snaked and spiralled up towards Wild Cane, then continued its ascent into the misty, mountainous region beyond, cutting a swathe through the dense vegetation like the track of a giant orange peel. All in all, it was a shortish ride, and Neville was actually disappointed when he noticed they'd turned into a gravel driveway that ran from the road up to the house.

It was a very large house – concrete, whitewashed, complete with the obligatory tiled veranda. It was located on an 'exclusive' plot, which was still evidently undergoing development, going by the mounds of earth, the unfinished houses, the dumper trucks, and the freshly dug irrigation channels.

Mrs Emmanuel came out to greet them. Tall and elegant,

with her slightly greying hair scraped back into a bun, she said: 'Mek haste, the food getting cold.'

The dining room was unnaturally cool, owing to the tiled floor, open French windows, and brass ceiling fan. The food was already on the table, and Neville wondered whether they always ate that early. There was white rice with oxtail; a salad of lettuce, skellion, tomatoes, and diced avocado pear (saturated in a home-made dressing); and for drinks there was sour-sop juice (Brenda's favourite) and a fruit punch laced with rum (Mr Emmanuel's favourite). Mrs Emmanuel said grace then invited everyone to help themselves.

For all their airs, the Emmanuels ate heartily, with relish, especially Mr Emmanuel, who put away copious amounts of food while hardly pausing for breath. By comparison, Neville's slow chewing and tiny mouthfuls made Mrs Emmanuel think he wasn't hungry, or, worse, wasn't enjoying the food. She said nothing, not wanting to embarrass him.

Afer dinner they went to sit on the veranda. The sun was still shining from a cloud-free sky, and it was reflected in the windows of the surrounding properties, around and beyond which lay a vast stretch of open land whose horizon shimmered like that of an arid desert. A few dogs barked in the distance. Mr and Mrs Emmanuel sat together on a cushioned swing-chair, while next to them Neville and Brenda sat on a small bench. Mrs Emmanuel had brought out some leftover sour-sop juice which she placed, with four tall glasses, on a small three-legged table. She invited the others to help themselves, but only Brenda took up the offer.

'Me could do with a Red Stripe, dear,' said Mr Emmanuel.

'Lord, man,' Mrs Emmanuel grumbled. 'How you gi' so much trouble? You wait till ah come all de way out 'ere before you talking 'bout beer. Chuh!' She sucked her teeth and went back inside.

Mr Emmanuel gave Brenda a victorious wink, but she failed to see the humour in her mother's humiliation, and so remained straight-faced. Mr Emmanuel noted her rebuff and turned to Neville. 'So, young man. You 'ave any brodda and sista?'

'Yes, sar. I 'ave a twin bredda name Joe.'

'Ah. A twin, eh? Identical?'

Neville nodded.

'Nice, nice,' said Mr Emmanuel. 'Jus' t'ink of all de fun you could have confusing people.'

Neville groaned. It was the standard reaction to his announcing he was a twin. People insisted on seeing the 'fun' side of it, while ignoring the drawbacks.

Feeling left out, Brenda rose to leave.

'Where you going?' asked Mr Emmanuel.

'To see wha' Mama doing.'

'Sit you ass down, girl. Every secon' you hitching up under you madder tail. She only gaan to de kitchen.'

Brenda sat down, pouting. Neville sensed a family storm brewing, and didn't want to be caught in it.

'Spoil rotten she is,' said Mr Emmanuel to Neville.

'Me not spoil,' said Brenda.

'Yes you is. Spoil. Spoil, spoil, spoil. Can't say nutten to you widout you push up you face. Jus' like you doing now.'

Mrs Emmanuel came back with the beer. Mr Emmanuel clapped and cheered and began singing a popular tune.

> 'Is a long time gyal me nevva see you
> Come Mek me hol' you han',
> Is a long time gyal me nevva see you
> Come mek me hol' you han', gyal
> Come mek me hol' you han' . . . .
>
> Peel head John Crow
> Siddung 'pon a tree top
> Pick out de blossooooom . . .
> Mek me hol' you han', gyal
> Mek me hol' you han' . . .'

'You stay dere,' said Mrs Emmanuel. 'Whatever sweet you going to sour you. Now move up!'

She shoved up next to him on the swing-chair, then noticed Brenda's sour expression.

'And wha' wrong wid you, young lady?'

Brenda didn't answer. Neville stared at his fingers. Mr Emmanuel sipped his beer from the bottle, and feigned ignorance.

'Is wha' you say to ar, Skip?' asked Mrs Emmanuel.

'Not a t'ing,' said Mr Emmanuel. He winked at Neville and started humming the tune from before.

'Hones'ly, man,' said Mrs Emmanuel. 'Me don' know why you mus' always trouble ar. Come, Brenda. Come to Mama.'

Brenda went over to her mother and sat on her lap.

'But would you look at dis, Lord?' cried Mr Emmanuel. 'Big, big twelve-year-ol' you babying like she jus' born dis afternoon. Dis is really too much.' He turned to Neville: 'You see, Neville. You see what ah mean? Spoil rotten.'

Neville smiled weakly. He wanted to go home.

'Never you min' him,' said Mrs Emmanuel to Brenda. 'You is Mama's likkle girl. No matter how big you is.' She stroked Brenda's ribboned plaits.

Brenda then did something which both Mr Emmanuel and Neville found utterly repellent. She started sucking her thumb.

'Oh, Brenda, please,' said Mr Emmanuel. 'Please, ah beg you, don' do dat. It don' look good.' He hid his eyes behind his hand.

'Leave her be,' said Mrs Emmanuel. 'She can suck ar finger all she want.'

'Ah gwine put some fowl doo-doo 'pon it one of dese days. Ah bet she never suck it again after that.'

'Ah 'ave to go home now,' said Neville, timidly.

'Come, Neville,' said Mr Emmanuel, happy to get away.

On the way home Neville reflected on the evening. He regretted going to the Emmanuels'. They were not his kind of people. He had only accepted the invitation because it promised intimacy with Brenda. As it turned out, she hadn't even spoken to him. Not that it would have made a difference, for the sight of her sucking her thumb had put him right off. He decided that when he got to school the following day, he would switch his attentions to Joyce Young.

The train pulled into Liverpool Street station. The young couple were up and at the door before it stopped, holding hands, eager to get off. The train finally screeched to a halt and they jumped off and started running along the platform, weaving in and out of the other passengers.

By contrast, Neville stepped tentatively from the train. He joined the procession down to the barriers, looking about the whole time. He was amazed by the vastness of the station, by all the trains. At the barriers, he was asked for his ticket. He produced it and asked about the train to Hackney Downs. Check the board, he was told, and rudely dismissed. He grumbled and stepped beyond the ticket inspector on to the main concourse. He got caught in a stampede of commuters, and found himself being pushed and shoved and jostled. 'Jesus Christ!' he shrieked. He stared up at the timetable, which he noticed was virtually in the roof. 'Why dem have to put de damn t'ing so high?' he whined.

Half an hour later he arrived at Hackney Downs, a station only marginally less desolate than the one he'd been at earlier. When he got outside, he suddenly realised he'd made a error. Lattie's was a club, which meant it was probably closed till nightfall. He checked his watch. Just gone five. Damn! He thought about calling Joyce, but decided she was probably at work. Which was just as well, since he was still unsure about going to see her. He would tackle each problem individually. First, find the place, which in itself should kill a bit of time. Afterwards, get something to eat. Beyond that . . . .

As he walked along he found himself nodding and smiling

at complete strangers. He was beginning to relax. After all, he was in London. What a place! If the boys knew, they'd be jealous as anything. Not that they'd show it. Especially not Freddie. 'Yes,' he could imagine Freddie saying, 'London all very well and good, but New Yaak, now dere's a town!' Neville smiled at the thought, then noticed a passer-by, an old black woman, staring at him. He wondered whether she'd mistaken him for a loony.

He came to a busy intersection. Traffic lights. Pelican crossings. Which way now? he thought. Just then he noticed some flyposters, stuck to a boarded-up shopfront. They were advertising all sorts of things, including reggae events. He recognised the names of some DJs from Jamaica. He smiled, unaware that these 'noisy' performers had any kind of following abroad. Well, well, he thought. He was about to move away when, to his sheer amazement, he saw a poster announcing an upcoming 'bashment' at none other than Lattie's Nightspot. There was an address, even bus numbers. Neville looked heavenward and gave silent thanks. He started ripping at the poster, drawing stares. Slapping his forehead, he got out his pen and pocket notepad, bought specially that afternoon. As he jotted down the details, his heart sank when he noticed the opening times: 10 p.m. till late.

On his way to view the place, aboard an open-back bus, he got into a conversation with the conductor. He was not only Jamaican, but hailed from Neville's parish. While the other passengers eavesdropped, they talked excitedly about all the places they knew. By a further coincidence, they learned that they had the same surname, and agreed that they might be distant relatives. Jokingly, they began calling each other 'cuz'. Neville asked if there were any decent places to eat in the vicinity. The conductor said that there was a West Indian takeaway only a few doors along from Lattie's. As an added incentive, he said that the cuisine was Jamaican, as opposed to 'smallie'. They laughed.

Neville finally reached his stop. Watching his step, he jumped down off the bus.

'Wha' you really name?' he asked.

'Eugene. You?'

'Neville.'

'Well, see you around, Neville. And good luck.'

'All right, cuz. You tek care now, you hear?'

Eugene pulled his cord-bell and the bus crawled away.

The club wasn't anything special. A single-storey building on a busy main road with 'Lattie's Nightspot' in yellow neon above the door. Neville studied it, up close and from a distance, then left to find the takeaway.

He whistled when he saw the queue. It stretched almost on to the pavement. It was evidently a popular haunt. Standing just inside the doorway, Neville felt that there was something disconcerting about the place. Initially he was stumped, and then it dawned: there were no white people.

At last he reached the head of the queue. He bought rice and peas and chicken, with a pineapple juice to wash it down. Normally he wouldn't have such a heavy lunch, but he thought that it might be his final meal of the day.

When he got outside he realised that he had nowhere to go and eat. A few of the other customers came out and he noticed that one or two had headed straight into the Ladbroke's next door. When in Rome, he thought.

The bookmaker's was noisy and smoky, and Neville almost turned tail and went out again. Fanning the smoke, he went and sat at a free table and began to open his silver foil containers. He kept expecting a member of staff to come and turf him out, but none appeared, so he ate his lunch in relative comfort.

When he'd finished, he disposed of his empties then stretched out and made himself at home. Only then did he really begin to take in what was happening around him.

It was the first time he'd been in a bookmaker's. He didn't

gamble, so had never had cause. Of course, he knew what went on there, but had never seen it with his own eyes. He couldn't believe the abandon with which the men were squandering their money. They seemed to have lost their minds. Some of them, he noticed, were clutching four and five betting slips at a time. Others were frantically studying their folded newspapers. While others still were rushing up to the counter and practically begging the harassed cashiers to take their money. Those that didn't get their bets on would lose their tempers and start swearing and carrying on in a way that Neville found really vulgar.

Someone clapped him hard on the back, almost knocking him out of his chair. Angered, he spun round. A man, roughly his own age, wearing a grey-coloured uniform, was grinning down at him.

'Well?' said the man, spreading his arms, as though wanting a hug. 'Cat get you tongue, Joe?'

Neville rolled his eyes.

'Not Joe. Neville.'

The man gasped, studied Neville wide-eyed and open-mouthed.

'Well I nevva,' he said. 'You mean to say you really exis'?'

Neville smiled. Feeling at a disadvantage, he stood up, offered his hand.

'And you name is?'

'Huh? Oh. Sorry. Art'ur, Art'ur.' He shook Neville's hand. 'Bwoy,' he said, 'you favour you bredda is a shame! You even wear de same clothes as him.'

Neville smiled.

'So. You's a Jamaican?' he asked.

'Born and raise,' said Arthur, proudly.

'Which part you come from?'

'Kingston.'

'Oh.'

Arthur grinned, revealing a row of crooked teeth.

'Me and you bredda used to joke 'bout the same t'ing. Used to call him country bwoy.'

'When las' you see him?'

'A good while now, you know? Mus' be a coupla year well.' Neville sighed. 'De man jus' stop come 'bout de place. Him gaan back a Yard or wha'?'

Neville told the story from the beginning. Arthur listened intently, stroking his bristly chin and nodding. When he'd heard everything, he said: 'Be careful when you go to Lattie tonight.'

'Why, is a rough place?'

'Yes, but not only dat. Joe have nuff enemy in deh.'

'Serious?'

'Serious.'

'Why, is wha' him do to dem?'

Arthur looked round, drew Neville in close. 'All kina t'ing. Sleep wid dem woman, borrow dem money an' run weh, bad mout' dem, all kina t'ing.'

'God know?'

Arthur put his hand to his heart.

Neville said: 'Ah don't tin'k ah will bodder wid it, den. After all, me not likely to fin' Joe in dere.'

'No. But ah know somebody who might know where you might fin' him.'

Again he looked round, drew Neville in. Her name was Michelle, and she and Joe . . .

By the time Arthur had finished, Neville had become almost tearful. Arthur put a consoling hand on his shoulder. 'Look,' he said. 'None of we is perfec', right? We all have we likkle weakness. Some man drink. Some sniff coke. Some fuck batty.' Neville's jaw dropped. 'Sorry. De point ah mekking is dis: dere was two t'ing you bredda couldn't resis' – white woman and gambling. Apart from dat, him's a genuine fella. Trus' me.'

'But what is dis, Lawd? You mean him tek up gambling as well?'

The more he discovered about Joe, the less recognisable he became. Gambling, for God's sake. If there was one thing he couldn't stand . . .

'Look,' said Arthur, 'ah have to rush back to work, but here, mek ah give you Michelle address.' He scribbled it down on a betting slip and handed it to Neville. 'Jus' say Art'ur sen' you.'

'Wait. Before you go. You know where dis place is?' Neville got out his notebook and turned to the front page. Arthur looked at it.

'Stamford Hill? Yes, is jus' up the road. 'Bout twenty minute by foot. You go out here, turn left, keep walking till you reach Stoke Newington High Street, then . . .'

A sprawling council estate, mostly high-rises. Neville was daunted by the sheer scale of the place. These were housing schemes such as he'd not seen before. The Kingston tenements were a collection of huts by comparison.

Clutching Arthur's note, he started wandering from block to block till eventually he found the right one. He entered the lift and stepped into a puddle. Initially he suspected a leak, but soon realised it was urine. 'God blin' it,' he cursed, then pressed the button for the twelfth floor. The door closed slowly and the lift suddenly jolted upward, unsettling his stomach.

On the twelfth floor, the lift opened on to a sign with arrows pointing left and right, the flat numbers beneath. Neville studied it for a moment, then turned left along the graffiti-covered landing.

He rapped softly on the door, self-conscious in front of the peep-hole. Within seconds a woman he took to be Michelle was standing before him, dressed in a green shell suit, her blond perm straggly, smoke-stained.

'Well, well,' she said, her left arm akimbo, her right holding the door open.

''Fore you say anyt'ing else, me name is Neville. Joe twin bredda.'

Michelle scrutinised him more closely. 'Bloody 'ell. You are an' all. He mentioned . . . . but . . . 'old on . . . don't you live in . . .' She leaned forward, looked up and down the landing. 'What're you doing 'ere? What's 'appened? Summing's 'appened, right? Where's Joe? What's he gone and done now? I don't want no trouble.'

'Me can come inside, please?' asked Neville.

They went through to the living room: second-hand furniture, woodchip wallpaper, old carpet.

'Can't offer you much,' said Michelle. 'Got tea.'

'Dat would be very nice,' said Neville, smiling through gritted teeth.

Michelle went out. Scanning the room, Neville noticed a row of photographs on the mantelpiece. In each of them, Michelle was surrounded by the same three children – two teenage boys and a girl no older than five, all mixed-race. The girl was quite pretty.

''Ere are,' said Michelle, re-entering the room. She handed Neville a mug of scalding tea, burning his fingers. 'You can sit down, you know.'

'T'ank you,' said Neville, and he lowered himself into a nearby armchair. Michelle sat opposite on the settee, crossing her legs. Neville noticed her red toenails poking out from the end of her furry slippers.

'So what's going on?'

Neville explained. When he'd finished Michelle said: 'Wouldn't worry about him too much. Prob'ly shacked up wiv some tart somewhere.'

'When las' you see him?'

'It'd be around the same time you say he went missing. Remember it well. Came round here dripping claret all over me bloomin' carpet.'

'Sorry, ah don' quite falla you. Dripping wha'?'

Michelle lit a cigarette. 'Blood,' she said, blowing smoke into the air.

'Him was bleeding!?'

'Yeah. From the 'ead. Said he got hit wiv a baseball bat. Nasty, it was. Real nasty.'

Neville groaned and stared into his tea-stained mug. 'Jesus,' he said. 'Sound like dem try to kill him.'

'Prob'ly. But you play wiv fire, gonna get burnt, intcha?'

'Wha' you mean?'

Michelle dragged on her cigarette, blew the smoke out. 'I mean he got himself mixed up wiv some real nutcases, the type you just don't mess wiv.'

'You know dese people?'

'No. And I don't wanna know 'em.'

Neville held her gaze and said: 'So de day Joe turn up 'ere bleeding, da's de last time you see him?'

'That's right.'

'You tek him to de hospital?'

'Like 'ell I did. Told 'im to sling his bleedin' 'ook. Bloody cheek. Don't see 'im for months then he shows up looking like that? Frightening the kids? Nah, sorry, weren't 'avin' it. Wouldn't be so bad if it was the first time, but I was always patchin' 'im up, always nursin' his bloody wounds. And what did I get in return? Sweet FA. Ain't as if I made any great demands on 'im. Far as I was concerned he could do what the hell he liked. Didn't even bother me that he was married.'

Neville did a double-take. Had his ears deceived him?

'You mean to say you did know 'bout Dilys?'

Michelle dragged on her cigarette. ''Course.'

'Good God in heaven! What sort of woman you is?'

'Now look 'ere, don't you take that tone wiv me. I . . .'

'Ah can't listen to no more,' said Neville, interrupting. 'In fact, ah going to leave now.'

'As you like.'

'Sorry to tek up so much of you time.' He stood up,

handed Michelle his mug. 'You people is jus' too much. Too much.'

'You going, or you gonna stand there beating yer gums all day?'

Neville shook his head then hurried from the room. Michelle escorted him out of the front door. As he walked off down the landing, she shouted: 'And if you do run into 'im, tell 'im not to bovver showing his face round 'ere again. I don't wanna see 'im, and 'is daughter certainly don't.'

Neville stopped in his tracks, thought briefly about turning round, but instead carried on down the landing.

On his way down in the lift, he tried to order his thoughts. How many more children had Joe sired, for how many different women? Neville wondered whether he had nieces and nephews scattered all over London. He might have passed a few in the street, for all he knew. The facts were mounting up, and a very clear picture was emerging. Joe hadn't changed at all. The evidence was overwhelming. Lies, deceit, adultery, illegitimate children, gambling, violence – the whole shebang. As ever, Neville thought of a fitting Jamaican phrase. *What a bam! bam!* In his letters, Joe had portrayed himself as a family man, cured of his wild ways by marriage and fatherhood. But in reality he was still the same Joe who'd caused his family so much grief as a teenager. Once again Neville found himself thinking about the Kingston episode, that period during which Joe had misbehaved to such an extent that his aunt had begun to fear for his life. He could still remember her heartfelt letter of complaint. His parents were illiterate, so he'd had to read it. It warned of Joe's increasingly unruly conduct, and expressed fears about where he was ultimately headed. Neville could recall it almost verbatim.

Dear Bunty,

Greetings in the name of Jesus, our soon-coming king. I hope this letter finds you in the best of health.

Well, where to begin? The first thing to say is that things not right here at home. It's Joe. I just don't know what get into him. It's like he lose his head. I just can't talk to him. Byron can't talk to him. He stop going to school. He take up with bad company. He don't come home. No amount of talking or beating have any use to him.

It all start one day when I get this letter from him school. They want to know if him sick because they don't see him for a week. One whole week. And me and Byron never know a thing about it. Well you can imagine how vex I was after reading this letter. I was so vex I could have burst. I walk up and down the house the whole day waiting for Joe to come home. I did make up my mind to wring him blasted neck.

When him finally come home and me show him the letter, him only have the wrenkness to tell me to leave him alone. I had no choice but to box him upside his head. And you know what the boy do? He only jump up off the settee like him did want to strike me.

Well, I tell you something, you see if him did touch me that day, so much as touch me . . . Luckily him see sense and put him arse back on the settee.

But you know what, I blame Byron for the way Joe carrying on. Because that evening, instead of the man drop two lick in the boy behind, him give him two feeble blow with the belt and tell him to behave himself. Even now me have to laugh when me think about it. Is no wonder Joe still playing up.

But that's just the start of it. Things soon get a lot worse. Byron suggest that me write you, but me just didn't want to worry you. Me tell myself that me could cope, and that Joe was only going through a phase.

Anyway, it seem me was wrong, because it wasn't long before me get another letter from the school. This time

they say they really concern about Joe, and that they
wanted to know what happen to him and all sorta horse
dead and cow fat. Me never bother show Byron the letter,
not at first. Instead me decide to follow Joe one morning
to find out where him was going all day, because him was
still getting up in the morning and pretending as if him
going to school. Me just don't know how the boy get so
deceitful.

Well, like me say, me decide to follow him. It wasn't
easy, because him not stupid. Me had to dodge behind a
whole loada car and tree so him wouldn't spot me. God
know how me manage it, but me get to find out that him
was spending all day at some downtown arcade owned
by a big old fat man name Ron. This Ron, apparently,
was a good-for-nothing cruff who encourage the children
them to spend all them money in him place while him full
up them head with all kinda foolish talk. Him tell them
that school is a waste of time, that them is all adults now
and should be thinking about earning money and having
children of them own. Me hear say him sleep with the
girls and send the boys them out on robbery, giving them
gun and everything.

It's then me decide to tell Byron about the letter. Me
just couldn't bear to think of Joe getting himself shot
on some robbery or other, maybe even by Byron. Well,
this time Byron never spare him. In fact me was really
frightened for Joe at one stage. But you know something,
water never once come to him eye. Not one drop. When
Byron finish beat him, him just stand there looking at we,
full of hatred. Him say that no matter what we do him
not going back to school. Byron was so vex the vein in
him neck nearly pop. Him rush Joe again but me had was
to get between them. Me don't know what him woulda
do to Joe.

And still that wasn't the end of it. You never going

*to believe what happen next. Me still can't believe it
meself.*

*Me had no idea what Byron was thinking of doing. Me
never believe him would go behind me back, not even
discuss it first. Anyway, that's exactly what him do. Him
go behind my back one day and pay this Ron fella a visit.
And this is where the story get a bit confuse.*

*According to Byron, Ron draw a gun on him and
him had was to defend himself. But according to some
eye-witness, it was Byron who draw first. According to
them, him just walk up and start firing. Anyway, Ron
end up dead and Byron get suspend, without pay, till him
superiors and them finish them investigation. Whatever
the truth is, Byron was damn foolish to go there in the
first place.*

*After that Joe don't come home for a week. Again
Byron pester me to write you, but me didn't want to get
you all fretty fretty. Specially since me didn't even know
where Joe was. One time me hear a rumour that him was
living with some other guys him own age and that they
does spend all day having orgy and smoking ganja and
doing all kinda thing. Every night me say a prayer for
him. Me beg Byron to go and look for him, but him say
him don't want nothing more to do with Joe.*

*Then one day, out of the blue, him show up. Him look
half dead, as if him don't eat or sleep for months. When
him come into the living room Byron didn't even look up
from the TV. Him simply tell Joe that for everybody sake,
him should go and never come back.*

*And that's why me writing. Me just can't take it no
more, sis. Please, please, me begging you, come and get
Joe before something really bad happen to him. Him not
such a bad boy, him just need guidance. Come and talk to
him, try and convince him to go back to the country. Him
won't come to no harm there. Some people just not cut out*

for city life. Please make haste, sis. Things getting critical here. So write back soon and make me know when you coming. Me look forward to your letter. In the meantime, take care of yourself and God bless you and keep you till me hear from you.

Your loving sister,
Dulcie

Granville and Bunty were on the next available bus, but it was a wasted journey. Joe (now living with a group of friends) refused to come back with them, and he stayed in Kingston till eventually he left for England. The family were sad to see him leave, and they fretted over what he might get up to overseas. But as the years passed, they were pleased not to receive any further reports of his bad behaviour. News of his marriage, and the subsequent birth of his son, finally convinced them that he'd reformed. But Neville now knew differently. He felt ashamed at Joe's antics, and tried to console himself with one simple fact: at least his parents had died ignorant of the truth.

It was time. He'd procrastinated long enough. What would he say to her? How would he explain? There was no getting round it. The truth, he decided, however unpalatable, would have to suffice.

Even to Neville's untrained eye, the house looked impressive. Three storeys, ivy-clad, on a quiet street. Later he discovered that Joyce occupied only the ground floor, and he was disappointed.

Joyce was shocked to see him. 'Good God!' she cried. When she'd recovered, she threw her arms around his neck and hugged him tight. They hadn't had physical contact in years, and Neville was embarrassed. He stood on the doorstep, his arms limp at his side, and allowed himself to be crushed.

'Why you never write?' said Joyce, releasing him. He shrugged. 'Never mind. Come inside, come inside.'

They walked through to the living room, which was warm and cosy and tastefully decorated.

'You hungry?' asked Joyce.

'No.'

'A drink, then. Me have beer.'

'Dat would be nice.'

Joyce left the room. Neville sat on the cream leather sofa, ill at ease. His thoughts turned to Dilys, and he felt a pang of guilt. Joyce returned with a four-pack of mini beer bottles, and two frosted glasses. She sat next to Neville on the sofa, too close for his liking.

They spent the next hour or so catching up. In the three months since her return, Joyce had been snowed under at work. She was sorry to be so boring, but that was the extent of her news. Neville gave a detailed update on life in Mount Moriah, complete with witty anecdotes, many of which featured Adlyn at her caustic best. Joyce lapped them up, often interrupting Neville to shout: 'That's my mama!' It then occurred to her that he had no luggage.

'Neville,' she said, 'please tell me you never come all this way with just the clothes on you back.'

The dreaded moment had arrived. Neville sipped his beer and began. As he'd expected, he found it hard going. Joyce listened without interruption, her expression becoming graver by the minute. Neville felt like the bearer of bad news, and he was relieved when he'd finished his speech. Joyce waited a moment before responding. She didn't think that Joe's running off was any great surprise: after all, he was, and had always been, the type to abandon his family. Instinctively, Neville leaped to his brother's defence. Joe would never do such a thing. Yes he would. No he wouldn't. A niggly exchange, before calm was restored.

'Almost a week in the country,' said Joyce, 'and not so much as a phone call. Imagine that.'

Neville sighed and slumped into the sofa. So he hadn't been spared after all. He should have known better.

'You better phone that woman,' said Joyce.

'Why?'

'So you can tell her you not coming back tonight, of course.'

Neville smiled. Five minutes later he was on the phone to Dilys, telling her not to wait up. She ticked him off for not taking an overnight bag, and said that she'd see him the following day.

Cyrian didn't react well to seeing Neville. He was cordial all right, but no more than that. At one point, during dinner, Neville asked him what he planned to do with himself after leaving school. He shrugged and said, 'Dunno.' Joyce was relieved when he eventually excused himself from the table. She couldn't understand why he was acting so strangely, so out of character. What was wrong with him? she wondered. Later that night she had her answer. He came into her room and said: 'Saw Dad today.'

'Oh, did you now?'

'Yeah. Came by the school.'

'The school? For what?'

'Gave me some money.'

Joyce shook her head. Bribery. The oldest trick in the book.

'How long's he staying?' asked Cyrian.

'Neville? One or two day, p'raps. Why?'

'Just wanted to know.'

CHAPTER SIX

The following evening Donovan and Michael showed up, accompanied by their wives. Neville hadn't seen them for years, and was taken aback by their facial hair and deep voices. Unlike Cyrian, they were pleased to see him, and they soon had him in conversation. Over dinner, they talked to him about Mount Moriah, saying how they hoped to revisit it some day soon. Cyrian groaned. Why, he asked, would anyone in their right mind want to visit such a place, never mind live there? He'd struck a discordant note, catching the others off guard. They stared at him agog.

'Who rattled your cage?' asked Donovan.

'Stay out of big people's business,' said Michael.

'But I'm asking a serious question,' said Cyrian.

'Shut up,' said Joyce. 'Just shut up and eat you food.'

For the next few days, Neville found himself alone in the house. To pass the time, he started going for walks. Initially, he confined himself to the immediate neighbourhood, a residential area with street after street of terraced houses and cars parked bumper to bumper. Each day he came across the same strange-looking men, going about in groups, all of them dressed in black from head to toe, with beards down to their chests. Confused, he asked Joyce for an explanation. She said that the men were Hasidic Jews, and that they didn't like black people and were to be avoided.

Little by little, then, he started venturing farther afield. One day he ended up on Stoke Newington High Street, where he became preoccupied by all the shops. Stuff, he thought. So much stuff. Loitering outside a hardware store, he heard: 'Is you dat, cuz?' He swivelled instantly, and saw Eugene leaning out of the back of his bus, which was stuck in traffic.

'How it a go, cuz?' he asked, excitedly.

'Working, working,' said Eugene. 'You know how it is.'

Neville smiled. Such was the traffic jam that they were able to catch up, exchange numbers and arrange to meet for a drink the following evening.

'Where?' asked Neville.

'Right there,' said Eugene, pointing at a nearby pub. Neville studied it. It was no different to every other pub he'd seen, with the usual silly name: The Rat and Parrot.

'Eight?' said Eugene.

'Eight,' said Neville.

Impatient to see his friend, he got to the pub half an hour early. The place was practically deserted, and he wondered whether he shouldn't go away and come back. Deciding to wait, he ordered a pint of Red Stripe from the barman and took it over to a secluded booth, which had cushioned leather seats. The first sip of his beer confirmed what he'd always imagined: Red Stripe abroad was inferior to Red Stripe back home. Still, he was filled with pride, for it was yet another thing that his tiny country had given the world. He ruminated on some of the others – reggae music, Bob Marley, Craven A.

He became restless, and started fiddling with the beer mats and the glass ashtray. There was a TV on in the far corner, set high on the wall, showing a live football match. Several black men sat beneath it, nursing their pints and staring up at the screen. Neville observed them for a while. Football. It wasn't his sport. He was a cricket man, and often went to see the West Indies play at Sabina Park in Kingston. In recent years he'd become disillusioned with their play, which he thought was dull and pedestrian. Brian Lara aside, he believed that the current generation of players were ordinary, not fit to kiss the boots of their more illustrious predecessors. Sir Garfield Sobers. Vivian

Richards. Michael Holding. As Freddie once put it: 'Any likkle pissin' tail country can beat de Windies now.'

When not watching cricket, Neville loved to play it. He was a member of his local side, which belonged to an inter-parish league. The team was no great shakes, but whenever they played at home the whole village would turn out to support them. Neville was one of the better players, adept with bat and ball alike. As a child he'd been very promising, if a little lacking in flair. Joe, on the other hand, was far more swashbuckling, with something of the Gordon Greenidge about him. At the crease, he could be a pitiless batsman, capable of winning matches on his own. Neville could remember one school match where he did just that. All afternoon he battered the opposition bowlers, shouting after each boundary: 'Six! Pick up sticks!' 'Four! Shut de door!', to the delight of his watching team-mates. The umpire was forced to speak to him. His conduct, he was told, was both unsporting and ungentlemanly. He curbed his outbursts, but still ended the day on an unbeaten eighty-five. From then on, big things were expected of him, and it was taken for granted that he would eventually go on and play for the national side, perhaps even the West Indies. Alas, he preferred football, which he was no good at. In Mount Moriah they still grieved over his wasted talent, no one more so than Neville.

Eugene finally walked in, still dressed in his conductor's uniform. He greeted Neville with a vigorous handshake, followed by a slap on the back. 'What's dat you drinking, cuz?' he asked.

'Red Stripe, cuz. Red Stripe.'

They chuckled, and Eugene left for the bar. While he ordered, Neville studied him. He was carrying a bit of weight, but carrying it well. The pub was obviously his local, for he not only shouted across to the men watching the football, he was quite friendly with the barman, too. He received the drinks and, trying not to spill any, walked carefully over to Neville. Squeezing himself into the booth, he raised his glass and said: 'Here's to St Ann. The best parish in all JA.'

'St Ann!' said Neville, and they clinked glasses.

They talked for hours, drawing innumerable comparisons between Jamaica and England. They agreed that the former was superior to the latter, except in one crucial area: the economy. For that reason, Eugene couldn't foresee a time when he'd repatriate. Neville sympathised, but said it was a huge price to pay for a better standard of living: the total rejection of your homeland. Eugene didn't see it that way. He was a Jamaican morning, noon and night, and didn't need to be living in Jamaica to prove it. Besides, he was a frequent visitor, unlike some he could mention.

'Like my bredda,' said Neville, and he proceeded to elaborate.

He told Eugene everything, then said that his hopes of finding Joe were fading fast. In response, Eugene waxed philosophical. He urged Neville not to give up, said that life had a habit of throwing up surprises, that the Lord worked in mysterious ways, and that you could never tell what might be around the next corner. Neville drew comfort from his words, then staggered off to order another round.

Too drunk to walk, they shared a minicab home. Neville was the first to be dropped off. Before he left the car he asked Eugene what his plans were for the following evening. Eugene grinned and said: 'Same time, same place?'

Joyce was already in bed when Neville got in. Relieved, he crept noisily to his room. He was in the middle of undressing when Joyce pushed the door open. Shaking her head, she watched as he tried to remove his trousers, hopping from foot to foot. 'Drink going to kill you one of these days,' she said, then left. As soon as she'd gone, Neville flopped face down on the bed. He was out in minutes, his trousers still round his ankles.

That night he had a recurring dream. The setting was Jamaica, and it featured himself and Joe as children.

It was a humid afternoon, and the threat of rain was evident from the vast black clouds obscuring the sun. Equipped with their slingshots, they set out for a nearby mango grove, which was seething with birds.

For a long time they sat beneath the trees and waited, in silence. Overhead, a gentle breeze rustled the leaves and swayed the branches. Now and then rays of light squeezed through the branches and impregnated the darkness below. The air was heavy with the cloying smell of rotting mangoes, many of which had ripened and fallen off the trees.

For a time there was no sign of any bird activity. Joe and Neville were becoming impatient, not to mention paranoid about duppies. They started whispering.

'Can't see nutten,' said Neville. 'You?'

'Nutten,' said Joe. 'Ah jus' don' understan' it.'

'Me nuh see not one bird yet,' said Neville.

'All right, all right, you jus' say dat.'

There was a loud thud behind them. They stiffened, but didn't look round.

'Is wha' dat?' asked Neville.

'How me mus' know,' Joe replied. 'Prob'ly mango.'

They resumed their vigil and for the next minute or so didn't speak. Neville began to get a neck ache. Moving his head from side to side, he said: 'You t'ink we should figet it fi tideh?'

'No!' said Joe, and he sucked his teeth.

'Oh, come aan, Joe, dis is a wasta time.'

'Hush up,' said Joe, annoyed by his brother's whining. 'Patient man ride donkey, remember? Look.'

He had spotted some half a dozen doctor-birds hovering above. He didn't like them because they were always hovering, difficult targets. Neville took aim, but Joe put out a restraining hand.

'Wait till dem in a group, eediot.'

The birds were now busy sucking the nectar from a cluster of blossom, using their needle-like beaks to get right inside the flowers. They appeared to be motionless, the beat of their wings too fast for the naked eye.

Stealthily, the boys stood up. Mindful of saboteur twigs, they gingerly manoeuvred themselves beneath the feeding birds. Then, raising his finger, Joe signalled for them to take aim. They pulled their slingshots back to snapping point. The doctor-birds, wary, continued to feed.

'Shit!' cried Neville suddenly.

'What? What?'

The doctor-birds soared away as one.

'Look,' said Neville, pointing at the ground. He was stamping up and down and brushing his legs and scratching his ankles.

'Ooo, eee, aaa,' said Joe, and he too began to brush his legs and dance about.

From the thigh down they were covered in red ants, the most devilish of all ants, capable of inflicting nasty little bites when provoked. The boys jigged around trying to get rid of them, but their numbers were too great and in the end they had to flee from under the trees.

At the edge of the mango grove they stopped to nurse their bites. Labouring the point, they swore revenge on all ants, their descendants, and their descendants' descendants. Thoroughly demoralised, they trudged off homeward. After a few hundred yards, it began to rain heavily. By the time they got home they were completely soaked through.

Eugene was first to the pub this time. Neville found him at the bar sipping a pint of Guinness with his nose in a battered copy of the *Sun*, which was opened on page three. Neville saw the nude photograph and frowned disapprovingly. He then ordered a round and he and Eugene went and sat at their booth from the previous day.

'So, cuz,' said Eugene. 'How you feeling?'

'Aaright. You?'

'Not so good. Head still sore from last night. Terrible day at work. Terrible. Just couldn't be assed. A whole heapa people get free ride today, I can tell you.'

Neville smiled and said: 'You better watch youself wid me, Eugene boy. De whole worl' know dat ah like a drink. You mustn't encourage me.'

Eugene smiled and sipped his Guinness.

'But you shouldn't be drinking dat,' said Neville.

'I know,' said Eugene. 'But there's only one cure for a hangover: hair of de dawg.'

'Ah beg you pardon?'

Eugene chuckled. For a moment they didn't speak, and were happy not to. Eventually Eugene said: 'You play darts, cuz?'

'Wha'?'

'Darts, man. Darts. Look.' He pointed. Neville was at a loss. He'd never before seen a dartboard. Eugene rose suddenly, walked up to the Kiwi barman, exchanged a few words with him, and was handed a set of darts.

Neville received a few lessons and soon caught the bug. Eugene then left him at the oche to practise alone.

'You's a natural,' joked Eugene. 'A natural. Keep it up and I might let you join me team.'

'Team?' said Neville.

Eugene explained. The pub ran a once-weekly team competition, on Fridays. There were three players to a team, with a maximum of five teams. Each player contributed twenty pounds to the pot, and the winning team took all. Neville did his maths, then whistled at the sum. 'You all mus' be very good,' he said.

'Good me raas,' said Eugene. 'We play for fun. Come Friday and see for youself.'

'I will,' said Neville, and he launched one of his 'arrows', as Eugene had called them. He'd aimed for the bull's-eye, but the dart landed in double nineteen. It was an odd game, he said. Yes it was, Eugene agreed, and a dying one. Once upon a time it dominated pub culture, but nowadays . . . actually, it was making a bit of a comeback, thanks to cable TV.

'You have cable?' asked Neville.

'Yes. I get it so I can watch de cricket.'

Neville paused mid-throw. 'Cricket, you say?'

'Yes,' said Eugene.

'Wha' sorta cricket? Tes' match and such?'

'Of course. De Windies down under as we speak.'

'Down where?'

'Australia. De other night I mussa stay up till t'ree watching de game.'

Neville didn't stand on ceremony. 'Ah could come and watch a likkle wid you?'

Eugene smiled and said: 'How 'bout tonight?'

Neville had assumed that Eugene was married, but one look at his flat (on the third floor of a high-rise) told him otherwise. The place was dark, cold, in need of decorating, with clothes scattered everywhere. Neville couldn't help turning up his nose, and he finally understood why people did the same when they visited his own place.

'Excuse the mess,' said Eugene. He cleared a space on the well-worn settee, then gestured for Neville to sit down.

'You on you own, den?' asked Neville, lowering himself on to the settee.

'You could say dat.'

'You don't have a . . .'

'You hungry?' said Eugene, interrupting.

'Erm . . . ahh . . . yes . . . I s'pose.'

'All right, den. You mek youself comfy. I going to rustle up somet'ing. You don't mind watching TV in de meantime?' Neville shook his head.

'De cricket not on for another hour, dat should give me plenty of time.' He switched on the TV (a portable), handed Neville the remote, then left the room.

Neville stared at the TV, which was showing adverts. At

the end of the ads, there was an announcement that the cricket would be on in an hour. Neville could barely contain his excitement. Looking at the remote, he tried to work out how to change the channels. There were no words, only confusing symbols. Recklessly, he pressed a button and the screen went blue, but the sound remained. 'Oh no,' he said, 'Ah break de man TV.' Panicking, he started pressing buttons indiscriminately. Eventually the picture was restored, but now the sound had gone. 'God blin' it,' he cursed, then started pressing buttons again. The sound returned, but he was on a different channel. More fiddling saw him return to the original channel, at which point he cursed modern technology and tossed the remote aside.

Eugene returned soon afterwards. 'You like fish?' he asked.

'More dan meat, sometimes.'

'Good. We having steam fish and white rice. Me speciality.' He looked at the TV and tutted. 'Snowboarding. What kinda sport is dat? Bring on de cricket, for heaven's sake.'

'You tek de words right outta me mout', cuz.'

They laughed and Eugene went out again. Neville was suddenly aware that he might be imposing, and he regretted having been so forthright in the pub. Normally he'd have shown more restraint, but the Windies were playing, and he'd forgotten himself. Besides, if he was any judge of character, Eugene looked as if he could do with the company.

The coverage was imminent, and Neville feared that Eugene might miss the start of it. He was about call out to him when Eugene entered the room carrying a tray laden with food and drink.

'Jus' in time,' said Neville.

'Oh. Good. You don't mind eating on you lap?'

'Lawd, man, shet you mout'. Dere's any odder way to eat?'

They laughed then settled down to watch the cricket. It was one in the morning.

By three o'clock, Eugene had fallen asleep in his favourite armchair, snoring lightly. Neville was wide awake, his eyes glued to the screen, a disgusted look on his face. The Windies were batting, and not faring too well. After a steady opening, there'd been a spectacular collapse, the middle-order batsmen barely putting on a hundred between them. Now the tail-enders were struggling to make the score respectable. When the final wickets fell, Neville couldn't help himself and swore loudly at the screen. Eugene woke with a start. 'What!?' he cried, his voice croaky. He quickly gathered his wits and squinted at the screen. 'How dem getting on?'

'All out.'

Eugene checked the scorecard. 'My God,' he said. 'What a useless setta man.' He kissed his teeth, scratched his groin, then consulted his watch. 'Raas! You know what time it is, cuz?'

Neville checked his watch, the one Joyce had given him.

'Me have to go to bed, Neville, boy. Work in de morning. What you want to do?'

'Erm . . .'

'You could stay here, of course. You more than welcome to de settee.'

Neville thought about it. He was imposing again, but given the lateness of the hour, plus the fact that he had no key to Joyce's place . . .

'Well,' he said, 'if you sure is no trouble . . .'

'None at all. Let me get you some bedclothes.'

Eugene rose and left the room. On screen, the pundits were busy analysing the West Indies' innings. The words 'shambolic', 'brittle' and 'capitulation' were mentioned. Neville picked up the remote and pressed every button until he'd switched off the TV.

A few hours later he was woken by Eugene, who was on his way to work. He'd asked to be roused in order to phone Joyce before she herself left for work. He just caught her, and launched into an explanation, for which Joyce had no time.

She said that she'd leave the spare key under the bin, and that she'd have appreciated a call. When she hung up Neville thought: like mother, like daughter.

He had a shower as soon as he got in, then changed into a set of old clothes belonging to Joyce's husband, Reggie. There was a tall mirror in his bedroom, in the wardrobe door, and for a moment he stood looking at himself. How had it come about that he was dressing in other men's clothes? He could almost justify wearing Joe's, but he felt undignified to be donning a stranger's. He'd been a fool to let Joyce talk him into it. With that thought in mind, he took his dirty clothes to the bathroom and washed them by hand, even though there was a washing machine that Joyce had taught him to use. Afterwards, he put the wet clothes in the airing cupboard to dry, determined to wear them again that day. If he must wear Reggie's stuff, let it only be for a few hours at a time.

Later that afternoon, he was relaxing in the front room listening to the radio when he heard the doorbell ring. Ever curious, he went and answered it. He was confronted by a man, about his age, snazzily dressed in an expensive-looking dark coat and scarf.

'Yes?' said Neville.

'It feel strange ringing me own doorbell,' said the man.

'Wha'?' Neville studied him. Might he be a madman? 'Sorry, but dere mus' be some kin'a mistake . . .'

'You must be Neville.'

Neville drew back.

'How you know my name? You's a friend of Joyce?'

The man laughed. 'I don't think she would say dat. De name's Reggie.'

Neville almost gasped.

'Pleased to meet you,' said Reggie, extending his hand. Neville pointedly refused it, and the snub established the tension that followed.

'You mind if me come inside?' said Reggie.

'Joyce not in at de moment.'

'That's all right. It's you I come to see.'

'Me?'

'Yes.'

Neville looked at him suspiciously.

'Well?' said Reggie, a smarmy smile on his face. Reluctantly, Neville stepped aside.

They walked through to the front room, Reggie leading the way. He was obviously familiar with the place, and that set Neville's teeth on edge. As soon as they entered the room, Neville said: 'So what you want?'

Reggie smiled. 'Relax,' he said, flopping down on the settee. 'Take the weight off.'

Neville remained standing, arms folded.

'Come on,' said Reggie. 'It won't kill you to siddung.'

Neville sighed audibly then sat on the arm of an armchair. 'Ah sitting.'

They held eye contact for a long time before Reggie said: 'So. You does come back to claims Joyce, eh?'

'Ah beg you pardon?'

'It's all right. I does know all about it. You's she one-time sweetheart, right?'

Neville sniffed contemptuously. 'Ah don' see dat as any business of yours.'

'I must say,' said Reggie, 'you leave it a bit late. Pretty as Joyce is, she not a spring chicken any more. She best days behind she now. She getting on a bit, putting on a few pounds here and there.'

Neville gritted his teeth. 'Look, Richard . . .'

'Reggie. De name's Reggie.'

'Whatever you name, exac'ly what it is you come here for, hmm? Come, man, speak up. Ah not in de habit of was'ing time. Say what you have to say den go 'bout you business.'

Reggie laughed bitterly. 'But we does live in a funny world these days, boy.' He shook his head. 'All you Jamaicans does be the same. Precisely where you get off ordering me around in me own house?'

'If is your house, how come you not living in it? Hmm? Oh, ah forget, Joyce t'row you out.'

Reggie sprang to his feet, as did Neville. They squared up.

'Now look here,' said Reggie. 'You best mind you tone with me.'

'Or else what?'

They continued to eyeball each other before Reggie threw his arms in the air and turned away. He walked over to the window and stood there, looking through the lace curtains on to the street. After a time he said: 'You really have some front. You cutting you ten in me house, wearing me clothes . . .'

'And sleeping wid you woman,' said Neville.

Reggie swivelled, enraged anew. 'What's that you say?'

'You deaf?'

Reggie sputtered, then finally managed to say: 'If you had any shame you would leave dis house right now.'

'Ah was t'inking de same t'ing 'bout you.'

Exasperated, Reggie said: 'Oh, go to hell,' then stormed out of the room. Neville followed and escorted him to the front door. Out on the doorstep Reggie turned and said: 'Stay away from me son, you hear, or as God is me witness . . .'

'Lawd, man, wha' you talking 'bout now?'

'Cyrian. I know you does be mistreating him. I warning you, leave he alone.'

Neville sighed. 'Ah don' know wha' Cyrian say to you, but if him claims ah mistreat him, den . . . den . . .' He couldn't think of what to say, so he slammed the door in Reggie's face.

He went straight to the airing cupboard and retrieved his still-damp clothes. He wasted no time getting into them, changing right where he stood in the hallway. He then put Reggie's clothes back where he found them and left the house.

Aboard the train, alone in his carriage, he reflected on his encounter with Reggie. He'd never felt so small, so humiliated.

It was all Joyce's fault. Damn the woman. Why had he gone to see her? In fact, when he stopped to think about it, why the hell had he even come to England? To look for Joe? If so, what efforts had he made? Apart from a few questions here and there, not much at all. Truth be known, he wasn't that bothered any more. So why keep up the pretence? Surely the gap was unbridgeable, the intervening period too long. Joe was as much a stranger to him as the graffitied names inside the carriage. In any case, with what he'd discovered, it wouldn't be possible for them to have any kind of relationship. It was time that he accepted the truth, that the brother he once knew and loved was gone for good. Perhaps even literally, since there was the very real possibility that Joe was dead. For a long while, he'd refused to entertain the notion. But now it was looking more than likely. And if it were true, how would it make him feel? He knew the answer even before he'd asked the question.

He'd forgotten how spooky the house was, and how damp. He almost gagged on the smell. Careful not to alert Major, he crept upstairs to his room. Dilys hadn't been in it while he'd been away, for there was a mound of Joe's old clothes on the floor where he'd left them. Gathering them up, he had a sudden realisation, as though the clothes themselves had spoken to him. If Joe had run off, surely he'd have packed a few items. Yet according to Dilys, he hadn't taken so much as a pair of socks. He'd left all his stuff behind, and she'd stored it away in the attic. What it all amounted to, Neville wasn't sure. But he did know one thing, and it partly explained why he'd been so reluctant to leave in the first place: whatever had happened to Joe had happened right there in the town. As these thoughts passed through his mind, a wry smile appeared on his face. Five minutes earlier he'd been indifferent to Joe's fate. Now here he was speculating on it.

Would he go back straight away? He had what he came

for, but perhaps he might sneak to the Crown for a swift one. He quickly dismissed the idea. Dilys was a few doors away at the launderette, and the risk of being spotted by her was too great. Besides, there'd be Madge to contend with. He stole away from the house and headed for the train station.

He got back about an hour before Joyce was due home. He decided not to mention Reggie's visit, or the fact that Cyrian had been stirring up trouble. He would, however, speak to her on another matter.

She came home weighed down with shopping bags. Pleased to find Neville in, she asked for his help in putting the groceries away. Neville couldn't believe the amount of stuff that she'd brought back. 'Good God, woman. You leave anyt'ing in de shop?'

Joyce laughed and started unloading the frozen foods. 'So, what you do with youself today, Mister?'

'Ah went and pick up a few clothes from Dilys.'

Joyce was surprised. 'You mean you go there and back today?'

'Yes.'

Joyce put some eggs in the fridge. She made a great show of it, and Neville sensed trouble. 'So why you never bring all you things with you?'

Neville didn't reply, so Joyce turned to him and said: 'Tell me something, what really going on 'tween you and that white woman?'

'Ah don' know wha' you taaking 'bout.'

'I mean if you rather you was there . . .'

'Look, who say anyt'ing 'bout . . .'

'Then why leave you things at her place? Hmm? And why you always phoning her?'

Neville thought about it. Why *had* he left his things? As an excuse to go back and see Dilys? Oh, for heaven's sake . . . 'Ah couldn't face lugging everyt'ing back here, dat's all. An' as for phoning ar, de woman was kin' enough to put me up. De leas' me can do is . . .'

Joyce slammed down a can of fruit. 'Finish!'

Things were a little calmer between them after dinner. Cyrian had gone to bed and they were relaxing in the front room watching TV. Neither could really engage with the film being shown, a sentimental family drama made for TV. To relieve the tedium, Neville said that he was sorry for not being around much lately. Joyce waved it aside, then apologised for her earlier outburst – though, jokingly, she still maintained that there was something going on between him and Dilys. Neville accused her of being jealous and threw a cushion at her. Horrified, she flung it back, and for the next few minutes it sailed to and fro, accompanied by a lot of giggling. The sound carried to Cyrian's room, and made him sad.

Neville then asked the question that he'd been meaning to for some time. Was Joyce considering moving back to Jamaica? Why had he asked? He thought she might be. And what had given him that idea? This and that, bits and pieces, a hunch. She paused before admitting it: yes, she was, but only considering it, mind. And if and when she did decide, it wasn't likely to happen for years. And even then she wouldn't dream of returning to Mount Moriah. It would have to be somewhere more civilised. One of the neighbouring big towns. Mandeville, perhaps. Or Christiana. Somewhere with running water. Somewhere with phone lines! They laughed, flung the cushion a few more times. Then Joyce said: 'So what about you?'

'Me?'

'No, Tom over there. Yes, you.'

'Wha' 'bout me?'

The question, thought Joyce, about summed him up. He had so much to offer the world, yet didn't know it. 'You shoulda come to England with me, you fool.'

Neville smiled and said: 'Maybe. From what ah can see, you certainly do awright for youself.'

'I not doing too bad. I comfortable. But it wasn't always like that, mind.'

Neville asked her to explain. It occurred to him that he knew very little about her life in England, and practically nothing about what it was like for her when she first arrived. The reason was simple enough: he'd never enquired, and Joyce hadn't volunteered the information. It was typical of their relationship.

Joyce said that the early years had been a real struggle. Jobs had been menial and low-paid, accommodation scarce. *No dogs. No Irish. No blacks.* Where many of her compatriots had given up and gone home, she'd soldiered on. After all, she was in the mother country, and things could only get better. And so it had proved. The days of sleeping four to a room were long behind her, and she was proud of all that she'd achieved since. Her one regret was the breakdown of her marriage, which she had thought she'd never get through. But the dust had settled, and she was still standing. Of course, her children had been affected, especially Cyrian. But she'd protected them as best she could, and her conscience was clear. As for the future, who could say? She was a single woman approaching fifty, and that held some fears for her. But she wasn't going to dwell on them, for being alone also had its compensations. She was free to do as she pleased, and there was no better feeling in the world.

Neville digested her words, then said: 'And what 'appen if you meet somebody tomorrah?'

Joyce pondered for a second, then smiled. 'I would fall at him feet and worship him.'

They laughed.

CHAPTER SEVEN

When Neville walked into the pub Eugene practically jumped on him. 'Lawd, cuz, I glad to see you.'

'Wha' 'appen?' said Neville, fearing the worst.

'The team short one man.'

'What? You mean . . . but . . .'

'Come,' said Eugene, grabbing his arm. 'I will pay you deposit.'

It was a busy night down at the Rat and Parrot, and noisy, with plenty of people Neville hadn't seen before. He was introduced to the individual members of each team, all black men his own age, the majority of them Eugene's work colleagues.

The competition lasted hours, and eventually Eugene's team triumphed by the narrowest of margins. To celebrate, they bought drinks for everyone, which made a sizable dent in their winnings. Neville and Eugene were soon drunk. Later, they went back to Eugene's to watch the Test match. It was the fourth day's play and the West Indies were being slaughtered, but it had no effect on Neville. He'd had a really good night, in good company, and not even a dismal showing by his beloved Windies could spoil that.

He'd been round the day before, to find that she wasn't in. He'd left feeling foolish and rash, and had decided to put her from his mind once and for all. Yet here he was again knocking on her door.

She answered this time, cigarette burning between her fingers. She was dressed in a faded white T-shirt and a pair of washed-out jeans.

'Go away,' she said, and slammed the door. Stunned, Neville stood there for a few seconds, then turned and headed off down the landing. He got as far as the lift when he heard: 'Oi!' He turned to see Michelle standing out on the landing, arms akimbo.

This time he declined the offer of tea, but Michelle still went off to the kitchen to make one for herself. While she was out of the room, Neville went up to the mantelpiece and studied the photographs. As on his first visit, he found himself drawn to the little girl; only this time he knew why.

Michelle came back, mug of tea in one hand, cigarette in the other.

'Summing wrong wimme chairs?'

'Beg you pardon?'

'You're standing aroun' like you did last time.'

'Oh. Sorry.'

They sat down, in the same seats as before, opposite one another. Michelle's toes, poking from the edge of her slippers, were not painted red this time, but black. 'Found 'im, then, 'ave ya?'

Neville shook his head. Michelle dragged on her cigarette, slurped her tea.

'I ain't seen 'im, if that's what yer 'oping.'

'Da's not why ah come here.'

'What, then?'

Good question, thought Neville. Just why had he come? He looked away from Michelle for a moment, towards the mantelpiece. The little girl in the picture smiled down at him.

'Wha's ar name?'

There was an ashtray on the floor by Michelle's feet. She stubbed her cigarette in it then kicked it to one side. 'Chantelle.'

Neville nodded. It was a nice name, suited the girl's features. 'How old she is?'

'Seven now. Four then.'

158

Michelle slurped her tea. Still looking at the photograph, Neville said: 'De las' time ah was 'ere, you say you did know 'bout Joe wife.'

'That's right.'

'So you mus' did know 'bout Sean as well.'

'Yeah? And?'

Neville faced her again. There was so much smoke in the room that he had to squint. He started making the point about Sean and Chantelle being brother and sister, and that in an ideal situation they'd get to know each other, and . . .

'Look,' said Michelle, interrupting. 'I know what you're gonna say, and I can tell you now, I don't give a monkey's. I only care about me and mine. Understand?'

Neville nodded, then looked at the picture again. Michelle lit another cigarette.

'Any chance ah could meet ar?'

'What for?'

'Would be nice. She's me niece, after all. De only one me 'ave . . .' And he paused before adding, '. . . far as me know.'

It was a loaded statement, a fact not lost on Michelle. She dragged on her cigarette, then said: 'I gotta pick her up round three. Come along if you want.'

Neville checked his watch. It was showing two o'clock. 'Ah would like dat very much,' he said.

'You mustn't come near her, though. I mean, she can't know you're there.'

'But why not?'

'Might think you're 'im, mightn't she? God knows why, but she loves 'im, still asks about 'im, misses 'im like no one's business. One look at you and . . .' She shook her head, slurped her tea. 'It's too much of a palaver, that's all.'

There was logic in her argument, thought Neville, albeit skewed. He agreed to keep out of sight.

He felt like an idiot standing across the road from the school, behind a tree. It was the height of the school run, and the gates were clogged with parents and children. Michelle stood smoking a cigarette, huddled into her puffa jacket against the increasingly cold weather. There was a lollipop lady escorting a few children across the street. Neville thought that she looked ridiculous standing in the middle of the zebra crossing holding her pole aloft. Just then he saw Chantelle, and his heart skipped a beat. She came out of the school grounds, in high spirits, and rushed up to her mother. Michelle, a little self-consciously, hugged and kissed her. They then linked hands and set off. After a few yards they stopped. Michelle stooped to adjust Chantelle's woolly hat and scarf, and to tie her shoelaces. Neville was able to get a good look at her, and it occurred to him that Michelle might have contrived this. Moments later mother and daughter continued on their way. Neville watched until they were dots in the distance.

Without knowing it, his time in London had acquired a certain rhythm. While Joyce was at work, he either stayed in watching TV or listening to the radio (talk radio, mostly), or he went for walks. Most evenings he was down the Rat and Parrot with Eugene.

He did things with Joyce, too. They managed to get out on a few 'dates', which included a couple of trips to the cinema. Neville hadn't been since he was a boy, and he found the experience wondrous. One day they attended a wedding together, or at least the reception. The daughter of one of Joyce's friends had got married, and she, the friend, had insisted on meeting Neville. It was a sumptuous bash, held in the function room of an expensive West End hotel. A good time was had by all. Neville got the thumbs-up from Joyce's friend, and he and Joyce danced the night away. Sadly, the evening ended on a sour note. Reggie was there, drunk, and he caused a scene by trying to pick a fight with Neville. He had to be shown the door.

One evening Eugene came over for dinner. Cyrian had been given prior warning, and the choice of whether to attend. He opted to spend the evening at a friend's.

Joyce prided herself on being a good hostess, and she really pushed the boat out. The table had been laid with her most expensive crockery, and she'd cooked a lavish three-course meal, the main dish being brown stewed fish. When Eugene saw the fuss she'd made, he told her that she needn't have bothered on his account. She said that he was worth it, and Neville felt a twinge of jealousy. He quickly put it from his mind, though, and they settled down to eat. A few minutes into the meal, Eugene said: 'I hope I not embarrassing you when I say this, but the two of you make a lovely couple. Hold on to her, cuz. Don't make dat Reggie fellow put you off.'

Neville grimaced. He'd told Eugene all about his encounter with Reggie, but had forgotten to swear him to secrecy. Fortunately for both of them, Joyce laughed it off.

'So,' she said. 'Neville tell me you's a single man, Eugene.'

Neville was instantly wary. Where was she taking that line?

'That's right,' said Eugene.

'But you have a sweetheart somewhere, right, good-looking man like you?'

Neville was jealous again. Eugene shifted in his seat, chewed his food too quickly.

'Come, come,' said Joyce, 'don't be shy. You's among friends. Who she is? I bet she young. Pass the salad, please, Neville.'

Neville did the honours. Eugene ate on, a coy smile on his face.

'So come on, Eugene, speak. What's the great mystery? You have a woman or not?'

'Lawd, Joyce,' said Neville. 'Not everybody tongue loose like yours.'

That tickled Eugene, and he sniggered childishly.

'Oh, shut you mout',' said Joyce to Neville. 'I just having a bit of fun.' She sipped her wine and said: 'Well, anyway, I have a theory. Maybe I wrong, but I think Eugene like man.'

Neville almost choked on a mouthful of rice. He started coughing and spluttering and had to have his back slapped by Eugene. This had little effect, so Joyce plied him with water. Still no improvement. He coughed and coughed, his eyes streaming. Eventually he had to flee the table. Eugene and Joyce heard him raking up in the bathroom. At one point Joyce shouted: 'You all right in there?' to which Neville responded with a fresh bout of coughing. Joyce smiled at Eugene, and, patting his arm, said: 'I was just joking. If I cause you any offence . . .'

Eugene waved it aside and said: 'Listen.'

Silence. A minute later Neville returned, eyes bloodshot, swallowing hard. Eugene and Joyce couldn't help themselves, and burst out laughing.

The evening ended, and Neville escorted his friend to the front door. He wished him a safe journey home, only to discover that Eugene wasn't planning on going home. He was heading off to a local shebeen, to listen to some music. It was Saturday, after all, and the night was young. He invited Neville along, but said that he'd understand if he wished to 'stay in for a little kissing and cuddling'. Neville reiterated that it wasn't like that between himself and Joyce, and said that he'd love to come out.

'Well,' said Eugene, 'what you waiting for?'

'But ah can't go out like dis. Me 'ave to change.'

Eugene kissed his teeth. 'Man, stop you foolishness. Dis is a sheebeen, not Buckingham Palace.'

Neville dashed to the kitchen to square it with Joyce. She told him to go and enjoy himself. Did she want to come? Thanks, but no. Her clubbing days were long behind her. Besides, she couldn't leave Cyrian alone.

'But him's a big enough bwoy can take care of himself.'

'Not in this country, he ain't. In the eyes of the law, him's a minor.'

That settled it for Neville. The law was the law, and he wouldn't be party to breaking it. 'See you later, den.'

'All right. You have you key?'

Neville patted his trouser pocket, and left.

The shebeen was in the basement of a run-down three-storey house. It was not at all what Neville had expected, and he was glad that he hadn't dressed up. There was a bored doorman, who stepped aside upon seeing Eugene.

Inside it was dark, and reeked of marijuana. Before them stretched a long corridor, with two rooms on the left, one on the right. The first room they passed was pitch black, and had music coming from it. The second was brightly lit and full of men standing around a gaming table shooting dice. The third had a pool table, with one or two people sitting around watching the game in progress. They finally came to the bar, a hole in the wall with a flap counter. Eugene exchanged a few pleasantries with the barman, who was called Strange. Neville wondered whether the name had anything to do with his manic stare. Eugene ordered a couple of bottled Red Stripes. 'So,' he said. 'What you think, cuz?'

Neville glanced around. There were a couple of old men standing downwind at the bar. The sight of them depressed him. 'You come here often?'

'Yes,' said Eugene. 'Is a good place to pass the time when you don't feel like going home.'

Neville knew what that felt like. Many a night Sam had to throw him out.

'Fancy a game of pool?' said Eugene.

'Erm . . . I never play before.'

Eugene laughed and said: 'Boy, you really live a sheltered life.'

'But ah can play billiard. Me frien' Sam . . .'

'Billiard, pool,' said Eugene, 'same difference. Come.'

In the pool room, Eugene was greeted by one or two of the men. Fishing some change from his pocket, he placed a couple of five-pence pieces on the side of the pool table, as 'markers'. There were other coins in front of theirs, as many as eight. It would be a long wait, said Eugene, so they went to check out the gambling room.

The game being played was seven-eleven, and the participants were shooting for high stakes. Most were clutching banknotes, and on the table itself there must have been hundreds of pounds. Men were squabbling for a throw of the dice. Gambling, thought Neville. He'd never understand the attraction if he lived to be a hundred. 'Madness,' he said.

'What?' said Eugene, caught up in the excitement of it all. He was craning his neck to get a better look.

'You go in for this sort of t'ing, cuz?' asked Neville.

'You mad? On my wages? No, no. I is stric'ly a watcher.'

Neville was relieved to hear it.

Soon they left to go and check out the music room. Once his eyes had adjusted to the darkness, Neville was surprised to see that there were as many women inside as men. He could make out couples slow-dancing, and he found it difficult not to stare. The DJ, calling himself Warrior, was in a neon-lit booth speaking softly into a microphone, warning the revellers that he intended to 'mad them' with music. He also claimed that his sound system – Damager Hi-Fi – was the best in the world. Neville was amused by his boasts, and, wishing to poke fun at him, he turned to Eugene, only to find that he was dancing with some woman. He managed to catch his eye, and was mortified to see that Eugene was indicating the woman standing next to him. He shook his head, but Eugene kept nodding at the woman, rolling his eyes in exasperation. Neville turned to the woman, whose air of desperation he found shocking to behold. He wondered what a woman of her age (she had to be at least the same age as Joyce, if not older) was doing in a place like this. Suddenly, the seediness of the whole scene began to disgust him, and he walked out.

A few minutes later, Eugene caught up with him at the bar. He cracked a few jokes based on Neville's bashfulness, then hauled him off to the pool room.

It was winner stay on, which disappointed Neville. He had hoped to play Eugene. Seeing the panic in his eyes, Eugene said: 'Don't worry. I will go first. Just watch me. It's a very simple game.'

Eugene lost, and Neville almost forfeited his turn rather than face the reigning champion. He had to be cajoled by Eugene.

As the game progressed, it became clear to Eugene that Neville had exaggerated his ability. He could barely hold the cue, forcing his opponent to remark: 'Yo, bredren. Better you go away an' practise.'

There were giggles from the onlookers. Neville, humiliated, slammed down his cue and went off to seek refuge at the bar. Once again, Eugene caught up with him. 'Don't worry,' he said. 'It's only a game.'

'Ah never wanted to play in de first place.'

Eugene soothed him, then went off to the loo. When he returned, he saw a large group of people forming a circle at the bar, but he couldn't see Neville. He fought his way through and discovered him lying on the floor, blood trickling from his nose, groaning and clutching his side. Strange and a group of others were crouched beside him. 'What de raas!' Eugene shrieked. He dropped to his knees. 'Cuz? Cuz?'

'Dere was three of them,' said Strange. 'Them jump him from behind.'

'Who?' said Eugene. 'Why?'

Strange shrugged and said: 'I don't know. Them just start kick and punch him.'

'Jesus Christ,' said Eugene. 'Cuz? Cuz? Talk to me, cuz.' Neville groaned. 'For heaven's sake, somebody call a ambulance!' He attempted to lift Neville's head, but Strange advised against it. A bystander got on his mobile and dialled 999. 'Cuz? It's me, Eugene. Talk to me. Where it hurting you?'

Neville grimaced and clutched his side; at the same time his eyes rolled back in his head. Eugene turned to Strange. Did he know the attackers? Strange said that they were regulars, but he couldn't put names to the faces. No one else knew them either, or if they did, they weren't saying.

'Him don't look in a good way,' said Strange.

Eugene wiped the blood from the corner of Neville's mouth, then shouted: 'Goddam it, where's that blasted ambulance?'

Neville groaned and clutched his side. The onlookers then started making idiotic suggestions. One said Neville should be given brandy. Another advised that he be stood up. One clever soul even thought that he might benefit from a snort of cocaine, and was prepared to donate a line. Eugene bawled him out and he went away grumbling.

The ambulance finally arrived. The attendants cut incongruous figures in their green uniforms. Everything stopped while they carried Neville out on a stretcher. Once they'd gone, however, things quickly returned to normal.

Eugene travelled in the ambulance to the hospital. Along the way he was asked to provide details of the incident. He couldn't, save the sketchy account given to him by Strange.

Soon the ambulance was pulling into the driveway of Homerton Hospital's A&E department. Neville was given a quick inspection by a harassed young doctor, force-fed some painkillers, then left on his stretcher to await a fuller examination. Eugene sat beside him for two hours, watching as the painkillers kicked in and lulled him into a fitful sleep.

He finally had his injuries confirmed by a senior doctor, a middle-aged woman wearing bifocals. Three broken ribs, severe concussion. He was, said the doctor, going to need expert medical attention. Eugene was asked to provide details of Neville's next of kin. He gave Joyce's name and telephone number. After that he was advised to go home, and told not to bother visiting for at least a couple of days, since Neville wouldn't be in a fit state to see anyone until then.

Two days later Joyce and Eugene came to see him, accompanied by Cyrian. They found him propped up in bed, dressed in hospital-issue pyjamas, with a bandage around his head, so drugged up he could hardly speak. His attackers, he said, had mistaken him for Joe. Joyce wanted to get the police involved, as did Eugene, but Neville said that it would be pointless.

That night he had a dream. In it, Joe attacked him, from behind, hitting him repeatedly over the head with a blunt instrument. The setting kept changing. First it seemed like the shebeen, then it began to resemble Dilys's bedroom, till finally it ended up looking like the woodland in Cuffie Ridge.

Because of the damage to his ribs, he didn't get out of bed for days. He was given bed-baths and regularly checked for bed-sores. Most of the time he slept, waking up at the oddest hours, often in the dead of night. If he did find himself awake during the day, he'd ask to be propped up so that he might observe something of hospital life. Which amounted to very little. One day he noticed a patient in the bed next to his, an elderly Asian woman with tubes in her nostrils. She was lying flat on her back, eyes closed, arms rigid by her side, with her thick grey locks splayed out across her pillow. He wondered what she might be suffering from. Looking at her, he was reminded of the state to which Charmaine had been reduced in her final days. At least she had spent that time at home, surrounded by loved ones, before passing on. This wretched creature next to him would no doubt suffer a more ignominious and lonely departure.

On another day, he woke up and spent the next few hours just watching the staff as they went about their business. He was struck by how numerous the black staff were, and by how many of them were in lowly positions. Aside from a few nurses (including the ward sister), the others were either porters or cleaners. Since arriving in the country, the only other place that he'd seen such a high concentration of black workers was on public transport. In an instant he saw what life for him in England would have been like. He'd have cleaned hospitals or driven buses. Next to that kind of work, being a small farmer didn't seem so bad.

He didn't make the best patient. Grumpy at the best of times, now he was positively querulous. The doctors treated him with brisk efficiency, that and condescension. The nurses were scared to go near him, for fear of being snapped at. They could never please him. His pillows were either too high, too low, too flat, or too lumpy. He complained of being ignored, of being treated like a child. Was it too much to ask for his bandage to be changed now and then? Wasn't there anything other than soup that he might eat? He became a real nuisance on the ward, and his fellow patients began to ask when he might be leaving. He was aware of the talk, which only made him more obstinate.

He mellowed only when Joyce and Eugene came to see him. At first they arranged for their visits to coincide, but after a while they began to show up on alternate days. Neville was pleased, because faced with both at once he could never relax. With Joyce, the visits lasted no more than half an hour at a time, mostly because she couldn't stand his whining. He was never sorry to see her leave. With Eugene it was different. Together they'd sit and make fun of the staff and the other patients. The only person to escape their tongue was Neville's neighbour. In all his time on the ward, she hadn't received a single visit, nor had she moved, except to open her eyes. Every so often she'd experience some crisis, and the doctors and nurses would dash to her bedside, drawing the curtain around them. Later they'd re-emerge, looking defeated. Many a time Neville thought she'd gone, and he'd look heavenward and mutter: 'In de midst of life . . .' But the old bird was more robust than she had any right to be, and confounded expectations time and again. Her desperate struggle for life reminded Neville of his own mortality, and made him depressed.

He was eventually told that his ribs had healed sufficiently for him to get out of bed and move around slightly. He had to be helped to his feet by a couple of nurses. With an arm around each, he tried to take a few steps, but his legs soon went and he had to be helped back into bed. He feared that he'd been crippled, but was told that his leg muscles had merely atrophied. He'd need to build them up again, which he could do by standing next to his bed for short periods each day. He was soon walking again, and two weeks after he was admitted, he was allowed home. The day before he left, his neighbour had a crisis, and didn't survive.

Neville's restless nature made him unsuited to convalescence. And for someone who'd lived alone so long, he was surprised at how much he hated his own company. With Joyce at work all day, he almost went out of his mind with boredom. At least at the hospital he could pass the time by haranguing the staff. Now he was forced to watch TV or listen to endless hours of radio. He started thinking about his parents, and marvelled at how keenly he felt their absence. He experienced headaches and dizziness, just as the doctors had warned him he would. He reflected daily on the viciousness of the attack and how close he'd come to dying. He grew fearful, and was tempted to go around the house locking all the doors and the windows. One day he became so afraid that he called Joyce at work. She had expressly asked him not to, unless in an emergency. When she got on the phone, after travelling from one end of the supermarket to the other, she couldn't believe her ears when he'd said that he just wanted a chat. When she got home they rowed, and she accused him of trying to get her the sack. It was for a similar reason that he called Dilys at the launderette. Unlike Joyce, she was pleased to hear from him. She said that she'd been wondering why he hadn't called. He told her about the attack, and about his stay in hospital. She was shocked by the news, and her concern touched and embarrassed him in equal measure. He reassured her that he was on the mend, and she asked if there was a possibility that she might see him some time soon. Yes, there was, he said, but didn't commit himself any further. After a heavy silence, he asked after Sean. Dilys said that he was 'preoccupied'.

Eugene came by most evenings, with cans of Red Stripe. He'd regale Neville with tales of life down at the bus garage. One evening, out of nowhere, he started complaining about how his work was getting him down, and that he was thinking of finding something else. After twenty-odd years on the buses, perhaps the time had come. Then again, at his age, with no expertise in any other field, it might be a risky move. Oh, for the day when he could retire and not have to worry about work. Neville asked him how he planned to spend said retirement, and whether he could see a special woman in those plans. He replied that he was a confirmed bachelor, and would be one till he died. For the record, he'd tried marriage, and it hadn't worked out. After twelve years his wife had upped and left, taking the kids with her. He couldn't be bothered to recount her reasons; suffice it to say that she wasn't happy. Ironically, years on, he could see her point. But that didn't stop the hurt, or alleviate the sense of betrayal, feelings he never wanted to go through again.

Neville thought about what he'd been told. Now he understood why Eugene had been so reticent on the subject of women. His wife leaving had clearly knocked the stuffing out of him. Neville knew something about that, and he felt a lot of sympathy towards his friend.

'Maybe you can fin' somebody else. Dere's plenty woman out dere looking for a good man like youself.'

Eugene laughed. 'I was thinking the same thing 'bout you, me frien'.'

'Wha' you mean by dat?'

'Joyce, of course. If you not careful, she going to slip through you fingers.'

Neville smiled crookedly, but didn't say anything.

It was over a week before Neville felt able to venture outdoors. One day he went for a walk around the block, passing many Jewish men on the way. On another day he found himself outside Chantelle's school. He loitered outside the gates for a while, drew a few suspicious glances, then ambled off.

When he felt up to it, he called Eugene and asked whether they could meet at the Rat and Parrot. Eugene wasn't sure. Joe's enemies were still at large, and there was no telling what might happen. Neville said that he wouldn't be scared into hiding, plus he was tired of being cooped up in the house. Privately, though, he was just as nervous as Eugene.

They got drunk that night, very drunk. In the cab home afterwards they sang Jamaica's national anthem. 'Eternal Father bless our land . . . guide us with thy mighty hand . . . keep us free from evil power . . .' The Nigerian cab-driver eyed them in his rear-view mirror, ready to turf them out at the first sign of any vomiting.

Before Neville got out of the car, he leaned across Eugene, bear-hugged him and said: 'You tek care of youself, you hear?'

'No, no, no, cuz,' said Eugene, and he hiccupped. 'You take care.'

They chuckled, shushed one another, chuckled again.

'No,' said Neville. 'Listen to me.' He burped.

The cab driver said: 'You going to leave the car or not?'

'Wait,' said Neville. He turned to Eugene. 'Cuz, you must listen to me. Seriously. Take care of youself, awright, and ah hope . . . ah hope . . .' He giggled.

'What,' said Eugene, 'what you hope?'

Neville laughed. The cab-driver rolled his eyes, drummed on his steering wheel.

'Ah hope,' said Neville, 'dat we meet again some day.'

Eugene looked at him, straight-faced, then burst out laughing. 'God blin' it, cuz,' he said, 'you's a real joker. Come, get outta the man car. Go on, shoo.' He practically shoved Neville out on to the pavement.

'But, but . . .' said Neville.

'Get inside, you fool. I not leaving till I see you push you key in that door. Now go on.'

Neville retrieved his key, swaying to and fro. The taxi-driver revved his engine. Reluctantly, smiling inanely, Neville staggered up to the house. He was just about to start fiddling with his key when Joyce opened the door. She waved to Eugene, then, grabbing Neville by the collar, dragged him inside.

He woke up at three the following afternoon, badly hung over. In the front room he found a note from Joyce. She wouldn't be home till late, possibly after nine. If he didn't mind, perhaps he might rustle up some dinner for himself and Cyrian.

Cyrian came home while he was in the shower. He came out of the bathroom, wrapped in a towel, and went and knocked on Cyrian's door. He had to knock long and hard to be heard above the music. Eventually the sound was lowered and Cyrian came to the door. 'What?'

'Don't what me, sonny Jim. Have manners. You modder never bring you up like dat.'

Cyrian leaned against the door frame, almost yawned. Neville informed him that his mother would be home late, and asked whether there was anything special that he'd like for dinner. 'No,' replied Cyrian, and with that he went back inside, slammed the door and turned the music up full blast.

'Awright, den,' said Neville, shouting at the door. 'Don' say me nevva awks.'

An hour later he was at the kitchen table polishing off a plate of saltfish and steam cabbage. It occurred to him that Cyrian was a spoilt brat, and would benefit from a good thrashing. A bit of discipline was what he needed. Joyce should assign him a few chores for when he got home from school. Neville remembered how his own childhood had been an endless round of chores: fetching water from the standpipe, retrieving the animals. But gathering wood had been the most arduous by far. Once a week he'd saddle Bones, the family donkey, and head off to the woodland in nearby Cuffie Ridge, renowned parish-wide as a place of striking beauty, boasting lush green hills and deep dark valleys. Yet the woodland itself was something of an eyesore on this otherwise flawless landscape. Accessible only by foot, and nestling in the centre of a shadowy ravine, it was a spooky place. Amongst the trees it was chilly and quiet, with a latticework of felled, ant-coated tree trunks covering a carpet of rotten wood chippings. The few trees still upright were free of leaves and dotted with vultures' nests, their barkless trunks intricately designed by legions of woodlice; and on the ground, darting about like harbingers of doom, was a dreadful infestation of chameleons. Neville remembered the overwhelming sense of death that prevailed, and he'd had an irrational aversion to the place that hadn't diminished with repeated visits.

In the middle of these recollections, Cyrian bowled into the kitchen and headed straight for the bread bin. Pointedly ignoring the pots on the cooker, he got out a couple of slices of bread and slotted them into the toaster. Neville observed him a while, then said: 'Cyrian. Don' be hard-headed. Dere's proper food right dere if you hungry.' Cyrian said nothing, so Neville kissed his teeth and left the kitchen. Outside he stopped and listened, and was soon sniggering to himself when he heard pots rattling.

Later, when Joyce came home, after she'd eaten and relaxed a bit, he made his announcement: he'd be leaving that very night. Joyce didn't fully comprehend, and for a moment she was speechless. Finally she said: 'Leave? Just like that?'

'I know. I know. Is sudden. But is de best way, Joyce. You know I doesn't go in for big send-off.'

'I don't care. You don't do things like that, Neville. It not right.' They were in the living room, and she started pacing up and down. 'My God. You's a real ungrateful so-and-so, you know that? You come here, me put you up, feed you, even give you clothes to wear, nurse you back to health, and . . . and . . . this is how you repay me? Eh? By running off into the blasted night? Well, go, then!' She was screaming now. 'Go! Go!' She pointed towards the door. 'Well? What you waiting for?' Neville stood rooted to the spot, dumbfounded. Joyce said: 'Ungrateful so-and-so,' then stormed from the room.

When she'd gone, Neville went and sat down. He felt indescribably guilty. He hadn't expected Joyce to be pleased, but the ferocity of her remarks had left him shell-shocked. He couldn't recall ever seeing her so angry. He felt a strong urge to go to her bedroom and apologise, but decided against it. He was still intent on leaving, and a penitent gesture at that stage, he reasoned, could be construed as a change of heart. In any case, he knew that her accusations of ungratefulness were merely a cover for her true feelings. In that respect, his conscience was clear. He hadn't promised her anything. He hadn't deceived her in any way. Yes, there'd been occasions when he'd thought about a reunion between them, he couldn't deny that. But he'd been very careful to keep those thoughts to himself. And he was pleased that he had, for he now knew that he and Joyce couldn't be together. The reasons were numerous. They were too old, too set in their ways, unwilling to compromise. They were carrying too much baggage, wanted different things from life. They even lived in different parts of the world. These were facts; cold, hard. Uncomfortable as they were, Neville knew that they had to be faced, accepted. And he'd be surprised if, deep down, Joyce didn't feel the same way.

He went to her bedroom and knocked softly on the door. She didn't answer, so he pushed the door open quietly, tentatively. Joyce was sitting on her bed, staring into space. Neville's heart grew heavy, and he lost his nerve. 'Look, ah can stay a few more days, if . . .'

'No. Please. Go now, Neville. Go now.'

The anger had gone, replaced by resignation. Neville remained in the doorway. Joyce did her best to fight back the tears. There was a long silence, which Joyce eventually broke.

'So you going back to the white woman?'

'Ah have to get me t'ings.'

Neville feared another outburst, but Joyce simply said: 'And what about Joe?'

Neville thought for all of two seconds. 'To hell wid him.'

CHAPTER EIGHT

It was past eleven when he arrived at Dilys's. Sean was already in bed, but Dilys had waited up. Neville found her in the living room watching TV.

'Hello,' She said. Neville could tell right away that she was upset. 'Expected you sooner. You said your train was due in at eight.'

Neville sat down. 'Yes. Ah know. Somet'ing happen and ah had to ketch a later one. Sorry.'

'I'd thought we might have dinner.'

'Really? Oh, no. Now me feel bad. Really bad. Forgive me.'

The apology was so heartfelt, Dilys couldn't help but smile. 'Well,' she said, 'if you're hungry, I could do you a little something.'

'Oh, no. It too late now. Ah will wait till breakfast.'

They studied one another, as though searching for changes, alterations.

'So how are you feeling?' asked Dilys.

'Fine, fine. Ah get dese headaches from time to time, but odder dan dat . . .' He waved his hand.

'Well, that's good,' said Dilys, and she paused. 'If you'd told me sooner, I'd have visited you in hospital.'

Neville didn't say anything. He'd forgotten how even her most innocent remarks sounded like reproaches.

After a brief silence, Dilys said: 'So you say it was an unprovoked attack?'

Neville had said exactly that on the phone, and he couldn't understand why she was asking again. It was almost as if she didn't believe him. 'Completely,' he said.

Dilys thought about it, then shook her head. 'Mindless. Absolutely mindless.'

Neville thought it was time that he changed the subject. 'So how you been?'

'All right. So you didn't find out anything about Joe's whereabouts?'

Neville sighed. 'No. Nutting at all.' He almost told her about Chantelle, just to see her reaction.

'Well, I must say, I always thought it was a long shot. I mean, it's not as if you had anything to go on.' She paused, then, smiling, added: 'I think your real intention was to see your old flame.'

'Very funny.'

A short silence, then Dilys said: 'I missed you, you know.'

Neville broke out in a cold sweat, fidgeted in his seat. He knew what he was expected to say next, but was reluctant to. Where might it lead? He couldn't go down that route. It was time he headed home. Oh, why did she have to . . .

'Well?' said Dilys.

'What?'

'Did you miss me?'

'Er, yes,' Neville replied, tentatively. The tension drained from Dilys's face; but it came back moments later when Neville said: 'An' Sean.'

There was a short silence, then Dilys said stiffly: 'So what are your plans now?'

'Wha' you mean, exac'ly?'

'I mean about finding Joe?'

Neville waited a moment, collected his thoughts, then said: 'Ah give up, Dilys. Joe is me twin bredda, and ah love him. Nutting will ever change dat. But . . .' He lowered his eyes, stared at his feet. '. . . he don't want anyt'ing to do wid me. He mek dat plain a long time ago. Da's somet'ing ah just have to accep'. It tek me a good while, over t'irty years, but ah finally get me head roun' it.'

He left it at that, omitting to say that he also thought Joe might be dead. He didn't think Dilys would want to hear that.

'Well,' she said, 'if you ask me, he doesn't deserve to have you as a brother.'

A sad smile from Neville. 'An' him don't deserve you as a wife.' He paused. 'In fac', is a wonder to me how you two ever get married in de firs' place.'

'I often wonder that myself. Did he ever tell you how we met?'

Neville shook his head. Dilys switched the TV off with the remote, pulled her feet up on to the settee. 'I remember it vividly,' she said. 'Summer of 1978. We met in the town centre, purely by chance. I don't know if he told you, but he used to drive a van.'

'Ah didn't know dat. Ah didn't even know him could drive.'

'Well, anyway, that's what he was doing here, making a delivery. I was coming out of the library weighed down with books, he was about to drop off a package. We were both daydreaming and bumped into each other. I spilled my books, he dropped his package. We stooped, our eyes met, and that was that.'

'Not love at firs' sight?' said Neville, mockingly.

'Don't be daft. No, we simply spent the rest of the afternoon together. He bought me lunch at the Crown and we talked and talked. I found out he was living in London. Before he left he asked for my number. I gave it to him and he said he'd call me in the next few days.'

Neville stifled a giggle. Loverman strikes again.

'By the time I got home I'd decided that I didn't want to hear from him, and I was really sorry I'd given him my number. He was just too smooth, too charming. He seemed like the type who had a girl in every town. I didn't want to become his latest conquest.'

'But you did, didn't you?' It was meant to be a joke, but it fell flat. 'Sorry. Go on.'

'He called that same night. He could sense something in me had changed, but he was determined and eventually broke down my resistance. We spent over an hour on the phone. He called me at least three times a week for the next month, practically begging to see me again. I must say, I found his desperation flattering, which is why I agreed to meet him.'

Bad move, thought Neville. Very bad move.

'We met regularly after that, always at the weekend, always in the town centre. It would have been nice to meet somewhere different for a change, but it was where I felt safe. I barely knew him, after all.'

'No, but by now you wanted to, right?'

Dilys thought about it, smiled. 'You could say that.'

Neville grinned knowingly.

'Anyway,' said Dilys. 'A pattern quickly developed. Lunch, followed by a walk, then off to the Crown for drinks. He was a Guinness man, couldn't half put them away.'

'Guinness. Yuk!'

'My thoughts exactly. He was so stubborn about it, wouldn't dream of trying anything else.' She shook away the digression, then continued: 'After the pub he'd walk me home, unable to keep his hands to himself.'

Neville sniggered.

Dilys smiled and said: 'Men. You're all the same. One-track minds.'

'But da's wha' you love 'bout we, right?'

'No!' said Dilys, smiling. 'Look, would you stop distracting me?'

'Awright, awright, ah won't say anodder word.' He drew an imaginary zip across his lips.

Dilys continued. 'Although I wanted to, I never invited him in. I was too worried about Dad's reaction. Plus I was nervous about . . .' She paused. 'Although I was twenty-eight at the time, I hadn't been with a man before.'

Neville whistled and said: 'Twenty-eight?'

'I know. It provoked a similar reaction in Joe. When I told him, he got turned on and suggested we go away for a dirty weekend. I told him I couldn't leave Dad alone. A stroke had made him bedridden and he needed my constant attention. Joe got frustrated, and I pitied him, but there it was.'

'Ah would imagine him was more dan jus' frustrated.'

They laughed, then Dilys said: 'Six months after we met, he proposed.'

'Wha'?'

'Exactly. I was just as surprised. We'd not discussed marriage, and I told him I'd need time to think about it. I was all over the place. Here I was, faced with the biggest decision of my life, with no one to discuss it with. I needed Mum then like never before. I had no experience with that kind of stuff, and became paralysed by indecision. Basically, I wasn't sure how I felt about Joe, or how he really felt about me. I wouldn't have said we were in love.'

'Really?'

'No. And I certainly couldn't conceive of a marriage based on anything else. There were other considerations, too. Before he proposed, I'd not seen his colour as an issue. But suddenly it seemed like the biggest obstacle to us getting married. Don't get me wrong. I'm no racist, but I'd be lying if I said it didn't cross my mind. And then there was Dad.'

'Mek me guess. Him didn't like black people?'

'Oh, no. Nothing like that. What I mean is, there was no way I was going to leave him to move in with Joe. And he wasn't going to take kindly to suddenly having another man about the house. Of course, there was the option of putting him into a home, but I'd made the decision a long time ago never to do that.

'Anyway, the upshot was I turned Joe down. When I gave

him my reasons he got angry and accused me of being a coward. I'd expected him to be disappointed, but wasn't prepared for his spite. It put me on the defensive, we had our first row, and didn't speak for a week. In that time I convinced myself that I was better off without him. I told myself that he was beneath me, that he lacked my intelligence. Suddenly we seemed worlds apart, with no common interests. For instance, he once told me he liked a flutter on the horses. At the time, wearing rose-coloured specs, it seemed quite innocent. But now that we weren't speaking, it looked to me like the confession of a chronic gambler. Not exactly the type I wanted to spend the rest of my life with. Know what I mean?'

'Ah wid you on dat one all de way. All de way.'

Dilys smiled. She hoped that she wasn't boring him. He seemed interested enough, but you never could tell. She hadn't realised till then just how much she needed to talk, to get stuff off her chest. That was one of the chief drawbacks of living alone, a lack of conversation. Neville could probably tell her a thing or two about that. Poor man.

'So come on,' said Neville. 'Wha' 'appen next?'

'Well, by the end of that week, I couldn't stand it any more and I called him.'

'*You* call *him*?'

'Yes.'

Neville was disappointed. He'd assumed it would be the other way round. That kind of thing would never happen back home. More's the pity. 'An' wha' you say to him?'

'"Let's get married, if you still want to."'

'Really? Jus' like dat?'

'Just like that.'

'An'wha' him say to dat?'

Dilys hesitated for a moment, laughed, then said: 'Put it this way. He couldn't understand my change of heart. But I told him it was a woman's prerogative.'

Neville smiled. How often had he heard that phrase? Charmaine had been very fond of it, had used it to justify her every caprice. 'So,' he said. 'You had you day in church, after all.'

Dilys looked at him. 'Joe tell you we got married in a church?'

'Yes.'

'He's a liar. Register office.'

Neville shook his head. He felt foolish.

'It was my idea. I've got nothing against church weddings, they're fine if you're a believer, but I'm not.'

Neville was scandalised. 'You mean you don' believe in God?'

'No, I don't. I take it you do.'

'Of course.'

'Good for you. We all need something to believe in. With me it's poetry. Always has been.'

Poetry, thought Neville, scornfully. How could someone put their faith in a set of rhymes? 'So I take it Joe wasn' too 'appy wid dis register office business.'

'He most certainly wasn't. There was tension between us even before we'd said our vows. He hadn't mentioned it, not on the day itself, but I knew he was upset at the low-key nature of the ceremony. Not only did he want the big church thing, he wanted to invite all his friends down from London. I fought him on that because I didn't want to compete with them for his attention. It was our day, and I know it sounds selfish, but I was loath to share it with anyone, least of all a bunch of his boozy mates.'

Neville remembered his own big day. What had made it extra special was having Sam and Freddie and all the others present. By contrast, Joe's wedding sounded like little more than 'I do, t'ank you very much, goodbye'. What a way to commit yourself to someone for the rest of your life. 'You couldn't let him have at leas' one frien', Dilys? Good God.'

'Yes. You're right. I've always regretted that. But don't worry, he never let me forget it. He beat me with that stick for years, I can tell you.'

Neville could imagine. Even as a child, Joe would hold grudges, sometimes for weeks. 'So where you go fah you 'oneymoon?'

Dilys laughed. 'What honeymoon? We came straight back here, had our tea and went to bed.' She thought for a moment, a smile spreading across her face. 'At least our first night together wasn't a let-down.'

Neville squirmed.

'Sorry. I've embarrassed you.'

'Don' be silly.' A lengthy silence. Then Neville said: 'So Joe move in wid you and you father?'

'Yes. And they were arguing almost from day one. As you can imagine, my loyalties were divided. They were always trying to make me choose between them. Dad's health didn't make it any easier. To this day I don't understand why my tending to him made Joe so jealous, but he acted as though I was having an affair.'

'Him was always a jealous one, Joe.'

'As I was finding out. Mind you, Dad's behaviour was equally juvenile. He tried to use his illness as a way to come between us. I'm ashamed to admit it, but there were times when I was tempted to put a pillow over his face.'

Neville widened his eyes.

'I know, I know, it sounds wicked, but you might think differently after I've told you what sort of man he was, what sort of dad. He was the biggest man I've ever known, a real man mountain. I've inherited his arms, as you can see. He was also very violent, and used to knock us about quite a bit, Mum and me. We lived in constant fear of him.'

I know, thought Neville.

'Him and Mum made the strangest couple. She was his complete opposite – small, timid, wouldn't say boo to a

184

goose. They met up north, in Mum's home town. He was a builder by trade and was working on some site up there. They got married very young. Guess how young?' Neville shook his head. 'He was twenty, she was eighteen.'

'What?'

'Practically children, right?'

'Goodness me.'

'After they got married, they moved to this house. Dad grew up in it. He lived here with his parents and three sisters. He was the eldest of the children. A year before he met Mum, he lost his family in a car accident. They were driving back from Skegness and were forced off the road by a drunk driver. Dad alone walked from the wreckage.'

Neville made a face; his blood ran cold. So that was the terrible event.

'Can you imagine anything so horrific? Dad was obviously badly affected by it, I can see that now, but as a child I was less than sympathetic to his suffering. I thought he used it to excuse his tyranny. Mum used to tell me I was wrong to think so, but I was too young and self-righteous to care.

'As for her, she spent her life trying to cure him, and I suspect that's why she married him. Personally, I think he should have carried on working. It would have been a useful distraction, and certainly preferable to moping about the house. But no, once he got his hands on the insurance settlement, he never left the house again.'

Insurance. That would explain it. Reading her diary, Neville had wondered how Dilys's parents had managed for money, since it was clear to him that neither of them worked. As for the father being cooped up indoors, he recalled what the factory supervisor had told him. Gossips. They never knew the half of it.

'Mus' have been tough times,' said Neville, eventually.

'They were. Especially for Mum. In the end Dad drove her to drink. Towards the end of her life she was a miserable wretch. When she finally died, aged thirty-five – thirty-five, for crying out loud – I was relieved. She was better off dead. When I think about her life it makes me sad.'

She paused. Neville could tell she was struggling. He was about say something, when Dilys continued.

'She lived without joy, my mother, without laughter. I hate to say it, but she was a victim. Life dealt her blow after blow. Did you know I had an older sister?'

Neville shook his head, and the lie forced him to avert his eyes. How he regretted having read her diary. What had possessed him?

'Megan, her name was. Welsh, like mine. She died at birth. Mum never got over it, and would visit her grave at all hours, often in the dead of night. For a long time I hated my sister, hated her for what she did to Mum. But we're reconciled now. After Mum went there was no longer a reason to be angry with her. I visit their graves and we talk. They're buried side by side in a cemetery not far from here. I've left instructions to be put next to them when I finally shuffle off.'

A dead sister. The thought hadn't even crossed his mind. The fleeting reference to her in the diary hadn't made it clear. The story was becoming more and more macabre, and he hoped that Dilys would soon finish. He'd asked about Joe, not about all this stuff. But he could see that Dilys was on a roll, unable to stop – might as well be talking to herself.

'When Mum died, Dad completely lost the plot. I must say, I was touched by the depth of his grief, and what little love I had for him began to grow. By the end he was little more than an infant, hopelessly dependent on me, shrunken beyond recognition. Two years after Joe and me were married, he died quietly in his sleep. He was seventy-two.' She shook her head. Neville thought that he detected a moistening of the eyes, but it could have been a trick of the light. 'I had him cremated, his wish, then sprinkled his ashes over the spot where his family died.' She smiled ruefully. 'I remember having to travel on the train, me and Sean, with his ashes. Weird.'

That had to be the end, thought Neville. He couldn't listen to much more.

'Now that it was just the two of us, the possibilities seemed endless for me and Joe.'

Joe. Neville had almost forgotten about him.

'We were free to do all the things we'd planned, such as travelling. I'd always dreamed of going to America, homeland of the great Emily Dickinson.'

'Who?'

'Poet. Joe wanted to take a cruise, but could never decide on a destination. Wherever we ended up first, we said we'd treat it as a belated honeymoon.'

She paused, with Neville on tenterhooks. 'So where you go?' he asked.

'Great Yarmouth.'

'Where's dat? America?'

'Seaside resort a few hundred miles from here.'

'Oh.'

'That's the furthest we ever reached. We spent a couple of weeks there one summer, a blissful couple of weeks, it must be said, but, sadly, that was the extent of our travelling. We simply couldn't afford it on Joe's salary alone. I offered to find a job, but he was adamant that no wife of his was ever going to work. When Sean arrived we became even more stretched and our dreams vanished overnight.'

Sean. He was someone else Neville had forgotten about.

'He was an accident, and it took us time to bond with him. Neither of us was prepared to admit it openly, but for a time we saw him as an unwanted burden. It was only after we realised that he wasn't like other children that our instincts as parents took over.'

Parental instincts. Neville was not an authority on the subject, which made him listen all the more keenly.

'My decision to take him out of school was the start of a running feud between me and Joe, and I would say it ultimately cost us our marriage. Once I found out that Sean was being bullied I made up my mind. His education would have to suffer, because only over my dead body was anyone going to mistreat him. I myself had been bullied at school, so I knew what he was going through, but Joe thought I'd overreacted and it provoked a series of bitter arguments between us. In the end I persuaded him to my way of thinking, though I had to promise to tutor Sean myself as best I could.'

'You do a very good job, from what ah see.'

She smiled. 'It's nice of you to say that. I know he can't speak French or explain Einstein's theories, but he can read and write and do basic maths. More importantly, his heart's bursting with love, and that's more than most people can say.' She nodded, as if to confirm her own assertion.

Neville waited a while, then said: 'So Joe was still working in London round dis time?'

'Oh, no. He was at the factory by then, started not long after Sean was born. Longest job he ever had. It was decent money, at least decent enough to live on, and for a time we were content. But Joe was never truly happy living in the town. He found it difficult to settle. Being the only black resident soon began to wear him down. He was too proud to say so, but I could tell because he escaped to London every chance he got. I'm not saying he had no friends here, just that they kept him at arm's length. They were little more than drinking companions, the type who'll spend every day with you down the pub, but won't think to invite you to their homes, and will make excuses if you invite them to yours.'

'So why de two of you didn' move?'

'We thought about it. At least Joe did. His patience finally ran out and he suggested we sell up and get out. I seriously considered it, more for his sake than mine, but in the end I told him I couldn't go through with it.'

'Why not?'

She pondered for a few seconds. 'This is my home, Neville, and I can't ever imagine a time when I'll leave it. I know that sounds odd, especially the state it's in, but there it is.'

Neville understood only too well. His father had once told him that a person's home was the place where they spent their childhood. To leave it is a wrench, and if it isn't, then there must be something in it driving you away; something or someone.

'I've never regretted not leaving,' said Dilys, 'but I was sorry about how my decision affected Joe. He withdrew into himself, shut down. The only way I could get him to talk to me was by engineering rows. Then he'd let out all his pent-up frustrations. He felt trapped, marrying me was a mistake, his son was a simpleton, and he longed to be among his own kind. Naturally, these were painful things for me to hear, and once they were out in the open, the solution seemed straightforward: divorce. Fear prevented us from mentioning the word, but I knew it was never far from our thoughts.'

'Might have been better, you know. Clean break an' all dat.'

'Yes, well, hindsight is a wonderful thing.' She looked towards the window, prompting Neville to do likewise. The headlamps of passing cars periodically lit up the room, momentarily blinding them. They faced each other once more.

'How you manage to keep sane t'rough all of dis?' Neville asked. He was referring to her childhood as much as her marriage.

'With great difficulty. The next couple of years were an absolute nightmare. We lived together, but effectively led separate lives. He'd go to work in the mornings and wouldn't get back till Sean and I were in bed. I'd lie awake waiting for him to get in, then pretend to be asleep when he did. He'd normally come home drunk, and would stumble into bed desperate for . . .' She caught herself, then went on. '. . . only to fall asleep on the job. His snoring, plus the smell of alcohol, would drive me to the spare room. I spent many a night in there, but unlike my parents we never officially had separate bedrooms. Maybe we should have tried it. We might still be together.'

Neville couldn't imagine anything less likely to save a marriage.

'Now the pressure was really on. While I was forced to stay here and tough it out, he'd go missing for a day or two, and I'd worry myself sick. Then he'd suddenly show up, offering no explanations. If I dared to ask where he'd been, he'd get angry and assert his right to privacy. I didn't like to imagine what he got up to, or who with. I suspected he was having an affair, but was too scared he'd hit me if I accused him of it. I must say, in all the time we were together, during all our problems, he never once laid a finger on me. But he had it in him. All men do, no matter what they say. Sorry, Neville, but I believe that.'

Neville gave it some thought. She was right, of course. He'd often felt the urge to let Charmaine feel the back of his hand.

'Sean,' said Dilys.

'Beg pardon?'

'He was my saviour. Without him I'd have lost my sanity. I clung to him for dear life.'

'It can't have been easy for de poor bwoy.'

'Actually, he showed no signs of being affected by it one way or the other. Of course, I kidded myself that I was shielding him, but with Sean you just never know. He has a capacity for letting things wash over him that I used to see as a curse but now see as a blessing.'

The Lord works in mysterious ways, thought Neville.

'Anyway,' said Dilys, 'while Sean and me got closer, Joe became even further removed from our lives. He even said I was trying to poison Sean's mind against him. I didn't need to. He was doing such a good job himself. He failed to understand that being a parent is about more than just the occasional kick-about in the back garden. I tried telling him this once, but he said that on top of everything else I was now accusing him of being a bad father. I'd obviously touched a nerve, though, because for a time he made more of an effort. He'd drag Sean away on all kinds of foolhardy . . .' She twiddled her fingers. '. . . "father-son" activities. I couldn't believe how long it took him to realise that Sean only agreed to his hare-brained schemes under duress from me. When he did, though, he dropped Sean like a bad habit, dismissing him as a hopeless mummy's boy.'

That was Joe all over, said Neville. Rough and tumble he could understand. Anything else confused him. As children, if they had a play fight, he was always too aggressive. And if he, Neville, so much as dared to cry, then . . .

'It was his loss. Sean completely rejected him. I mean completely, wouldn't even speak to him. And that, more than anything else, was what tipped him over the edge. He started gambling seriously, and it quickly became an addiction. I'd find betting slips all over the house, for huge sums. God knows where he got all that money from. I do know he started stealing money from me, from the very housekeeping that he himself provided. No matter where I'd hide it, he'd sniff it out. I accused him once of being no better than a common thief. He flared up and said he couldn't steal what already belonged to him. When he spoke like that, I just didn't know him. And on top of all that, he started going missing for days at a time, and would turn up looking as though he'd been in the wars. He'd have cuts and bruises all over, even the odd broken bone. He'd never say how he got them, and of course I knew better than to ask. If he was in a particularly bad way, I'd do what I could for him, but mechanically, without feeling or without love. And then came the phone calls.'

She paused for effect. Sure enough, Neville said: 'Wha' you mean?'

'Phone calls, as many as three a week, threatening ones.'

'Dey t'reaten you?' Neville wondered whether it was the same thugs who'd jumped him.

'They threatened me *and* Sean. I never did find out who made those calls, but I knew they were somehow connected to Joe's shady dealings. Thank God my fears came to nothing, but at the time I felt as though the two of us were in real danger.'

The danger is real enough, thought Neville. Real enough. Michelle's words popped into his head. *He got himself mixed up wiv some real nutcases, the type you just don't mess wiv.*

'Well,' said Dilys, 'by that stage I'd reached the end of my tether. Those calls really were the final straw.'

'You tell Joe 'bout dem?'

'Too right I did, and I demanded he move out. I prayed to God he'd see sense and do the decent thing, but he flatly refused. I tried everything. I begged, I pleaded. In the end I had to resort to emotional blackmail. I said that if he had any feelings for Sean whatsoever then he'd pack his bags and go. Again my pleas fell on deaf ears. Then, just as I was getting myself ready for a long-drawn-out affair, he went. Just like that. After a month, I knew he wasn't coming back. I haven't seen or heard from him since, and I hope and pray I never set eyes on him again.'

Neville didn't know where to put his face. He shifted about in his seat and kept looking anxiously towards the window. Whenever a headlamp shone in his eyes, he'd turn back to Dilys to find her staring at him intently. He was in an awkward situation. Dilys clearly thought that she'd exposed him to a few home truths about his brother, yet she hadn't revealed anything about Joe that he didn't already know or hadn't already suspected. Lest his silence be misconstrued as sympathy for Joe, he felt that he should say something to make

Dilys understand where his loyalties lay. Finally he said: 'You better off widout him.'

Dilys looked at him searchingly, in that way that always made him nervous. He was relieved when he saw a thin smile appear around her mouth. 'You and me both, eh?'

Neville smiled, and, involuntarily, it turned into a yawn.

'I'm sorry. I've talked your ears off.'

Neville suddenly felt dog tired.

'You look as if you're about ready for bed, mister.'

'My, ah piece a tiredness jus' hit me, you see.'

'You should go up.'

'You wouldn' min'?'

'Not at all,' said Dilys.

Neville rose, stretched luxuriantly, yawned again. 'You staying up?' he asked.

'For a bit. All that talking's left me feeling wide awake.' She reached for the remote and switched on the TV. They'd been talking by the soft light of a table lamp, and the brightness from the TV screen lit up the room, the harshness of it forcing Neville to shield his eyes. He started heading for the door.

'By the way,' said Dilys. Neville stopped and turned and faced her. 'Sean and me have been invited to Sunday lunch at the Bishops' tomorrow. I don't really want to go, but I will for Sean's sake. I'd like it very much if you came with us.'

Put like that, he could hardly refuse. 'All right, den.'

'Thanks. Night-night.'

'Goodnight, Dilys. An' min' you don' stay up too late.'

And with that he left the room.

CHAPTER NINE

They paused outside the wrought-iron gates, waiting while Neville studied their intricate design. He might have been outside Buckingham Palace.

'It's just a gate,' said Dilys, eager to get the thing over with. Neville was surprised by her marital tone.

They set off again, along the gravelled avenue, which was flanked by immaculate lawns.

The Bishops were waiting to greet them, standing on the portico, sandwiched between two enormous stone pillars.

'Hello,' said Margaret.

'So pleased you could make it,' said Edward.

Handshakes all round, except for Sean, who had his head patted.

They walked through the vast entrance hall (the women's shoes clack-clacking against the flagstones) and into the dining room. Neville could hardly believe his eyes. Where he came from, there were houses smaller. There was a two-tier Jacobean chimney piece and a formidable sideboard recess lined with velvet, above which was a huge ornate mirror. In the centre of the room, five Victorian rococo chairs covered in claret leather were positioned around a sturdy-looking mahogany table, which had already been set for lunch. They arranged themselves around it, Neville befuddled by all the cutlery. How many forks does one person need? he wondered.

Lunch was uninspiring. Soup, lamb, lemon tart. Afterwards, Edward took Neville off for the guided tour, the highlight for Neville being the library. The sheer ostentation of the room took his breath away. Silk rugs, ancestral portraits, a piano-forte, antique furniture, bookshelves lined with leather-bound volumes, marble statues, porcelain vases.

Meanwhile, Margaret and Dilys had decided to take a stroll around the grounds. Margaret was soon tired, and was forced to sit on a stone bench. Dilys sat next to her, conscious of the older woman's frailty. She could hear her rasping breath, which sounded dangerously asthmatic. Before them stretched acres of rolling lawns, fringed on either side by huge poplars.

'I never get tired of that view,' said Margaret.

'Hmm,' said Dilys, nodding. 'It is very pretty.'

It was the first time that she had actually set foot on the property. Until then, the closest she'd come was on the first day of Sean's employment. As he'd made his way along the avenue, inching along nervously, she had stood outside, looking in through the open gates. 'I wonder where Sean's got to,' she said.

'Oh, he's around somewhere,' said Margaret. 'Exploring, no doubt. Probably in the woods.' She smiled, thought for a second. 'He really is a wonder, that boy of yours. I absolutely adore him. We both do. You're a very lucky woman, you know that?'

Dilys smiled. The sun disappeared behind a cloud, casting a shadow over the landscape and lowering the temperature slightly. Margaret buttoned her quilted overcoat, Dilys her cardigan.

'May I ask you something, Dilys?'

They faced each other.

'What is it?'

'Please don't think I'm prying.'

Dilys prepared herself for some prying. 'I'm listening.'

Margaret played nervously with her hands. Finally she said: 'We're worried about Sean.'

'Sean? Why?'

'He just hasn't been himself lately.'

Dilys immediately feared the worse. 'What's happened?'

'Nothing's happened, as such. I mean, he's been a bit absent-minded of late, unable to concentrate . . .' She paused before adding, 'One might even say sad.'

Oh, might one? thought Dilys. It broke her heart to think of Sean being unhappy. She didn't want to believe it, even though she knew it to be true. Sean was, and would always be, unhappy. 'Things are a bit unsettled at home. That might explain it.'

'Yes, we were wondering about that,' said Margaret.

I bet you were, thought Dilys.

Margaret said: 'His uncle showing up out of the blue can't have helped. My, he's the mirror image of Joe, isn't he?' She thought for a second. 'Any news on him, by the way?'

Dilys shook her head. 'It's my fault,' she said.

'Sorry?'

'Sean. I've been ignoring him a bit lately.'

Margaret didn't want to comment on that, even though she and Edward had discussed it in some detail.

'You have to understand,' said Dilys. 'It's not easy for me. Sean can be a real . . .' She searched for the right word. '. . . burden.'

'I can imagine,' said Margaret, speaking almost in a whisper.

Dilys shook her head. 'No offence, but you can't even begin to imagine.'

Margaret felt chastised. 'No,' she said. 'Of course not. You're right. That was presumptuous of me.'

The two men emerged from the house, waved at the women, then went off to tour the grounds.

'He seems like a nice man, Neville.'

'He is. I enjoy having him around. At first it was difficult, as you can probably guess.' Margaret nodded. She knew all about Dilys and Joe. 'But then a funny thing happened.'

Dilys thought about it, then said: 'Oh, I shouldn't be telling you this.'

'I wish you would. I promise to be the soul of discretion,' said Margaret.

Dilys turned and faced her. How had it come about that she was confiding in Margaret Bishop? Here was a woman she had always regarded as a figure of fun. The lady of the manor was how she and Joe used to describe her. Indeed, that was how many people in the town referred to her. 'He went up to London recently to see an old girlfriend.'

Margaret gasped in mock horror.

'It's OK. I don't think there's anything between them any more. They knew each other in Jamaica, and she's been living here for over thirty years.'

'Oh. Hardly a rival, then. Let's dismiss her. Poof. She's gone. OK. So he went up to the smoke, and?'

'And while he was gone . . .' Dilys paused. 'I found myself thinking about him night and day.'

Margaret smiled. 'You must tell him how you feel.'

'Impossible.'

'Nothing's impossible.'

'I couldn't.'

'Why, what are you afraid of?'

Good question. She'd never considered herself to be afraid of anything. The sun re-emerged from behind the cloud, forcing them to squint. 'What if he doesn't feel the same?' asked Dilys.

'Then you have nothing to lose, and everything to gain.'

And at that point Dilys came back to earth. She said she could never allow anyone to come between herself and Sean.

'It doesn't have to be like that,' said Margaret.

'It's always like that. In life, I've found that you have to choose. You can't have everything. Sacrifices have to be made.'

'Now you listen to me for a moment, and listen carefully.

There's no inviolate law that says we must always put our children's happiness before our own. I've raised three of them, so I know what I'm talking about. Our job is to look after them, love them, and prepare them to go out into the world. Then we have to let them go. Do you understand?'

'Yes, but Sean's different. I can't ever see him "going out into the world" as you put it.'

'Why not? He's more than capable. And besides, what's the alternative? He can't stay with you for the rest of his life. If you really love him, and I know how much you do, then you must force him out. It's absolutely imperative that he stand on his own two feet. You can't protect him for ever.'

Dilys was about to say something when she noticed that the men were approaching. Margaret patted her on the arm and said: 'Don't worry. We'll finish this conversation another time.'

Later that afternoon, Neville was relaxing in his room when he heard the front door slam. Curious, he went downstairs to investigate. He opened the front door and saw Dilys walking away from the house. Where could she be going on a Sunday? 'Going for a walk?' he shouted.

Dilys stopped, turned round.

'Er . . . sort of. Want to come along?'

Neville slammed the door and hurried to join her.

A short while later they were in the town centre. Dilys stopped at a florist and bought two bunches of flowers. 'For the girls,' she said.

The church, called St Mary the Virgin, was not very far away, down one of the many lanes leading off the main thoroughfare. It was old, dating back to the fifteenth century. It had a spire and stained-glass windows running along both sides. To the rear was a sizable graveyard, full of headstones, most of them so old the names had been eroded. Some were lopsided, others covered in lichen. One or two of the plots had dead or wilting flowers.

Dilys, adopting a solemn air, went up to her mother's grave first. She crouched, removed the old flowers from the vase, and replaced them with a new bunch. She spent a fair amount of time arranging them. Neville watched her. It occurred to him that he had never put flowers on Charmaine's grave. The thought had never even crossed his mind. When he got back that would be the first thing he'd do. And, like Dilys, he'd make a ritual of it thereafter.

Dilys then went up to her sister's grave, which was diagonally opposite her mother's. The same routine – old flowers for new. Such was her deference, Neville wondered whether she hadn't been less than honest about her religious beliefs. After all, she was on sanctified ground, had indeed chosen it as her final resting place. He wanted to challenge her on the matter, but since it was neither the time nor place, he kept quiet.

Afterwards, he invited her to the Crown. She declined, so he made sure that she didn't mind walking back by herself, then went for a quick one on his own.

Being a Sunday, the place was even more dead than usual. The clientèle numbered three men; two sitting together, one on his own. The solitary man had a sheepdog dozing at his feet. Madge looked about ready to die from boredom, which accounted for her excitement at seeing Neville.

'Hello,' she said, beaming.

'Madge.'

He eased himself up on to a stool, aware of the other men watching him.

'Pint?' said Madge.

Neville hesitated. Pints of beer. How quickly he'd gotten used to the habit. 'You have any stout?'

'Of course,' said Madge, and she reeled off a list, which included Guinness.

'Well, you can forget dat for a start.'

He opted for something more obscure. When Madge poured

it, he was pleasantly surprised. She leaned across the counter and said: 'So come on, don't keep me in suspense. You find him or not?'

Neville groaned. He didn't want to think about Joe. He sipped his beer and looked at Madge over the rim of the glass. If she covered up her cleavage, he thought, and removed the false nails, she could look half decent. 'No.'

'What? Did you go to Lattie's, like I told you?' Neville shook his head. 'But why not?'

'Look, Madge, you don' understand, an' ah can't bodder to explain. Ah didn't fin' Joe and da's dat.'

Madge stood up straight. 'Well, excuse me for breathing,' she said.

Neville shook his head. He'd never met anyone as easy to offend as Madge. In his village there were children with thicker skins. He sighed heavily and said: 'Sorry. Ah know you mean well, but . . .'

'It's all right. If you don't want to talk, fine.'

'Don' be like dat. Come, have a drink wid me.'

Madge put her nose in the air, turned her head away. 'Don't know that I care to.'

'Oh, go on. Please. Please.' He tried to catch her eye, but Madge refused to look at him. 'Go on. You know you love me, really. Stop preten'.'

Madge couldn't hold out. She smiled, then poured herself a white wine spritzer. Once again she leaned across the bar, so close to Neville that he could see the beads of mascara on her eyelashes. She raised her glass and said: 'To Joe. May he be safe, wherever he is.'

Neville raised his glass half-heartedly, and didn't say anything.

On her return from the cemetery Dilys went straight into the living room. She'd noticed from outside that the curtains were still open and had gone in to draw them. She didn't bother switching on the light, even though darkness was imminent. As she walked across the room she saw a vague shape in one of the easy chairs. She stood still for a moment, giving her eyes time to adjust to the gloom.

'Can't sleep?' she asked.

He got up, walked over, and threw his arms around her waist. She hugged him to her bosom, squeezing him tightly; too tightly, in fact, for she heard him groan. 'Sorry,' she said. 'Don't know my own strength, eh, love?'

He brought his hand up and started stroking her breast, in a downward motion, ever so lightly, as though he were smoothing creases from her dress. She indulged him for a few seconds, then grabbed his wrists, gently but firmly. 'Time for bed, I think.'

He humphed, stamped his feet.

'Yes,' said Dilys. 'Now go on. Upstairs. If you go right now I promise I'll come up and tuck you in.'

Sean raced from the room. Dilys went over and drew the curtains.

Walking through the town centre on his way home from the pub, Neville saw Joe staring at him from an off-licence window. His face was on a poster for missing persons, which was sandwiched between special offers for Löwenbräu and Miller Lite. It was a blown up version of the picture that Neville had given to Sergeant Pettifer, with a caption that read: *Have You Seen This Man?* No, said Neville to himself, and continued on his way.

It was dark when he got back, and he didn't notice Valerie standing in her doorway until he was almost upon her. There was no light on in her hallway and she gave him a real fright.

'Evening,' she said.

'Well, well. Good evening,' said Neville.

'Been for a walk, have we?'

'Yes. And very pleasant it was, too.'

'Haven't seen you since the day you left for London.'

'Yes. Ah spen' a likkle time up dere.'

'All right for some. Got time for a cuppa?'

Neville thought for a moment, a mischievous glint in his eye. 'You 'ave anyt'ing stronger?'

Valerie smiled and held the door open.

CHAPTER TEN

'Whisky do you?'

'Dat will do jus' fine.'

They were in the front room, Neville sitting in his 'favourite' armchair. The room was dimly lit by one of the tasselled standard lamps. Whatever the bulb's wattage, Neville thought it was too low. Valerie handed him his drink, then, clutching one of her own, went and sat on the settee opposite.

'Cheers,' she said, raising her glass.

''Cheers,' said Neville, and he sipped his drink, shuddering when it hit his stomach. For a while they just sat there observing each other in the half-light. It was Neville who spoke first. 'How long?'

'I'm sorry?'

'How long?'

Valerie looked at him askance.

'What do you mean?'

'You and Joe.'

Valerie froze for a second; then, holding Neville's gaze, she took the tiniest sip from her glass. She then started to run her finger around the rim. Neville watched her finger going round and round, round and round. 'Who told you?' she asked, finally.

'Nobody. Jus' a guess.'

'But what made you guess?'

'Ah simply put two and two togedder.'

'What do you mean?'

'De widow and de womaniser. It 'ave a certain ring to it, right?'

Valerie became thoughtful, her eyes fixed on a spot above Neville's head. He downed the rest of his drink and watched her. When she looked at him again, she had a smirk on her face. Neville hadn't expected that. She said: 'Good, huh?'

'Wha'?'

'The drink.'

'Oh. Yes. Very.'

'H left bottles of the stuff. I'm slowly working my way through them. He'd have been proud of me.' She giggled. 'Fancy another?'

Neville nodded and handed her his empty glass. She took it and went over to the mobile bar in the corner, which she'd wheeled in specially. She filled Neville's glass. 'That should keep you going for a while,' she said, returning. She sat down again. 'Getting involved with your brother was the biggest mistake of my life.'

Neville was caught off guard, precisely what Valerie had hoped for. She sipped her drink and let him think about it. She wanted him to say something, to try to defend Joe somehow. When it became clear that he wasn't going to speak, she said: 'I still don't know how I let myself be taken in by him.'

'Don't be so 'ard on youself. Dat bredda of mine could seduce a nun.'

That raised a half-smile. Neville was pleased.

'Maybe I was flattered that he could actually find someone like me attractive.'

'Oh, don' say dat. Don' do youself down. You not exac'ly ugly.'

'Nevertheless, at my age . . .' She paused. 'Well, let's just say that I'd almost given up hope of finding happiness with another man.' She sipped her drink. 'Not that I was looking, mind. I didn't think any man could ever measure up to my Harry.'

She fell silent, rolled her glass between her palms. Neville could see her brain working.

'Right from the start I had no concern for Dilys. I've always hated her. And I know she hates me.'

'Yes, but why?'

'Damned if I could tell you. And I bet she couldn't either. I know one thing, though: seeing Joe behind her back made me feel ten feet tall. Ha!'

Neville found the flourish excessive, and he immediately transferred his sympathy to Dilys.

'Six months,' said Valerie.

'Wha'?'

'That's how long it went on for. And for the whole of that period we carried on right under her nose.'

She was boasting now, and if there was one thing Neville couldn't stand . . .

'I was constantly worried we'd be caught. But not Joe. He had a reckless way about him that I found both infuriating and attractive. For example, one time, he was sat in the back garden with Dilys and Sean, when suddenly he gets up, says he's going for a pee, then runs round here and starts groping me. I mean, can you imagine? When he hears Dilys calling he scurries back, grumbling about how a man can't use the toilet in peace in his own house.'

With each new disclosure, Neville was tempted to leave. He could do without hearing the sordid details of yet another of Joe's conquests. So why didn't he just get up and go?

Meanwhile, Valerie was well into her stride.

She described how she and Joe used to go to out-of-town B&Bs. He could never stay more than a night, and one of them would have to return before the other. She didn't know what excuses he gave Dilys, and she didn't care. It didn't matter anyway, for by this stage Dilys wasn't bothered about where he was.

'How you know dat?' asked Neville.

'That's what he told me.'

Neville snorted dismissively and said: 'And him tell you how much him love you, right?'

'He told me he loved me, yes.'

'An' you believe him?'

'Yes, I did. And I loved him.'

Neville laughed bitterly. So much for Harry being her one and only.

She had asked Joe to leave Dilys. He said he would, eventually, but that it wasn't just a question of walking out. He said that there was Sean to consider, but she thought he was simply making excuses. What she saw was a man trapped in a loveless marriage but too cowardly to do anything about it. Of course, she was being totally selfish, and she knew it at the time, but she didn't care. Besides, it wasn't about her and Joe any more. It had become a battle between her and Dilys.

Things came to a head when she fell pregnant.

'Him get you pregnant?'

'Yes.'

'Jeezas Christ! But wha' in heaven . . .'

He had to leave it, because Valerie was away again.

She had been scared stiff. Not only because of the risks involved in having a child at forty-five, but also because she knew that Joe didn't want any more children. Which was odd, given that they hadn't been taking precautions.

When Joe found out, he immediately suggested that she have an abortion. He gave her a choice: him or the baby. Although it was a reaction that she'd expected, she was hurt beyond measure. He was just so cold about the whole thing. She thought about having the baby out of spite, but in the end she opted for a termination. She'd regretted it ever since.

'Is a funny, funny worl',' said Neville. 'Some people can't 'ave baby, and some t'rowing dem away.'

Valerie wasn't listening. She was staring into her glass, hardly blinking. When she spoke again, she did so softly.

Nothing was the same after the abortion, she said. Though she and Joe carried on seeing each other, it was all very forced, spoiled. She started pestering him more and more to leave Dilys. As she saw it, she'd made the ultimate sacrifice for him. She'd demonstrated her commitment. Now it was time for him to do the same. She was to be disappointed. It slowly began to dawn on her that he was never going to leave Dilys, and out of sheer frustration she threatened to tell her rival everything. 'Goodness me! I'd never seen him so angry. He said some things to me that day which I can't bring myself to repeat, but the bottom line was if I said anything to Dilys he'd kill me. I knew it wasn't an idle threat.'

By now, Neville's face was set in a permanent scowl. The whole thing sounded repugnant. Impatiently, he said: 'Why you never jus' walk away, Valerie? No man wort' all dat.'

She'd wanted to, but instead she and Joe got together to try to sort things out. He took the day off specially, knowing Dilys was visiting her uncle up north. They sat in Valerie's front room for hours, talking in circles. She knew that they'd come to the end of the road, but a part of her still hoped that they might make it work.

All afternoon she pleaded with Joe to give the relationship one last try. She urged him to leave Dilys and move away with her, start afresh. But Joe wasn't interested. In fact, he'd decided to try to make a go of his marriage, and was planning to tell Dilys the good news when she came back from her trip up north. He made the announcement, then waltzed out.

'I cried and cried till there wasn't a tear left in me. I mean, I was literally dry. Then, afterwards, I felt . . . I felt . . . I don't know what I felt. Angry's too puny a word. It was more like . . . vengeful . . . no . . . murderous.'

Neville stood up. He'd heard enough.

'Where are you going?'

'I can't listen to no more. Ah feel sorry for you an' all dat, but . . .'

In a calm, quiet voice, Valerie said: 'But don't you see? You can't go. You must hear everything. Every last detail. That's why you've travelled all this way, isn't it?' She paused, then added: 'You do want to hear what happened to your brother, don't you?'

Neville looked at her. She appeared composed, even serene, but there was fire in her eyes. Neville became fearful. The gloomy light wasn't helping; neither was the whisky he'd drunk. Paranoia then kicked in. Had he been drugged? He'd heard of such things. Finally he said: 'Wha' you taaking 'bout, woman?'

'Sit down and I'll tell you.'

Neville gave her a last lingering stare, then slowly lowered himself back into his seat.

'That's it. Now where was I?'

She resumed her story.

Once she'd cried herself out, she got up, walked calmly over to the fireplace, and picked up one of the logs. She recalled weighing it in her hand and thinking: no, too heavy, too unwieldy. So she put it down and picked up the poker instead.

'I went out the back, stepped over the fence and walked straight into that stupid mutt. For a minute we just stood there sizing each other up. I wasn't frightened in the least. In fact I know I'd have bludgeoned him to death had he attacked me. He must have sensed this because eventually, without so much as a whimper, he moved out of my way and went and lay down in his kennel.'

Neville's heart was pounding. He could see it beating under his shirt. Another whisky. That would settle him. But dare he ask?

'By now I was so focused on the job in hand it was almost like being in a trance. I distinctly remember how quiet it was.'

Now Neville's throat was dry. He swallowed, hard, but there was very little saliva.

'I looked in through the kitchen window and saw no sign of life. I wondered if he might have gone out, but then I heard a noise, so I crept in through the back door.

'Although I'd never been in the house, I knew the layout well enough, since it's identical to mine and all the others in this row. I sneaked into the front room and was almost beside myself with rage when I saw that he wasn't there. To calm myself, I took a few deep breaths, then started climbing the stairs.

'I may as well have been floating, because I made not a sound. Not one. Up on the landing, I got confused. I knew he had to be in one of the three rooms, more than likely his bedroom, but I didn't know which one that was. So I stood and listened, hoping to hear him moving about. Sure enough, I heard a noise coming from the room furthest along the landing. I crept towards it.

'When I got there I noticed that the door was half open. I walked up and put my eye to the crack between the door and the frame. Within seconds I'd spotted him. He was on his hands and knees, with his head buried in the wardrobe, rooting around looking for something. I thought he must have been trying to find Dilys's housekeeping money. The thought of what he was planning to do – go down the bookies' for heaven's sake, after what he'd just done to me – well, let's just say that I was enraged all over again.'

Neville felt faint, on the brink of passing out. Air. He needed air or he might die.

'I crept in and went and stood directly behind him. He carried on rummaging in the wardrobe for a few seconds before he noticed me. He tried to say something, or maybe he tried to get up. I don't remember. Anyway, I hit him twice with the poker, using all my strength. He groaned and toppled over on to his side. I stood there looking at him, half tempted to hit him again. Then I noticed the blood seeping from his wound. It was dark, rich. I watched it soaking into the carpet, watched the pool spreading wider and wider. Then I turned and calmly walked out.'

Neville stood up, swooned, then fell back into his chair. Breathe, he told himself. Just breathe. As he sucked oxygen into his lungs, his mind began to drift. Fragments of a childhood memory began flitting in and out of his mind. He grabbed after them, trying to piece them together, but they were proving as elusive as dandelion seeds.

He had been about nine, or ten. He couldn't remember how, or where, but he'd injured himself – nothing serious, a gashed knee, perhaps a stubbed toe. He'd gone crying to his mother, or it may have been a visiting aunt. He'd had his injury treated with iodine, or was it Dettol? Either way it had stung like hell. Afterwards, in a whispery voice, the nurse told him something, something spooky. *Be careful*, she said. *Don't you know that when you hurt yourself you hurt your brother as well? Never forget that as twins you feel each other's pain.*

Now it all made sense. What he had dismissed as a dream had in fact been a vision.

He stood up, staggered towards the door.

'Where are you going?' asked Valerie. 'Come back here. What are you going to do?'

She was talking to herself. Neville had gone.

Outside, he leaned against a lamppost, gulping air greedily. His legs wouldn't support him, so he slid down and sat on the pavement. It was a good while before he was able to stand again. When he did finally get to his feet, he headed off towards the town centre.

'You believe her?' asked Sergeant Pettifer.

'Of course!' said Neville, shrieking. 'Why de hell she would lie about a t'ing like dat?'

'Any number of reasons. Attention, for one. She sounds like a very lonely woman.'

'Oh, come now, Sergeant, nobody dat lonely. For God's

sake!' His eyes were bulging from their sockets. 'De woman confess to killing me bredda an' all you can do is sit dere 'pon you ass taaking all kin'a fart. Come, man. Stir youself.'

'But can't you see? It's almost farcical.'

'Almos' wha'? Look, man, don' bandy words wid me. If . . .'

'All right, all right. Calm down. Let's look at it, shall we?' Sergeant Pettifer spread the fingers of one hand, in readiness to count them off. 'One, if she did kill him, and it's a big if, how did she get rid of the body? Eh? Don't tell me she got it out of the house all by herself, in broad daylight.'

Neville gasped, held his forehead.

'What is it?' asked Sergeant Pettifer. 'Hold on . . . where're you . . . wait . . . Neville!'

He didn't find her downstairs, so he ran upstairs and burst into her bedroom.

'Neville, what the . . .'

'Wha' you do wid him, Dilys?'

'I beg your pardon?'

'Joe. Where you bury him?'

Dilys looked at him, looked over his shoulder, as though she thought he might have company. She was sitting on the edge of her bed, in the process of removing her shoes. Eventually she said: 'Come in and close the door.'

Neville slammed the door. 'Ansa me, woman!'

'Please. Lower your voice. I don't want Sean to hear any of this.' She paused, then added: 'Look, Neville, whatever it is you're accusing me of . . .'

'Valerie tell me de whole story.'

Had he blinked he'd have missed her reaction, it was that subtle. She rubbed her feet, eased them into her slippers. Her movements were slow, deliberate, provocative. There was a faint knocking on the door. 'Bed, Sean. Right now!'

Neville pictured Sean sloping off down the landing, his

shoulders hunched. Dilys went and stood at the window. 'Sit down, Neville.'

'Ah don' want to.'

'You won't get a word out of me if you don't.'

Neville hesitated for all of two seconds, then went and sat in the wicker chair.

'Now then,' said Dilys. 'What exactly did that woman tell you?'

'Evert'ing. Excep' where you and she bury the body.'

A short silence, then she said: 'Maybe we didn't bury it.'

'Wha'!?' Neville was appalled. He began to imagine all sorts of grisly goings-on. 'But . . .'

Dilys opened the window, leaned out. Major heard her and began to whine. She shushed him. Neville slouched in his chair, at a loss. Looking at Dilys's broad behind, he felt a sudden urge to push her out of the window. He imagined her landing and breaking her neck. The image soothed him, comforted him. Funny, but he hadn't felt anything like as vengeful towards Valerie. As though she were reading his thoughts, Dilys pulled herself in and shut the window.

'Ah don' know how you can jus' be so calm 'bout de whole t'ing.'

She turned and faced him, rested her bottom against the windowsill.

'Two years is a long time, Neville.'

Neville stood up, paced to and fro, sat down again. 'Why, Dilys? For heaven sake, why you never jus' call de police?'

'I almost did. When I came home and saw the scene, that was my first reaction. I ran downstairs with the intention of doing just that, but as I got to the phone it started ringing. I answered it and was shocked to hear her voice. In my state of mind it didn't even occur to me to put the two things together. Anyway, she calmed me down and explained what had happened, begging me not to call the police before she'd had her say. Dazed, I hung up the phone and went round to see her.'

She walked over to her dressing table, sat down, then began to apply some night cream. Neville was astonished at her composure.

'When I got there, she plied me with some of Harry's stale whisky then confessed the whole pathetic tale: how long it had been going on, where they went, the things he promised her, what they said about me, the abortion, everything. She was so ashamed, so full of remorse and guilt, that at no point did she look me in the eye. This from a woman who'd spent years giving me withering stares. When she'd finished I didn't know whether to throw my drink in her face or give her a hug.'

She finished applying her cream, then went and sat on her bed. Neville half expected her to lie down.

'So there it was. Her fate lay in my hands. And as much as I hate that cow, I didn't think she deserved to go to prison. After all she'd been through, it didn't seem fair, somehow. What she did will be on her conscience for the rest of her life. I think that's punishment enough.'

She paused, studied Neville. He had a crazed look in his eyes, and for a moment, for a fraction of a second, she was afraid that he might try to harm her.

'After that,' she said, 'the logistics were fairly straight-forward. Under cover of darkness we disposed of the body and the bloodstained carpet. The how and where is a secret we swore to take to our graves.'

Neville had been listening with his head in his hands, unable to believe all the lies that he'd been told. It occurred to him that Dilys had been lying to him from day one, lying and smiling with it, she and Valerie. Lying to cover up their wickedness. But God wasn't sleeping, and as sure as night followed day, they would get theirs. Without looking up he said: 'So where Sean was while all dis going on?'

The question was so unrelated, Dilys had to think about

it. 'He stayed on at my uncle's for an extra couple of days. Thank God.'

'And wha' you tell him when him come home?'

'The truth, after a fashion. I told him that his father had gone away and wouldn't ever be coming back. And d'you know what? He smiled.'

That did it. Neville broke down and wept, quietly, head forward, almost between his knees. Dilys watched him for a while, not sure what to do, what to say. In the end, she walked over to him and rested her hand on his back. As soon as he felt her touch, he shot up from his chair. Dilys backed away, convinced that he was about to strike her, but he merely walked out. Shortly afterwards she heard the front door slam.

Neville got to the Crown just in time to see Madge locking up.

'Ah, Neville,' she said. 'Too late, I'm afraid. Pubs close early on Sundays.'

'Dat's not wha' me come about.'

'No? What, then?'

'Dat room of yours still available?'

Madge smiled and said: 'Yes. You need it?'

Neville nodded.

'When?'

'Tonight.'

'Tonight?!' She noticed his woebegone appearance. 'Oh my God! What's happened?'

'Mek we go to your place and ah will tell you.'

Madge couldn't finish locking up fast enough.

She lived on the Gorswood estate, which was much derided by the local snobs. So, too, were the residents, who were made to feel like second-class citizens.

Madge had some beer in her fridge, six cans of Stella. She grabbed a couple and she and Neville went through to the front room.

Neville told her everything, then immediately regretted doing so. He may have unburdened himself, but Madge was a gossip, and he couldn't bear the thought of his dirty laundry being aired in public. Then again, if Dilys and Valerie were exposed, and ultimately brought to justice, perhaps it would be no bad thing. But was that truly his wish, to see the women locked up? After all, were they not victims themselves?

'Jesus Christ,' said Madge, shaking her head. She sipped her beer, from the can. 'Of all the evil, wicked . . . told you about her, didn't I?' She pondered for a moment. 'Poor Joe. Poor, poor Joe.' She looked at Neville. Reclining on the sofa, he looked totally worn out, his eyes puffy, bloodshot. 'There must be something we can do.'

'Wha'?'

'I don't know. Something.' She racked her brain for a few seconds, then gave up.

A door slammed somewhere in the house. Moments later Billy entered the room, swinging his keys. He seemed every inch the yob – close-cropped hair, cheap gold jewellery, check shirt, blue jeans, white trainers – and he confirmed it seconds later when he said: 'What's he doing 'ere?'

'You mind your manners,' said Madge, enraged.

'Fuck manners. What's this nig-nog doing in the house?'

Madge leaped up and slapped him. Neville noticed a pattern. So far every boy he'd met had taken exception to him. First Cyrian, then Sean, now Billy.

'Look,' he said. 'Maybe ah should leave.'

'You stay right where you are, Neville,' said Madge. She turned to Billy, who was rubbing his cheek. 'You gonna apologise?'

'Like fuck I am.'

'Then get out.'

'What?'

'You heard me. Get out of this house right now.'

'But where'm I gonna go?'

Madge didn't answer. She snatched his keys and frog-marched him from the room and out of the house. When she came back, Neville was standing up, all set to leave. 'Really,' he said, 'Ah t'ink is best if ah . . .'

'Would you sit down? This is my house. You're my guest. Besides, what are you going to do? Go back to that woman?'

Neville thought about it, then sat down. Madge went out and quickly returned with two more beers.

Half an hour later they'd relaxed again.

'Where him father is?' asked Neville.

'Inside.'

'Inside?'

'Prison.'

'Raas! For what?'

'GBH. Beat the living daylights out of some guy at a football match.'

Neville became pensive. More violence. It was beginning to look like a common feature of English life.

'Kids,' said Madge. 'You give them everything and they turn round and break your heart. I'm at my wits' end with that boy.'

'How old him is now?'

'Eighteen. He's going exactly the way of his old man. And there doesn't seem to be a thing I can do about it.'

'Is not too late for him to change. You jus' 'ave to put you trus' an' faith in de Lord.'

'You religious, then?'

Not another unbeliever, thought Neville. On the whole, he'd found England to be quite a godless place. No wonder it had so many problems.

'Ah believe in de Faader, de Son, and de Holy Ghost.'

'Me too,' said Madge. Neville was relieved. 'You've got to. Otherwise . . .' She didn't finish it, for she'd noticed how intensely Neville was staring at her. 'What?'

Neville didn't know what to say, or do. It had been a long

time since he'd made a pass at a woman, and countless years since he'd had sex. The desire had all but left him, and he was surprised to find himself wanting Madge of all people. They maintained eye contact for a while, until Madge came to his rescue. 'Let's go upstairs.'

Afterwards they lay in bed, staring up at the ceiling, lost in their separate thoughts. Madge was thinking about Billy, and where he might possibly be. Neville was rating his performance, and scoring it not very high. He'd flagged badly a couple of times, and Madge had been forced to take pity on him. They heard the phone ring downstairs, and instinctively checked their watches. It was after two.

'Is a bit late for people to be calling,' said Neville.

'It's probably Billy wanting to come home. Let him sweat.'

The phone rang a couple more times, then stopped.

'You sure you want to leave him out dere? Is a cold night.'

'It's OK. He won't wander the streets. I'm not that cruel. He'll probably go round to Becky Marshall's. He's best mates with her son, Daniel. They live just across the way.'

'Oh. Him all right, den.'

'Yes,' replied Madge. She rolled on to her side, facing Neville. 'So. You recovered yet, old man?'

Neville looked at her. 'You not serious?'

Madge raised her brows lewdly. Neville groaned.

Later he had a nightmare. Not surprisingly, it featured Joe. It was a continuation of his previous dream, only this time, instead of being bludgeoned by Joe, it was the other way around. He woke with a start, in a cold sweat. Beside him, Madge was snoring. Appalled, he sneaked out of bed and crept downstairs.

Sitting at the kitchen table, he had two cups of tea, then cursed himself for falling into the habit. He couldn't wait to get back home to enjoy his usual morning tipple – fresh peppermint, or scalding hot chocolate with the consistency of crude oil. In fact, of the two, the latter had to be his favourite.

STEPHEN THOMPSON

He could drink mug after mug of the stuff, accompanied by hunks of hard dough bread. Funny the things you miss about home, he thought.

Now he was wide awake, and he began to analyse events. He'd come a long way, done many things, seen another kind of life. And what did it all amount to? Not very much. He hadn't found what he'd been searching for, and now it was time to go home. Did he regret coming? No. Would he miss anyone after he'd gone? Of course. Eugene, Joyce, but mostly Dilys. As for Joe, though it pained him to think it, and he prayed that God would forgive him for doing so, Joe deserved everything he'd got.

CHAPTER ELEVEN

Neville felt anxious on his way to see Dilys that morning. But it couldn't be avoided. He needed to get his things. He was planning on staying at Madge's for a few days before booking his flight home.

He met Dilys at the gate. They both froze on seeing one another. It was Dilys who spoke first. She said that she was on her way to the police station. Neville immediately thought that it had something to do with Joe.

'De police station? Why?'

'It's Sean. He's been arrested.'

'Sean! Arrested!? For wha'?'

'Something to do with Billy Winters. I don't know the details. They wouldn't tell me over the phone. They just said it's serious.' She pushed past him and headed off down the road.

'Wait,' said Neville. 'Ah coming wid you.'

At the front desk was the same surly officer who Neville had met on his first visit. In a disinterested tone, he told them that Sean had been arrested in connection with an assault on one William Winters. He couldn't say more, and they would have to wait while he went and got the arresting officers. He buzzed them through to the small side room.

Minutes later, Sergeant Pettifer came in. 'Hello, Neville,' he said. 'And you must be Dilys.'

'What's happened?' she asked, frantic.

'Well, I wasn't the arresting officer, but under the cir-cumstances . . .' He looked at Neville. '. . . I thought it best if I came and spoke with you.' He paused, then added: 'I'm afraid it's serious. Very serious. Billy Winters is in hospital, suffering from a fractured skull. He fell into a brief coma, but is out of it now.' He looked at Dilys. 'He says your boy attacked him last night, says he jumped him from behind and just kept pounding his head against the pavement.'

'Impossible,' said Dilys. 'Sean was at home all last night. When was this supposed to have happened?'

'About one-thirty this morning.'

Neville remembered the phone call from the night before. It must have been the police, or the hospital.

'No way,' said Dilys. 'Sean was in bed by then.'

'So why would Billy Winters finger him?'

'It's obvious,' said Dilys. 'He's had it in for Sean since they were at school. He's a well-known racist.'

'So you're saying Sean was at home all last night?'

'Yes. He went to bed before me. Isn't that right, Neville?' Neville nodded.

'And you'd both swear to that in court?'

'YES!!!' they chorused.

'And there's no chance he might have left the house again without you knowing?'

Neville and Dilys looked at each other. He certainly couldn't swear to that, since he'd spent the night elsewhere; and neither could she, in all honesty. Sean might easily have sneaked out without her knowledge; though it was highly unlikely, she thought. 'When did you arrest him?' she asked.

'Around seven this morning. A couple of officers were on their way to your place when they saw him leaving the house. Where was he going so early?'

'He works,' said Dilys distractedly.

'Hol' on,' said Neville. 'Mek ah get dis straight. You saying him beat up de bwoy, go back home to bed, sleep, wake up, den set out for work as usual?'

'It would appear so,' said Sergeant Pettifer.

Neville shook his head. He could hardly credit it.

'I don't believe it,' said Dilys. 'Sean isn't that calculating. Where is he? Can I see him?'

'Sure.'

Sean wasn't answering any questions. He sat on his bunk staring at the ground, catatonic. Dilys begged and pleaded with him to say whether he'd left the house, but he remained silent. Then Neville had a go, but he might as well have been talking to the cell walls.

'That's how he's been since we picked him up,' said Sergeant Pettifer. 'If he is innocent, not talking won't help. Is he always like this?'

'So what happens now?' asked Dilys.

'The case officers are still making up their minds whether to charge him. It's simply a question of whether they believe Billy Winters. There's no other evidence to consider.'

All three stood looking at Sean.

'It's a waiting game now,' said Sergeant Pettifer. 'There's nothing more you can do here. You might as well go home. You'll know by this evening one way or the other. They'll have to charge him or release him.'

Outside the station, Dilys announced that she was going to the hospital.

'You sure 'bout dat?' asked Neville.

'I have to talk to Billy. I know he's lying.'

The hospital was forty-five minutes away by bus, in the middle of nowhere, next to a busy dual carriageway. It was set in expansive grounds, with a vast carpark out front. There was a main building, and lots of outbuildings, none more than two storeys high. To Neville, it looked more like a small village than a hospital.

Despite detailed directions from the receptionist, they got lost. As they wandered around in ever-decreasing circles, Neville was reminded of his own recent hospitalisation, and he wished he hadn't come. Finally, after consulting a porter, they found the right ward. As they approached Billy's bed, Dilys noticed Madge sitting beside it. She immediately realised her error, and whispered to Neville: 'Let's get out of here.'

'Good idea.'

The ward being so quiet, Madge overheard them. 'Oi, you!' She ran up to Dilys and would have hit her had Neville not stepped between them. She proceeded to shout obscenities, drawing stares from all the other people on the ward. She called Sean all sorts of names and said that he would pay for what he did. Dilys retaliated, calling Billy 'racist scum' who 'had it coming to him'. Madge responded by calling Dilys a murderer and promised that she and Valerie would get no peace in the town. She took another swipe at Dilys, before being led away by a couple of male doctors. Dilys and Neville exited immediately afterwards.

As they made their way to the bus stop, Dilys kept repeating to herself: 'Bitch. Bitch.' She then turned on Neville. 'And where do you think you're going? Go away. I don't want you anywhere near me.' Neville ignored her remarks and continued to walk beside her, his head bowed, guilt-ridden.

A few hours later Dilys got the call she'd been waiting for. Sean had been charged with GBH and was scheduled to appear before the local magistrate the following morning. At least he hadn't been charged with attempted murder, Sergeant Pettifer said, trying to soften the blow. When she heard the news, Dilys let the phone drop and walked from the room. Neville, who'd been waiting anxiously near by, picked up the receiver.

'Hello?'

'Neville? Is that you?'

'Yes, is me, Sergeant. Wha' 'appen?'

Sergeant Pettifer repeated what he'd told Dilys.

'My oh my,' said Neville.

'Tough break,' said Sergeant Pettifer. He paused before continuing. 'Listen, Neville, about that other thing; just so's you know, I passed on what you told me to the CID boys and they said they'd look into it. So there might be movement on that some time soon.'

'Movement?' said Neville. 'Wha' you mean by "movement"?'

'Well, I'm not sure. But my guess is that they'll want to question the neighbour. Depending on how that goes, they might want to take a look around her place. If what she says is true, and she's still got that poker, there might still be blood on it, even after two years. Then there's your sister-in-law.'

'Dilys? Wha' 'bout ar?'

'Again, depending on how things go, they might want to look around her bedroom. These forensic boys, nothing gets past them. If there's a hair under the skirting board they'll find it.'

Neville thought for a few seconds, looked over his shoulder to make sure Dilys hadn't wandered back into the room. 'Look, Sergeant,' he whispered. 'Ah was going to come and tell you in person, but ah might as well tell you now. Don't was'e any more of you time. It finish. Over. You unnerstan'?' The line went quiet for a moment. 'You still dere?'

'Yes, I'm still here. What are you saying exactly?'

'Ah fin' Joe.' Again the line went quiet. 'Hello.'

'I'm still here. You found him, you say?'

'Yes. Him call here dis morning, from London.'

'I see. Well, I'm happy for you, Neville. I really am. You're one of the lucky ones.'

'So it over, right?'

A short pause. 'Not quite.'

Neville panicked. 'Wha' you mean, Sergeant?'

'You'll have to come in and do it officially, I'm afraid; make another statement to the effect that you've found your brother and that you no longer wish us to continue our search for his whereabouts.'

Neville sighed with relief. 'As soon as ah can, ah will come down. See you den.'

'Er, Neville, just before you go.'

'Yes, Sergeant.'

'Do you see now how ridiculous that woman's story was?'

Neville thanked him for all his efforts and hung up.

Sean cut a pathetic figure in the defendant's box. With his head bowed, he was asked to enter a plea. Guilty or not guilty. Dilys and Neville looked on from the gallery, fretting. The Bishops sat next to them, looking concerned. The magistrate, a stern old woman with a clipped voice, again asked Sean to enter a plea: guilty or not guilty. He raised his head, looked round at Dilys, turned back to the magistrate and, in a loud, clear voice, said: 'Guilty.'

Dilys broke down.

Sean was remanded on conditional bail prior to sentencing, the date for which was set three weeks hence. The condition of his bail was that he didn't go within a half mile radius of the Winters' house, which, by a geographical quirk, meant that he couldn't go to work. Confined to the house, he resumed work on his bird. One day Neville observed him at it, and marvelled at the dexterity with which he used his mallet and chisel. He definitely had gifted hands, Neville thought.

For the next few days an air of despondency pervaded the house. Sean moped around a lot, and spent a good deal of time on his sculpture. Dilys had been given indefinite leave by her employers, and was determined to spend it catching up on her reading. Neville had booked his return ticket and was now simply killing time, which he did, for the most part, by holing up in his room. Every so often he'd come down for a drink, or a snack, then sneak back upstairs.

One afternoon he was lying on his bed daydreaming when he heard a knock on the door.

'Come in.'

Dilys entered and said: 'Didn't mean to disturb you, but I thought you might want to see this.'

She walked over to the window, followed by Neville.

'Well, bless me soul,' said Neville.

'Beautiful, isn't it?'

It was snowing, heavily. The garden was already covered. Major was prancing around, spoiling the effect with his paw prints.

'So da's wha' it look like.'

'You're lucky. Haven't had snow like this for years.'

'Wait till ah tell de bwoys 'bout dis. Dey nevva going to believe me.'

Dilys felt her heart sink. She said: 'Looking forward to getting back?'

'Yes, very much.'

Nothing to lose, everything to gain. 'Stay,' said Dilys.

Neville sighed, shook his head. 'Ah can't do dat, Dilys.'

'Why not?'

'You really wan' me to explain?'

A long silence, then Dilys said: 'I don't see that there's anything back there for you.'

She couldn't disguise the anger in her voice. Neville thought it best not to say anything.

'You're going back to take care of that old woman, aren't you?'

'Dat ol' woman 'ave a name. Adlyn.'

'Whatever her name is, she's not your responsibility.'

'Please, Dilys, don' tell me wha' my responsibility is. I's a grown man.'

They saw Sean walk out into the garden, carrying Lucky in his fist.

'What the bloody hell's he playing at now?' said Dilys, and she banged on the windowpane. Sean heard the sound, but ignored it. Dilys banged some more. 'Get inside!' she shouted. 'Sean! Get inside right now!'

'But dat bwoy really mad,' said Neville. 'Him will catch him det in dat wedder.'

Sean raised his arm above his head, opened his hand, but Lucky wasn't going anywhere. It was a surreal image: the falling snow, Sean with his arm in the air, Lucky a miniature ball in his outstretched palm. Suddenly, he hurled the frightened creature high into the air. Immediately she started flapping her wings, but that didn't prevent her downward trajectory. Sean positioned himself, ready to catch her. Neville and Dilys held their breath, fearing the worst. They needn't have worried. Lucky's survival instincts took over, and she flapped her tiny wings as hard as she could and flew away. Sean, his face covered in snow, watched until she disappeared.

Finally the day came for Neville to leave. The taxi waited while he said his goodbyes to Dilys and Sean in the front room.

'Sure you don't want us to come to the airport with you?' said Dilys.

'No. Ah really can't stand dat type a t'ing.' He paused, then said: 'Well, goodbye, Dilys.'

'Take care of yourself.'

An awkward embrace. When they broke, Neville turned to Sean. 'Goodbye, young man. You look after you modder now, you hear?'

Sean stared at his feet. The adults talked around him for a while.

'Don' worry too much 'bout de court case.'

'I am worried. I'm very worried. He'll never survive a custodial sentence.'

'Dat won' 'appen. De Lawd is watching.'

Dilys smiled.

Neville said: 'OK, den, ah better get going.'

'Write, won't you?'

And suddenly he remembered the question that had been bugging him since the first day.

'Taak 'bout write. Wha' ever 'appen to all dem letter ah sen' Joe?'

Dilys thought for a moment, a shadow of guilt passing across her face. She wasn't sure which ones he meant. Those that Joe had received, or the handful that had arrived in the two years after his death? Not that it mattered, since they had all suffered the same fate. 'I burned them,' she said.

Neville gave a knowing nod. He'd thought as much. It made

sense. In her position, he'd probably have done the same thing. But there was still one question remaining. Had she read the letters before setting fire to them? He decided not to ask, and instead made his way out to the front door. Dilys escorted him, dragging a reluctant Sean with her.

Neville's suitcases were already in the boot of the taxi. Dilys and Sean watched him get into the back seat. A final flurry of waves, then the taxi moved off. As he drove past it, Neville gave Valerie's house one final look, paying extra attention to the For Sale sign.

Toy Soldiers
STEPHEN THOMPSON

When Gabriel checks into a rehab in west London he thinks his problems are over. With a fractured life behind him, a father he never knew, teenage years lost to petty crime and an increasing dependency on crack, all that the future can possibly offer is hope. Then he is forced to confront his demons, aided by Marcia, the enigmatic hostel worker with whom he falls in love. Unflinching, warm and lovingly crafted, *Toy Soldiers* combines a love story with a brilliant account of a life brought back from the brink of extinction.

'Beautifully written, painfully honest and deeply affecting'
Hanif Kureishi

'Accessibly psychological, gripping and just the right side of confrontational'
i-D

'Sensitive, subtle and fascinating'
The Times

'A compelling urban tale, gritty yet filled with inspired prose and characters you can reach out and touch'
Courttia Newland

'A gem of a book that all too many people can relate to . . . a book that gives us all hope'
Pride

'Beautifully honest . . . dark and challenging'
Independent on Sunday

'In a cool plain prose without fuss or melodrama, he manages the astonishing task of making his young alter ego – the crack-dealing, violent, hate-filled Gabriel – hugely sympathetic'
Evening Standard

'Stephen Thompson's vital, gritty and gripping novel reads like a kind of *Trainspotting* in Hackney. Ali G could only wish for Staines to be this real'
19

SCEPTRE

Gringo Soup
J. B. ASPINALL

You couldn't tell which would be the wise-crackers, the grumblers, the claustrophobics, the cheer-leaders, the thugs, the wannabes, the enigmas. All you could be sure of was that they would be a bit worse than the last group. They always were . . .

As tour leader Lisa anticipates supervising the new arrivals on a trip around Mexico, she is finding it hard to summon up any degree of professional good will. But then her passengers aren't exactly ecstatic either – and not only with the performance of their 'rep'. As we discover in the course of witnessing each day from a different perspective, those on the trip are less than happy both with their travelling companions and, in most cases, with the cards life has dealt them.

'A darkly funny look at package holiday hell that makes for perfect summer reading'
Mirror

'Immensely vivacious . . . very, very funny indeed'
Pete Davies, *Open Book*, BBC Radio 4

'Deadpan delivery ensures that this novel, set against a background of tour-guiding in Mexico, really hits the mark . . . Entertaining, informative and occasionally laugh-out-loud funny, this is an ambitious, well-written novel that equates the disappointments of tourism with the crashing disarray of life itself.'
Marie Claire

'The curious, Big Brother-like concept of the group package tour is exploited to darkly comic effect . . . a brisk, entertaining tale'
Daily Mail

SCEPTRE

Pig
ANDREW COWAN

When his grandmother dies, and his grandfather is removed to a home, fifteen-year-old Danny determines to look after their elderly pig and ramshackle garden. Here, on the ragged edge of a blighted new town, Danny and his Indian girlfriend Surinder create a fragile haven from the enclosing world of racist neighbours and stifling families, a summer's refuge from the precariousness of their future.

'A poignant but often tenderly comic romance of urban decay'
Jonathan Keates, *Observer* Books of the Year

'A first novel of extraordinary poise and accomplishment, treating a boy's coming of age amid the squalid realities of the new British underclass with a delicacy and lyricism which is both gripping and moving'
Michael Dibdin

'A coming-of-age story as strange and surprising, in its way, as *The Catcher in the Rye*'
New York Times

'Danny's relationship with Surinder is delicately observed in its tenderness, sensuality and awkwardness, as is the stubbornness and wisdom of adolescence. This is a wholly satisfying book, quietly beautiful and inescapably ominous'
David Buckley, *Observer*

'The detail is immaculately recorded; the effect is heartbreaking'
Louisa Young, *Sunday Times*

'Beautifully evoked . . . Cowan writes with a deceptive simplicity'
Amanda Craig, *The Times*

'A wonderful first novel'
Christopher Hart, *Daily Telegraph*

'Cowan writes with a deeply impressive grace and economy'
Boyd Tonkin, *New Statesman & Society*

'Honest, charming and extremely moving, it is a real treat'
Rachel Thomson, *Tribune*

SCEPTRE

A selection of other books from Sceptre

Toy Soldiers	Stephen Thompson	0 340 75147 9	£6.99	☐
Gringo Soup	J. B. Aspinall	0 340 73378 0	£6.99	☐
Pig	Andrew Cowan	0 340 82412 3	£6.99	☐
He Kills Coppers	Jake Arnott	0 340 74880 X	£6.99	☐
Too Small for Basketball	Kris Kenway	0 340 79272 8	£6.99	☐

All Hodder & Stoughton books are available at your local bookshop or newsagent, or can be ordered direct from the publisher. Just tick the titles you want and fill in the form below. Prices and availability subject to change without notice.

Hodder & Stoughton Books, Cash Sales Department, Bookpoint, 39 Milton Park, Abingdon, OXON, OX14 4TD, UK. E-mail address: orders@bookpoint.co.uk. If you have a credit card you may order by telephone – (01235) 400414.

Please enclose a cheque or postal order made payable to Bookpoint Ltd to the value of the cover price and allow the following for postage and packing:
UK & BFPO: £1.00 for the first book, 50p for the second book and 30p for each additional book ordered up to a maximum charge of £3.00.
OVERSEAS & EIRE: £2.00 for the first book, £1.00 for the second book and 50p for each additional book.

Name . . . .

Address . . . .

. . . .

. . . .

If you would prefer to pay by credit card, please complete:
Please debit my Visa / Access / Diner's Club / American Express (delete as applicable) card no:

Signature . . . .

Expiry Date . . . .

If you would NOT like to receive further information on our products please tick the box. ☐